Highland Shifter

by

Catherine Bybee

Highland Shifter

Cover Art by Crystal Posey

Visit the author at www.catherinebybee.com

Publishing History
First Edition, 2012
Published by Catherine Bybee
Print ISBN 978-0-9850888-0-4

Published in the United States of America

Dedication

For Tammy.
My first true fan and my harshest critic.
I'm truly blooood to call you my friend.

Acknowledgements

I want to thank and acknowledge all of you, my readers. If it wasn't for your response to the first three time travel books about the MacCoinnich's, I would never have written Simon's story. My fans on Goodreads and Facebook have been relentless, clamoring for Simon, Amber, and Cian's stories. I can't blame you. I love these characters so much they feel like my own children. Although I enjoy the happily ever after ending, I still want to see a glimpse or two of these characters as they ride through life.

Thank you all for giving this writer a need to finish this series so we can all see how Simon, Amber, and Cian turn out.

Chapter One

Current Day, Los Angeles
Energy buzzed down Helen's spine until she
shivered with the electrical current her gift created. The
information she sought was close enough to taste, all
she needed to do was touch it and she'd be one step
closer to finding the missing boy.

Helen Adams shifted onto the balls of her feet,
reached well beyond her five-foot six frame, and tipped
the old leather bound text into her hands. As the book
slid from its comfortable position on the top shelf in
Mrs. Dawson's library, dust plumed off the sill in a
cloud. The zap she'd been feeling for the last half hour
eased into a nice, steady hum. The blanket of warmth
that only came when she'd found what she sought
brought a rare smile to her face.

"There you are," she whispered to the ancient book
as if it were alive.

"Did you find what you're looking for?" Mrs. Dawson
limped into the room, leaning heavily on the cane.
Nearing her eighty-fourth birthday, Mrs. Dawson's
battered, frail body appeared as if it wanted nothing
more than to lie down and rest forever.

"I think so." Helen gently blew the layer of dust off
the book and peered close to determine the title.
Embossed into the leather was an old Celtic design. The
scent of a fresh meadow after a cleansing rain settled
over her. Helen closed her eyes and grasped the text
hard. She heard the hooves of horses, smelled the sweet
scent of horseflesh. None of this experience came from
the room where she stood, but from the book she held in
her hands.

1

As the scents dissipated, Helen opened her eyes and gazed at the book in wonder. How could a book this old hold any relevance on a missing child's case in the twenty-first century?

"Do you have any idea where this originally came from?" Helen asked as she moved to the table and turned on a light to view the pages inside the book.

"My late husband collected boxes of books like that when he was alive. As you can judge by the dust, they've not been touched since his death." Mrs. Dawson eased herself into a chair, cringing as she sat. Helen knew her friend's arthritis would be acting up with the sour weather pounding the window outside. Helen also knew Mrs. Dawson wouldn't accept anything more than a sympathetic smile if Helen were to ask if she could help her sit or stand.

"Well, let's see what you have there."

Judging by the cover, Helen expected the text to be in either Celtic or Italian. She was wrong.

The title of Folklore, writing in a beautiful script font, splashed the front page of the book.

The book was written in English.

Helen glanced at the opening credits to see the publication date.

"This is over two hundred years old," Helen said, confused.

"What does it have to do with that boy?" Mrs. Dawson asked.

"I've no idea."

Mrs. Dawson was the only person who knew the extent of Helen's gift. Well, the only person Helen had told who hadn't laughed at her and passed her off as crazy.

Her work at a local antique shop had led her down this path to Mrs. Dawson's library in search of a missing teenage boy, Simon McAllister. What the boy and the book in her hands had in common, Helen hadn't a clue.

Helen gently turned the pages and skimmed the text. From what she could tell, several different storytellers wrote the content. Illustrations dotted the pages with small captions explaining the pictures.

There were illustrations of Celtic symbols, Scottish kilts, warriors with broadswords, and women wearing long, flowing dresses.

What any of it had to do with Simon McAllister disappearing off the face of the earth without a trace was a mystery to Helen.

Releasing a long-suffering sigh, she flattened her hand on the table and twisted away in frustration. "This is useless."

Mrs. Dawson cocked her head to the side in a motion of concern. One of the shutters on the outside of the house ripped free of its lock and swung back, hitting the side of the old house with an angry bang.

Helen and Mrs. Dawson jumped at the noise and swiveled toward it.

Cold air blew into the room, and the drapes around the window flapped in protest from the outside elements.

An eerie screech whistled through the crack in the window, and the book to Helen's side started fluttering through pages like a deck of cards being shuffled in Vegas. The pages moved in a rapid pace, but the current of air in the room barely brushed her skin.

Unable to pull her gaze away, Helen watched as the pages of the book came to a sudden stop.

The air on her back blew colder, harder, but the pages no longer rustled.

Her chocolate brown hair started to come loose from the tight bun on her head, but she ignored the tendrils falling in her face. Instead, Helen inched closer.

Two illustrations covered the pages. On the left was a Scottish warrior, broad shouldered and dressed in his plaid, as would any proud Scot of centuries past. In the corner of the illustration flew a hawk or maybe it was a falcon. Helen couldn't be sure.

The warrior's hand extended toward the opposite page, his face solemn with an expression of absolute desperation.

Helen let her eyes travel to the right page and time suddenly stood still.

"My God," Mrs. Dawson exclaimed.

My God indeed.

"That's you."

Helen peered closer, stared at the image, which certainly looked like her. The woman in the picture wore her hair long, past her waist. She wore a floor length dress with long, flowing sleeves.

Yes, it could have been a distant relative of Helen's. That alone gave her a sense of familiarity she had never experienced any other time in her life. Abandoned at a young age, Helen never knew her parents or any other relative.

Helen took in the features of the woman's face and gasped when her gaze landed on the pendant around the woman's neck.

Reaching a hand to her own neck, she pulled out an identical replica of the necklace in the picture from under her turtleneck sweater.

The breeze from the window stopped and the room started to warm.

"This lady must be one of your relatives," Mrs. Dawson said.

Helen nodded but couldn't voice any words. The necklace wasn't an heirloom. What did the picture mean? Who was the man on the opposite page, and what did it have to do with the missing boy she felt a need to find?

She had more questions than answers. Glancing at her watch, Helen realized how late it was. "I should leave so you can rest. Do you mind if I hold onto this book for a while?"

Mrs. Dawson patted her hand. "Of course not, dear. It appears to belong to you anyway."

Helen reached for the book, but Mrs. Dawson stopped her hand midway. Frail, wrinkled fingers touched the backside of Helen's hand and fiddled with the watch surrounding her wrist. Mrs. Dawson tapped the watch then lowered her same finger to the picture of the woman in the book.

There, in the pages of an ancient text, was a very similar timepiece on the wrist of the woman.

"Perhaps not a relative after all."

"What are you suggesting?"

"She looks exactly like you, Helen. That necklace, where did you get it?"

"I found it in a thrift shop." Her love for all things old brought her into thrift shops in search of hidden treasures. Lots of people threw their possessions away instead of treasuring them. The pendant had Celtic markings with a polished stone dead center. It was simply a well-polished rock set in a common metal. But the stone felt warm against Helen's skin when she'd put it on. Somewhere inside of her soul, she knew she was meant to own the necklace.

"This woman is wearing a watch. Your watch."

"That's ridiculous. It's probably a bracelet."

Mrs. Dawson pressed her reading glasses close to her eyes and peered down. "I see numbers."

Helen noticed them, too. But it wasn't possible. "What are you suggesting?" The woman in the picture was clearly garbed in a dress right out of medieval times, a time when watches weren't part of any woman's wardrobe. In fact, Helen knew wristwatches weren't invented until the early nineteenth century.

Mrs. Dawson stared deep into her eyes before she spoke. "To coin a phrase, 'a picture is worth a thousand words.'"

"Now you're throwing riddles at me." Her curiosity spiked, however, and she decided a Google search was definitely in order. What was the exact date the wristwatch was invented, and who were the authors of this book?

Glancing back at the curtains, Mrs. Dawson said, "Seems something else is throwing riddles at you, dear. I just happen to be the one holding the book with the answers."

* * * *

1596 Scotland

An unrelenting desire surged into the tips of Simon's fingers. If only he could toss a ball of fire onto the ass of his opponent's horse. But no, that would be cheating, and why hurt the innocent horse. Using his powers would be like bringing a gun to a knife fight. Besides, the warrior's sword arm was tiring. Simon felt it the last time the man's broadsword hit his shield.

Metal clashed against metal behind him, and smoke plumed above the fires in the encampment of the invaders who threatened MacCoinnich Keep. Night crept around the edges of light being cast off by the flames, bringing finality to the fight at hand.

Simon's opponent dug his heels into the flanks of the horse he rode, his sword aiming straight at Simon's chest.

Hold still, he whispered mentally to his horse. This skill, the one where he talked to animals, was one he'd mastered at the tender age of thirteen. Now, nearly thirty, Simon had complete command of any animal he came in contact with. Or, as his mother often said, he was a regular Doctor Doolittle.

The warrior charging him released an angry cry, his blade poised for a deathblow.

Simon waited, one hand holding his own weapon firmly, the other cradling a shield with the family crest engraved upon it.

A little closer.

Within a hair's breadth of the sword reaching his personal space, Simon urged his mount to lunge. With that momentum, he knocked the other man's sword aside and pierced his enemy's chest, laying it wide open, spilling the man's lifeblood.

A set of stunned eyes caught Simon's as the warrior slid from his horse on his final descent from life.

Simon paused for only a second to watch him topple

before quickly spinning around to assess his next threat.

The enemy retreated to the west, fleeing the losing battle so they could fight another day. Duncan, his uncle by marriage, stood beside his horse, his chest heaving heated breaths as his brother, Cian, circled the fallen. He would determine if any still lived.

The bloody battlefield stunk of unwashed flesh and dying men.

"Do any still breathe?" Duncan called out to Cian.

Cian slid from his horse and carefully rolled one of their enemies over. Even from Simon's distance, he could see death on the man's face.

"Nay. None."

Several other battle-weary men gathered and awaited direction from Duncan.

"I'll send hands from the Keep to aid in the burial of these men," he told his men. "Did anyone see a leader?"

Simon shook his head. "No one stood out among them."

"None." A chorus of denial rose.

"Mayhap ye should send scouts to follow those who fled."

"Aye." Duncan's gaze settled briefly on Simon. An unspoken request lit his eyes. They would scout, but not with men on horses. Sending a small party, easily outnumbered and ambushed, was not the answer.

"I'll ride ahead and report to Ian."

This excuse would go unquestioned by the men. Ian was Laird of the MacCoinnich clan, and he would want to know the outcome of this battle. Instead of returning to the Keep, Simon would scout ahead alone and return without anyone knowing that he watched.

Duncan lifted his chin. "Tell my Tara I'm well."

Simon nodded, knowing he didn't need to say a thing to his aunt. Duncan and Tara had a special mental bond that made it possible for the two of them to communicate with their thoughts. Tara was probably in Duncan's head right now asking about his well-being.

Simon and his extended family were Druids, all of

them. Each possessed special gifts—Druid gifts that aided them in life and allowed them to defeat their enemies, magical and mortal alike. He'd take the latter any day of the week. Magical enemies were much harder to fight.

Keeping to the forest, Simon reined in his horse away from any watchful eyes and slid to the ground.

He quickly removed each layer of armor and clothing and stacked them against a tree. "Keep an eye on my things, won't you, Kong?" Simon had named his very first horse King, a massive animal that served him well. Kong was King's son. The names were a constant joke between his twenty-first century family members.

Kong sniffed the air before moving to a patch of grass to graze. The horse was hungry and tired after the battle. Most likely, he'd eat and rest until Simon returned.

Stepping away from his horse, Simon spread his arms wide, closed his eyes, and envisioned the falcon.

Familiar energy gathered around him. The air crackled and the world started to pitch.

His limbs shortened and his skin erupted and morphed.

Pain started at his head and spread to his feet, but it was brief and gone before Simon could blink an eye. The entire change took only a few seconds before Simon became the falcon.

Kong offered a passing glance before returning to his meal.

Simon took to the sky.

Above the trees, Simon returned to the direction of battle. He noted the battlefield and Cian helping with the dead.

Simon let a falcon's cry fill the air and saw Duncan and Cian both turn their heads his way.

Duncan nodded at him then continued with his duty as Cian waved a mock salute.

Leaving his family behind, Simon followed the trail the enemy left behind in search of answers.

Chapter Two

Without an invitation, Helen walked into her boss's office of the Auction House and gently placed the book she'd found the day before on his desk. "Look what I found."

She'd spent most of the previous night mulling over its pages and found herself more confused than ever by why her gift led her to this particular tome.

"What is it?" Philip lifted his dark eyes to hers briefly before glancing at the book in front of him.

Helen leaned a hip against the side of her boss's desk and crossed her arms over her chest. "It's about Scottish folklore."

"Is it valuable?" He ran a hand over his firm, attractive jaw, the way he always did when intrigued. She had his attention.

"It might be." Though she doubted it. "It's what I found inside that has me puzzled."

Philip Lyons, owner of The Auction House and Magazine, and her boss, encouraged her to follow her gut instincts when it came to finding valuable antiques. A couple of months before, two ornate candlesticks were brought into the auction house to be sold on commission. As the house photographer, and occasional buyer, Helen's entire body sizzled with excitement when she encountered the twelfth century works of art. She knew there was more to the candlesticks than a common sale to a collector. Philip knew it too.

He opened the pages of the book with care and skimmed the words. "What am I looking for?"

Helen leaned in and scooted the book closer. She

opened to the page of the Highland warrior and the lady who looked a whole hell of a lot like her.

Philip paused.

"Quick. What's your first thought?" she asked him, not wanting him to filter his words.

He paused, and then said, "She looks like you."

Not your first thought.

Helen wasn't sure how she knew Philip held his first impression back, only that he did.

"What else do you notice?"

Philip ran his finger over the page, stopping at the pendant around the woman's neck. "That's your necklace."

The necklace Helen wore even now. Philip's gaze traveled to her neck. His eye twitched and a smile started to spread over his face. "How's that possible?"

"I told you I had funny feelings about things."

Philip reached out and touched the pendant. His cool fingers sent a tiny jolt over her skin and she shivered.

Philip leaned forward to examine the necklace. His proximity suddenly felt too personal, and Helen shifted back.

Letting his hand drift to the desk, Philip narrowed his eyes to hers. "Maybe I should appraise your necklace."

"I've already checked. It's not worth much of anything." Besides, the thought of removing it and handing it to anyone actually left her ill.

Philip's eyes skirted over the necklace and dipped lower. After a brief pause on her breasts, they returned to the book.

Men and their wandering eyes.

Helen would have been offended if she hadn't already detected a desire from her boss to get to know her better. Something she wouldn't have minded exploring if he wasn't in charge of her paycheck.

He was five years older than her, financially stable, and pleasing to the eye. His dark brown hair was military short and his jaw always clean-shaven. Though, if Helen had to guess, she'd swear he'd worn a beard at some point in his life. She constantly caught him stroking his chin and upper lip, a habit men with facial hair acquired. At six feet, he had five inches on her and though she'd seen him only in a suit and tie, she didn't think he was a stranger to the gym.

...but he was her boss. That meant off limits as far as she was concerned.

"What do *you* think it all means, Helen?"

"I'm not sure, but I'm hoping you'll give me a couple of days off to look into it."

"A couple of days off? That's all?"

Now came the tricky part. "A week, actually."

Philip didn't say a word, just continued to stare at her.

"...and a plane ticket to Scotland."

* * * *

Twenty-two hours later, Helen finished unpacking her suitcase at a Holiday Inn outside of Dundee, Scotland and after renting a car, she started driving north. Where to, she hadn't a clue.

Part of her couldn't believe she was even here, another part, a nagging little itch, felt as if she was coming home. Which was stupid, because Helen had never had a home? The closest she'd ever come was Mrs. Webber's foster care where she'd spent four years housed in a small room with three other girls. At seventeen, Helen emancipated herself from the system by running away and never looking back. Smart thing, too, the other girls she'd roomed with all ended up either pregnant, in jail, or strung out on some cheap drug. Not the sort of life Helen envisioned for herself.

Feeling at home in a country where she'd never been was as foreign as driving on the wrong side of the road. Even the gimped up car they'd loaned her didn't have the controls in the right place.

Still, the strange sense of peace had washed over her the minute she'd walked off the airplane.

11

Philip had given her the time off and the ticket abroad. He'd have been stupid not to. The last time she asked for such a thing, she delivered the location of a stolen Vermeer.

While on assignment in a Boston museum, Helen photographed several pieces that were going to auction. When she scraped her hands along a wall, she'd felt a current of electricity similar to one she'd experienced when touching the book of Scottish folklore.

Apparently, a Vermeer had been heisted from the spot long ago. Helen called Philip and asked him to research the museum and tell her everything he could find out about the missing art. In addition to looking into the past theft, Philip flew to Boston and stood beside her as she followed her gift tracking the painting around the city. One week and hundreds of miles later, on an island off the Florida Keys, Helen led her boss to a collector who had the art in his possession.

The museum in Boston credited Philip's Auction house for the retrieval of the art. As a result, his standing in the art community elevated to amazing heights. Philip attributed her gift, her ability to follow objects and find missing things, to intuition. There was a lot more to it than intuition. That she knew. But why was this path now leading her toward a missing boy?

"The answer is out here somewhere," she said to herself as she dodged a crater-sized pothole in the road.

The roadside signs pointed off in all directions to castles dating back hundreds of years. The desire to drive up to the nearest one and pull out her camera was strong, but the feeling that doing so would slow down her search stopped her.

As she approached a four way stop, her right hand started to tingle. If she hadn't been waiting for the sensation, she would have missed it. At the stop she veered northeast onto a tiny two lane road. According to her map, the road would eventually run out and become nothing but dirt. Yet while her hand hummed, turning away wasn't an option.

Ten miles later the road turned to dust, and weeds of neglect crowded the lane. A large rut forced her from the car. She still had several hours of daylight and a backpack full of snacks and water.

Outside the car, humidity hung in the air like a blanket. Helen rolled up her short sleeved shirt to catch some of the wind blowing off the eastern coast. Following the rolling tingle along her skin, she moved away from the deserted road toward the sound of the ocean. She didn't think she was that close to the shore, so the noise caused her to pause.

A strange, panicky sensation rolled down her spine, forcing Helen to spin in a circle, searching for the cause. She was alone, but the feeling of being watched made her question the sanity of venturing off the marked road in a foreign country. Anyone could come along and do, God knew what, and never be caught. The only person who even knew she was in Scotland was Philip, and he wasn't expecting an update for a couple of days.

Hoisting her backpack higher, she pushed aside her unease and tried to walk closer to the noise of crashing waves.

A low stone wall peaked above the grassy field a good two miles from her car. She took a moment to rest and removed a bottle of water from her pack. After taking a long drink, Helen closed her eyes and leaned against the stones. She realized then the ocean sound hadn't changed since she'd stepped from the car. It hadn't gotten louder, or softer. It was as if she were walking along a coast, yet the coast wasn't there.

Her entire body began to hum. A small vibration told her she was close to whatever clue came next. "What the hell am I looking for?" she called out to the empty field. She removed the objects from her pack that led her this far, hoping to find her answer.

First was a picture of the candlesticks. Twelfth century pieces of art sold on consignment at Graystones, a rival auction house. They'd stayed in the possession of the owner for nearly a year before the said owner sent them to Philip to be resold. Apparently, the current economic crisis wasn't limited to the poor.

When Helen had touched the candlesticks every nerve ending in her body lit up. When an insatiable need to find out more about them rivaled breathing, she decided to discover all there was to find out about their history.

A woman by the name of Myra Doe consigned the candlesticks. Lord, the name Doe put up so many red flags Helen couldn't see straight. It was worse than Smith or Adams, for that matter. Still, a real live person brought in the candlesticks to sell. Yet when the sale took place, the money was put in another woman's name. Elizabeth McAllister.

Elizabeth was the mother of Simon. Both of whom simply disappeared without a trace nearly two years ago.

Helen thought she'd reached a dead end. The missing persons' case was cold. It didn't seem like anyone cared about these two people vanishing. On further study, Helen learned of another sister who'd gone missing. It was then Helen found herself in the halls of a favorite haunt, the public library. Then she explained her plight to her oldest friend, and only real family-like person in Helen's life, Mrs. Dawson.

Now the book from Mrs. Dawson's library warmed her palm as she opened it to the pages of the man with the woman who looked like her. Under their pictures was a simple passage. *Love is Timeless.* Whoever wrote the book was either a poet or a romantic.

A school picture of Simon dropped from one of the pages. Helen gripped the familiar photo, the same one that had been plastered in newspapers and on milk cartons for months. Even though his mother disappeared at the same time, the authorities always obtained more tips about missing children than missing adults.

Helen didn't know what to think. Only that her gift was pointing toward the child and not the mother. But something told her if she found one, she'd likely find the other. She shoved her things back in her bag and pushed herself to her feet.

A flicker of white caught her eye. The picture of Simon lifted with a breeze, floating away on the wind.

With bag in hand, she ran after the photograph. She tripped once, scraping her palms on the jagged surface of the rocks, and then took off running again. When the wind calmed for a moment the picture dropped and caught in a weed.

Helen pounced on it.

Out of breath, she placed her stinging hand on her chest, and held the picture with the other. A smudge of dirt layered the picture. Helen brushed the filth aside and left a trail of blood on the image.

"Dammit."

Her hands were a mess, full of embedded gravel and dirt with just enough blood to cake it all together.

She shook the picture. "See, here. I'm bleeding to find you, Simon McAllister. So stop trying to fly away."

The words no sooner left her lips before the sound of the ocean simply turned off. The air around her crackled and rushed out of her lungs.

The colors of the sky disappeared in a swirling tornado. The grass around her flickered and went black.

Panic rose in her throat in a scream, but when she opened her lips the sound didn't escape. Gravity sucked her down and pushed her back up.

All Helen could do was sit hopelessly by and pray the world found its axis soon.

Wind swirled around her and a loud thunderous roar replaced the nothing.

When Helen's stomach threatened to rebel, she closed her eyes and crushed her hands to her ears.

I don't want to die.

As fast as the world shifted around her, it came to a stunning halt.

Squeezing her eyes shut, Helen held perfectly still, fearing any movement would start the tornado again.

Her skin chilled. The temperature felt almost frigid, and the smell of the air had changed.

The sound of a horse neighing forced her eyes to spring open.

She was in a forest, a lush green forest with dew dripping off the trees. A massive black horse stood a couple of yards away and eyed her with curiosity.

"Well now, what have we here?" A deep, tender voice rumbled behind her.

Helen jumped to her feet and let loose the scream that had been lodged in her throat before. Now filling every inch of the surrounding forest with her shock, she spun, dropping her backpack at her feet.

There, standing in the middle of the forest and draped in only a kilt, stood the man from the book. Only this man was massive, huge in a way a picture could never describe. Thick arms and a bare chest so ripped with muscles, Helen couldn't help thinking he could do some serious damage to anyone if he had a mind to.

And she was alone with him.

Her head reeled.

It was too much. Everything had happened so quickly. She started to back away from the stranger, her foot caught on her pack, and down she went.

Fine with her. Maybe she'd hit her head and wake up in her bed and all of this was nothing but a dream.

Chapter Three

Simon lunged to catch this stunning traveler before she hit the ground, but he couldn't move fast enough. Kneeling beside her, he carefully pushed a lock of her hair from her forehead. Her eyes were shut, her breathing slow and steady. "Come now, lass. Wake for me."

She didn't. With gentle fingers, he brushed through her hair and felt for any lumps or tender patches. Finding none, he lifted her head, rested it on his knee, and waited for her to wake.

"When?" From when did she travel, and why? She wore a cotton shirt with perfect stitching. His eye traveled to her thigh and stuck there. Shorts were from a time in which he'd once lived. Memories of days running in the park, or on the playground with others in similar clothing, were etched so deeply in his past he had to close his eyes to reach it.

Forever ago.

It seemed it had been a lifetime since he saw this woman's garb worn by anyone. Even his own mother and aunt didn't bother any longer. Lizzy, his mother, rebelled against the clothing of this century for nearly five years before giving up the fight. His Aunt Tara gave up shortly after Simon and his mother arrived. Either way, Simon wasn't used to seeing women with their legs bare for anyone to gaze upon.

He liked it.

In a strange way, he missed it. Her sun kissed skin was free of any hair. Smooth. His hand itched to feel the silky surface. But before his fingers made contact, the woman winced and shuddered as she came awake, jarring him from his thoughts. If she'd been any other girl, he'd worry about the impropriety of her head being in his lap. This girl was from a different time, and he doubted she'd be shocked at his closeness. Well, at least not as much as a common lass from this time.

"There you are," Simon whispered.

Her jaw tightened, and her body went rigid.

"You're still here."

It wasn't a question. It was a statement that brought a smile to Simon's lips. "Aye."

"Where am I?"

Anyone else, he would have scoffed at the question. "Scotland."

She nodded, eyes still closed.

"That's good."

"You are not from Scotland." Easily deduced from her lack of accent.

"No."

"America then?" It was a trick question since America was little more than an unexplored land full of Indians at this date in time.

The girl nodded, smiled. "Yeah, California." Her eyes were still closed.

"Who's the leader...? I mean president?"

Her brow pitched together before her eyes sprung open. "Obama. Geez, I didn't hit my head that hard."

Bright blue eyes met his.

Beautiful.

Obama. Not a name he recognized. This woman must be from a future he hadn't experienced. The confusion marring the expression on her face as it searched his made him wonder if she knew what she'd done.

She gazed at him for several seconds with a multitude of emotions filling her eyes. "You're him," she finally said.

Simon held his tongue. If there was one thing he'd learned in this time, it was to let others speak their

18

piece before he offered his own. Patience was something he'd learned through the years. Not something practiced in this woman's America.

She knew him, but Simon knew nothing of her. Maybe she was sent from the future with a message. A warning. Lord knew he'd had plenty of them.

"What's your name, lass?"

"Helen."

When she didn't offer more, he asked. "You were looking for me?"

Helen shook her head.

It was his turn to look confused.

"You're not looking for me?"

"I'm looking for a child. Y-you look like someone I've seen before."

Her gaze moved to his plaid, her cheek was firm against his thigh. Helen scrambled to remove herself from his lap, but her eyes never left his. "Who are you?"

"'Tis you who showed up from nowhere, and you who needs to answer my questions. Where did you come from?"

She took in the woods around her, her eyes pitching together again. "I was walking in a…. I don't know, meadow, I guess. I dropped something." Helen glanced down at her hand. In it was a paper crushed within her palm. She uncoiled her fingers and flattened the paper to her other hand. "Then everything went crazy."

"A meadow?" Simon glanced at the trees above their heads.

"Maybe I did hit my head."

Simon didn't think the confusion on her face was false, but he didn't dare say anything that would damn him or his family. Better to keep quiet and learn.

Kong, he called his horse in his head.

The massive animal started toward them. Helen's focus changed from the woods to the animal.

"Where did he come from? Where did *you* come from?" Helen backed up a few steps.

Simon took a step toward her, and she scrambled

out of his reach. Stopping, he placed a hand in the air.

"I'll not hurt you, lass."

"You weren't here. None of this was here."

"Right. You were in a meadow, chasing that paper, then noise erupted, and darkness fell."

She was nodding now, eyes full of hope. "Right."

"Then everything stopped, and you were standing here."

Helen's head bobbed on her neck. "Exactly."

"Only you don't know where here is, do you?"

"Scotland. You said Scotland."

Where wasn't the right question, but Simon wasn't about to ask her the harder one.

"Helen?" He approached her slowly, as he would a child. His hand lifted to hers.

"What the hell is going on?"

Spunk, he loved a woman with passion. "I have answers, but I think you'd feel better in the presence of other women."

Even from her time, a woman alone in the woods with a man would be frightening. Unless the woman was a fighter, or police officer. This one looked soft and vulnerable. It was a very good thing he'd come upon her instead of any other medieval man.

"You're not a woman."

He laughed. "Nay. That I'm not. But my family is full of them. They can help."

* * * *

Helen had never been on a horse in her life, let alone with a man as solid as Fort Knox at her back. Yet here she was sitting ram-rod-straight on a huge horse with a huge man flush against her.

He looked nothing like any man she'd ever seen. Every ounce of his body looked as if it had been carved from stone, every muscle firmly in place. Dark locks of hair draped around his face, a scruff of facial hair afforded him a mysterious look any woman would appreciate.

The skin on her bare arms tingled, not in the way it

should considering she had no idea where she was, or more importantly, how she'd come to be there. It was because of the man whose muscular legs tensed against hers as they rode.

Somewhere in the back of her mind, Helen thought she knew him. A strange sense of déjà vu washed over her every time he spoke. She supposed it was like thinking you knew a celebrity simply because you've seen them on the big screen. Yes, that had to be it. The picture in the book resembled the man at her back, therefore she thought she knew him.

Get your head out of that book, she chastised herself. She ought to be thinking about where she was, or where her car had disappeared to. Maybe she'd fallen when she'd reached for the picture and hit her head when she fell. That would explain a lot.

Helen reached for the top of her skull, feeling for a knot.

Nothing.

"You didn't hit your head."

Statement, not a question.

"Excuse me?"

"You've not hit your head. Everything you see from this moment on is real. Remarkable, but real." His deep voice rumbled in his chest and stroked upon her back in a hauntingly familiar caress.

"How do you know my thoughts?"

He laughed. "I've been where you are."

The horse under her stuttered in his step.

"What's your name?"

He leaned back on the reins. The horse stopped.

Every noise in the forest waited for her next breath. Without being told, Helen lowered her voice. "What is it?" she whispered.

The man behind her went rigid. The reins in his hand fell to the side of the horse, raising alarm in Helen's blood. *What if the horse bolted without its master holding him tight?*

Helen bent over the horse, grasping for the leather.

"Shhh."

Crouched over the animal, Helen's gaze wandered beyond the trees, deeper into the forest. A forest that hadn't been there before the strange storm swept her away.

Heat inched up the right side of her face. She turned toward it and caught movement in the wood.

The man beside her turned his head to follow hers. His hand drew the sword strapped to the costume he wore.

The same clothing the man in the picture wore.

"What is—?"

His free hand clamped around her mouth, silencing her.

Every nerve in her body stood on end waiting for release.

Helen held still when the man behind her let go of her mouth and reached into a small pouch strapped to his thigh. He drew a jewel-encrusted dagger and pressed the hilt of it into her palm.

She started to tremble. Helen couldn't help her body's shudder any more than she could stop blinking her eyes. The forest seemed to wait, quiet with anticipation. Her breath held in the back of her throat for some sort of action.

Nothing prepared her for what she saw when it came.

On their right, three men bounded from the forest, two on horses, and the other on foot. They wielded swords and wore armor that should have been in a museum instead of on their backs. Still, they filled the air with battle cries and charged toward them.

The horse she rode stood perfectly still. Helen would have run for the nearest exit. Only when the closest man fell on them did the animal move. When it did, it backed away, and her dark hero took aim at their enemy's sword.

Metal scratched against metal while Helen grasped the dagger in her palm and held onto the horse's mane for balance.

This wasn't happening. Couldn't be happening. No one fought with swords any longer. The closest thing she could recall was knife fighting, like with the one in her hand.

Without looking, she knew this knife wasn't like any she'd held. And before her misguided youth decided on her current path, she'd held plenty. She now turned to that instinct. The one that had kept her alive on the streets of Hollywood when she'd run from the last foster home.

The men charging them meant to hurt them.

From the force of their strikes, they meant to kill them.

Helen refused to fall victim to anyone before she had answers to the many questions burning inside her head.

While her hero beat down one man with a sword, another descended upon them. Hardly fair, but these giant men didn't seem to care.

Black eyes met hers and skimmed to her legs astride the horse.

Helen couldn't see the expression on the man's face because of the strange mask he wore, but laughter lit his eyes.

She drew the knife in her hand in front of her, ever mindful of the man behind her beating his sword against the man trying to kill him.

The horse bolted forward, and Helen held on for dear life.

An arrow caught in a tree to her side, right as the horse skidded to a stop. It missed her by inches.

Three more men bolted from the forest, all more dire than the next.

Six to two.

Within seconds, they were surrounded.

The horse she rode stamped his foot on the ground.

Helen held her dagger in a fist, knuckles white.

"Hold your tongue," her hero breathed into her ear.

Not that she needed the advice. If there was ever a time in her life to close her mouth and open her ears it was now. These men stepped from the pages of time, each of them regarding her with a mixture of lust and speculation.

Helen had an uncanny desire to pull her shorts lower on her legs.

"MacCoinnich?" one of the men shouted.

Her hero shifted his gaze toward the voice.

"Looks like we've captured one after all."

The men circling them started to laugh.

The sound grated on her nerves.

"And with a lassie, too."

What was up with the *lass* thing? Unlike any time the man at her back had used the term, the man stating it now did so with vulgar intent.

Her hero sensed it too, or so she thought as she felt his body move closer to hers. Without thinking, Helen moved her hand from her thigh to his in acknowledgment. Hold your tongue, he'd told her.

She could do that.

"Put down your sword, MacCoinnich, and we'll let you live to see another day."

The man's accent was English, not the thick, Scottish brogue she'd heard since arriving in Scotland.

The animal under them pranced.

Helen held her breath.

A fight would be futile. They'd die. The men surrounding them were similar in stature to her hero, yet all of them had a deadened gaze behind their eyes. Haunting.

One man aimed an arrow straight at her chest. The thought of outrunning it would mean suicide.

"What do you want?" MacCoinnich asked.

"You, to start with. And then your companion. She appears quite inviting dressed as she is. Wouldn't you say, men?"

The leader led the laughter erupting around her. She knotted her fist into MacCoinnich's thigh.

This was bad. Very, very bad.

MacCoinnich's breath brushed against her ear. "Follow Kong, my horse," he uttered.

Maybe he had a plan. A plan of escape.

Yet as the thought solidified in her mind, their enemies drew closer.

Her hero lowered his sword, but his body screamed with tension.

The predatory cry of a bird filled the air and several of the men shot their attention above their heads. The horse carrying the warrior holding the bow pitched onto his back legs, forcing the man to lose his aim to stay on the animal.

MacCoinnich drew his sword high, and wrapped his free arm tightly around Helen.

All the horses started to prance, their riders struggled to get them under control.

Kong leapt toward an opening between the men, and it was all Helen could do to stay mounted. The other horses didn't seem to be able to move, but that didn't stop the men from fighting. One threw himself off his horse and clashed swords with MacCoinnich.

"Grab the girl!"

Kong's exit was blocked and the horse spun around.

Helen's gaze collided with one of the men trying to kill them. From the ground, he reached for her leg. She pulled her leg back, retreating from his fingers. And when he moved closer, she thrust her heel as hard as she could at the side of the man's head. When he fell back, another man took his place. This one slashed at her with a sword. The skin on her leg started to burn.

"Hold on, Helen," MacCoinnich said behind her. "Trust me."

The words left his mouth and the sky started buzzing with noise.

The man who'd sliced her leg open didn't stop to glance at the sky. He descended with death in his eyes.

Suddenly, her hero jumped off the horse, and Kong ran at breakneck speed into the forest with Helen crouched low over his back. She tightened her legs around his flanks, but still didn't think she could hold her seat. The voices behind her started to fade, but Helen didn't feel any relief from it. She didn't dare look back.

This was a nightmare.

Dammit, she wanted to wake up.

Kong's gait shifted from a full run to a slower gallop. The change jarred Helen and sent her tumbling off the side of the horse.

Air rushed from her lungs when she hit the ground.

Kong continued to run away, leaving Helen less than a half a mile from the fighting men and struggling for breath. Alone on an open path, she stumbled to her feet, ignoring the pain in her leg, and scrambled behind a large tree.

She needed to focus. Her breath came in short gasping pants, while her heart raced in her chest so quickly she could hear her own blood gushing through her veins.

The knife MacCoinnich had pressed into her hand was her only defense if the men returned. Helen held it in front of her, and her eyes darted, following every noise in the forest.

As adrenaline started to subside, the pain from her leg started to scream. Unable to avoid facing the injury any longer, Helen glanced down at the three-inch gash on her calf. It wasn't horribly deep, but it hurt like hell. Some gauze and an antibiotic was all she needed. She colored herself lucky since the sword that did the damage was large enough to amputate her leg with a single blow.

Using the knife, Helen cut away a portion of her shirt and pressed the cloth into her wound. With blood seeping through her fingers, she wondered if the scent would attract animals from the woods.

She had to keep moving. But where?

With the loose ends of the cotton tied together, she attempted to stand. Everything hurt.

After moving only a few yards in the direction the horse had run, Helen tripped on a stump.

Anger and frustration welled inside, threatening tears. "Dammit!"

Boy, did she want to sob big fat tears that would serve no purpose.

She didn't. Instead, she picked herself up off the ground and began walking again.

A twig behind her snapped.

She spun.

Two sets of angry eyes, belonging to two equally angry men, stared at her.

If these two managed to follow her, Helen couldn't help but wonder if MacCoinnich had died in the fight.

The thought of her life ending in a foreign land, at the hands of men dressed in ancient warrior garb, had her blinking back tears. One managed to escape, trickling down her cheek.

At the sight of her weakness, the men laughed. "No need to fret," one of the men said as he stepped closer to her.

"Oh, she should fret," said the other man who'd met her foot with his face. He didn't hold back his anger.

Helen backed up with each of their advancing steps.

Why had she left home?

More tears clouded her eyes.

She thought she heard a growl in the woods behind her, but couldn't risk turning away from the men to look.

Instead, Helen curled her arms into her chest and wept, "I want to go home. Please, just let me go home."

The world around her tilted and once again fell away.

Chapter Four

Amber MacCoinnich cried out in physical pain. "Not again." Grief swelled in her gut, doubling her over until she had to sit or risk falling. Her empathic gift suffocated her. The loss of Simon blanketed her with sorrow. She'd only experienced this feeling once before in her short life. It had happened years ago, when Grainna cursed her older brother Fin and his wife, Lizzy, sending them into the future. The memory of that loss swelled in her mind, even though Lizzy and Fin eventually made their way home.

The door to her room sprung open, her sister-in-law Lizzy tumbled through. "Simon's gone."

"Aye."

Her body ached with his loss. The void of a loved one's death was the only thing that compared.

Desperation marred Lizzy's face. Her son was gone. In a heartbeat, in a one blink of an eye—gone.

Amber closed her eyes and willed the pain gripping her stomach to recede. She focused her gift, reaching for some hope. But she didn't feel any. She had no way of knowing if Simon was dead, or swept away by some magical force.

She prayed it was the latter. The family would depend on her to reveal hope of Simon's safety. And each year her empathy grew, nearly crippling her.

"Mother?" Selma MacCoinnich pulled at Lizzy's skirts. The ten-year-old's blue eyes clouded with unshed tears. "What is it?"

Lizzy shook her head and patted her daughter's head. "It's okay. Find your grandmother and aunts."

28

Selma ran off and Lizzy closed the door behind her staring blankly at Amber with fear etched in her face.

Amber pulled Lizzy into a chair, although the physical connection caused Amber more pain. Her empathic gift felt like a curse during times of grief. It was as if she harbored the misery of everyone around her.

"Can you feel him at all?" Amber asked. Lizzy and her son shared a bond that once allowed them to speak to each other in their heads. As Simon grew, that bond severed. Left in its wake was what Lizzy described as a simple hum. A buzzing sensation told her, her son was well.

"No."

Amber didn't press. Soon her mother Lora and sister Myra rushed into the room. "What happened?"

Tara was fast on their heels.

"'Tis Simon. Lizzy can't feel him."

Lizzy sobbed. For Amber, the sound renewed her deepest fear, for Lizzy never cried. She was as strong as any Highland warrior.

Lora knelt beside Lizzy and gathered their hands together. "Shh."

"I can't feel him."

"I know, lass, but hold hope. I've not had any premonitions of death."

"If not death, then what?" Tara asked.

Myra ran her palm over her swollen belly as she spoke. "Could he have turned himself into an animal so small you're not able to sense him?"

Lizzy shook her head.

"What if he used the stones?" Amber posed the question, and the women all turned to stare at her.

"Did he ever say he wanted to?"

"Nay. But perhaps—"

Lizzy shot from the chair and fled the room. Amber knew her sister-in-law would search all the hiding spaces around the Keep where they'd hidden the stones. After Tara and Myra left, going in different directions,

Amber joined the search up the spiraled staircase to the tallest tower and into what appeared to be an abandoned room.

Behind a hidden door was a space occupied by one of the sacred stones—the stones the ancients charged her family with for their safekeeping—the time traveling stones, that hadn't been used for over a decade.

When Amber's fingertips touched the stone, it started to glow. She lifted it out of its home intending to take it to the others as proof.

As she started to stand, the stone in her hand grew hot. Fearing she'd drop it, Amber set it on the floor. Before her eyes, the stone split into several pieces. Light cascaded over the stone and created a searing heat. Amber backed away and watched as the broken stone mended itself back together.

When the light faded, and the temperature in the room dropped, the stone appeared unharmed, but beside it was a thumb size piece of the rock.

Determining the stones wouldn't burn her palm, Amber gathered them and searched out the women in her family.

She found them in her father's study, each with a bewildered expression on their face. Amber lifted both stones up. When she did, Lizzy and Myra pointed to the table on which they'd placed the other stones. Once Lora returned to the room all five stones sat beside smaller pieces.

"Should we look in the trunk?" Myra asked.

"Simon would never take that one." Lizzy said.

The trunk Lizzy spoke of housed the sixth stone. Safely tucked away to be used some 500 years in the future. Simon would die before compromising that one.

Lizzy fingered the smaller stones. "They had babies."

Myra, six months pregnant with her third child, laughed.

"What do you suppose it means?" Tara laid an arm

over Lizzy's shoulders.

"I've no idea." Lizzy lifted one of the tiny stones and inspected it closer. "There's writing on it."

Amber crowded her, taking a better look.

"Aye. 'Tis the same as the larger stones."

At the doorway to the study, the patter of small feet crowded in. Amber smiled into the faces of her nieces and nephews. Briac, Tara's oldest son, stepped forward, a strange pack dangled from his hand.

"Grandpa asked me to rush this inside," Briac said.

Lizzy gasped, and Tara walked to her son.

"What is it?" Amber didn't recognize the material or design.

"It's a backpack."

Amber still had no idea of what her sister-in-law spoke.

"Where did it come from?"

Selma stepped away from the other children and placed her hand into her mother's palm. "Simon's horse arrived without him."

* * * *

Simon wrapped his arms around the lass and braced for the fall.

A scream ripped from Helen's lips the moment gravity crushed them to the earth's surface.

They landed on something soft. The air around his body no longer felt cool or permeated with the smells of the forest. Simon jerked his head up, but kept the lass firmly within his hold. Protecting her from whomever may have followed them in the vortex.

Looking from side to side, he recognized the inside of a home similar to the one he'd spent the first decade of his life.

Under the trembling girl was a sofa. To the side of the couch was an end table and lamp. A mechanical noise filled the room and a high-pitched beep repeated every few seconds. Other than the noises of the apartment, there were none.

Simon sighed with relief and closed his eyes. No

bloodthirsty warrior had tumbled with them through time. But this was not how he thought his day would end when he awoke this morning. Ah, but the woman under him was wonderfully soft in all the right places,

"Get. Off. Me."

Simon had no desire to move. But move he must. And explain.

Helen's small fist pounded against his chest, her legs started to kick out from under him.

"Calm down, lass. I'm moving."

As soon as his weight lifted from hers, like a frightened rabbit, she scurried several feet away.

Simon stood to his six-foot-two height and glanced around the room.

"You're naked!"

A necessary evil when shifting from animal to man. Much like an animal wearing only its fur, Simon felt no shame in his nudity.

The woman in the room had other thoughts.

Simon watched a blush rush to her cheeks. The glow brought much-needed color to her face. Her eyes left a fiery path, as she looked her fill. When her eyes settled south of his stomach, his body responded.

Helen gasped and turned away.

Simon chuckled. A small throw blanket sat on the couch. He wrapped his hips into the material before saying, "I'm decent now."

Helen glanced over her shoulder briefly before turning back toward him. It was then he noticed the blood flowing down her leg beneath the makeshift bandage. Renewed concern for her wellbeing filled him.

"You're bleeding."

She glanced at her leg and laughed. "It wasn't a dream."

"I'm afraid not."

Simon stepped toward her and she pulled away. His dirk rose before her.

He lifted his hands. "Do you really believe I'll hurt you, lass?"

"I-I don't know what—"

"Come now. We need to clean that before an infection seeps in." Besides, giving the girl a task would put her mind to work and keep her from falling apart.

She nodded, and started walking toward another room. Simon caught her arm when her body tilted after applying weight on her swelling leg.

Inside the small bathroom, she turned on a light. The action brought a smile to his face. Electricity was a beautiful thing. He remembered it now.

Helen sat on the side of the tub, and lifted her leg to remove her shoes.

"I'm going crazy, aren't I?" She asked the question but never stopped her task.

"You're not crazy."

Simon helped her remove her sock and twisted the knob at the faucet. Water flowed through the pipes. Only when the water started to warm did he ease her leg to the tub. With a gentle hand, he untied the bloody rag and tossed it to the side.

"I was in Scotland this morning."

"As was I." Simon found a washcloth and pressed it under the water. Helen stared at the back wall and let him tend to her wound.

"We were in the woods a few minutes ago."

"That's right." She flinched when he placed the cloth on her leg.

"We're in my apartment. Now. In California."

So that's where they were. "This will hurt." Dirt had caked into her wound, and Simon started to scrub slowly away at the grime.

"How did we get here?"

Her question answered a few of his. She had travelled through time, but had no idea how she'd done so. Earlier, when a flash of light and a roar created by the fabric of time being stretched had detoured him from his task of returning to the Keep, Helen emerged from the fog. Never being sure who, or why, a person would travel from the future to sixteenth century

Scotland, Simon had kept his guard high.

This woman, who now held perfectly still while Simon ministered to her leg, must have sought something in the past. And she must also be Druid.

He wondered if she knew that last fact.

"I'm not entirely sure how you managed to move us here."

"I didn't do it." Her voice rose in defense.

Well, I certainly didn't do it. The time traveling stones were safely tucked away in the Keep and couldn't have been responsible for their travels.

"What were you thinking about right before we ended up here?" Simon continued to scrub her leg while they spoke.

"I thought I was going to die."

"Aye, what else?"

She shook her head and shivered, no doubt thinking of the men who chased her. "That's it. I was going to be killed in a Scottish forest by a bunch of freaks wearing costumes."

Simon reached back in his own memories of his childhood—to a time when he had believed he would die at the hands of evil. All he had wanted was to go home. Run to his mother and go home. "Did you beg to go home?"

"Yeah, I guess. Anywhere but there."

In his knowledge, no Druid was able to shift in time by merely wishing it so. There had to be stronger powers at work.

"Before you arrived in the forest," he kept questioning. The bleeding on her leg had stopped and his hand rested on her knee. "You were chasing a paper, right?"

She nodded and then jumped in alarm. "My backpack, the book."

Her shoulders slumped. "Things. I'm worried about things and I nearly died today."

Simon took her hands in his urging her to sit back down. He noticed gravel embedded in her palms and renewed his attention to her skin.

"Where were you before you ended up in the forest with me?"

"Just outside of Dundee. I pulled off the side of the road and was walking."

"Were you looking for something, or simply enjoying the day?"

Her eyes skirted across his briefly before pulling her hands away and reaching for a cake of soap. "Both."

"What were you looking for?"

"It's not important."

"I'll be the judge of that."

Helen pushed away from the tub and hobbled to a cabinet where she removed bandages. "I was following a hunch."

"A hunch?"

"Looking for a missing person."

"Are you a police officer?" Simon knew one personally. His pseudo uncle, Todd, spoke of hunches all the time.

"No."

"Were you looking for a loved one?"

"Just a kid."

Her own child, perhaps?

"No one I know. It doesn't matter." She lifted her leg up onto the countertop and covered her wound with ointment from a tube. "I'll never follow a hunch again. It isn't like I even know any of Simon McAllister's family or anything."

Everything inside Simon grew still.

At least he knew why Helen practically landed in his lap. She was looking for a child, however, not a man. He needed more answers. "How long has this child been missing?"

"Two and a half years. It's a cold case. None of the authorities are putting much effort into finding him."

That hurt. A missing teenage boy meant so little to this world. Simon blew out a long breath. Some pieces of the puzzle were snapping together.

"What is it?"

"Excuse me?" he asked.

Helen ran a hand over her arm as if chasing away the cold. "You know something."

Definitely Druid. The lass displayed a sixth sense that helped her *read* people. The women in his family were far better at it than the men.

With as much dignity as one could manage when wrapped in a blanket, Simon stood and made a grand gesture of bowing. "My lady, Helen, allow me to introduce myself."

She held perfectly still, waiting.

"Simon McAllister, at your service."

Chapter Five

Helen laughed in his face. "Right. Dude, you are *not* a fourteen year old kid."

"True. But Simon McAllister I am."

"The men in the woods called you MacCoinnich."

"A name my stepfather honored me with when he married my mother, Elizabeth McAllister, now Elizabeth MacCoinnich."

"You're not fourteen." So far away from fourteen, in fact, Helen needed to remind herself to keep her eyes glued to his or risk licking her lips while gazing at his very manly chest.

"You've just traveled from a forest in the Highlands to your apartment in California in only minutes. Believing I am the Simon McAllister you're searching for can't be impossible.

One crisis at a time. Emergencies were tumbling over themselves screaming for attention, but she could only deal with one drama at a time.

This would be easier with wine.

Without another word, Helen walked around the massive man in her bathroom and made a beeline for the kitchen. She found an unopened bottle of Cabernet and set it on the counter with a plop. The man watched her every move, but she didn't bother with explanations or even conversation. Not yet.

Scotland. They'd both been in Scotland an hour ago.

She rummaged through a drawer and found a corkscrew. Maybe she was dreaming. Yeah, that must be it. She was asleep. Why on earth would any dream of hers with a man draped in nothing but a throw, involve men slicing through her leg with swords? And, why the hell did it hurt so much?

Helen struggled with the cork for a couple of seconds before it popped free from the bottle. She poured a generous portion of wine into a tall, plastic glass before lifting it to her lips for a long drink.

She probably should have tried something stronger. Whisky. Leaning a hip along the counter, she watched the man in her apartment settle his very sexy ass on the backside of her sofa and regard her without saying a word.

Simon?

The boy in her picture had dark hair and blue eyes.

Helen went ahead and allowed her gaze to settle on her guest's face.

Dark hair, blue eyes.

Big deal. Half the men in this country had those characteristics.

After another drink, Helen let her shoulders relax. She couldn't completely. Her body was too charged to let go of the energy of the day. Humming. She was positively humming and had been since she'd first laid eyes on this man. That same hum had sizzled when he touched her.

Even his innocent touch while tending to her leg felt like a thousand butterfly wings brushing against her skin—similar to the buzz she'd felt before she'd found the book in Mrs. Dawson's library, and the same buzz that had struck when she'd first seen the picture of Simon.

What did that say?

If the man in front of her wasn't Simon, what would he gain by saying he was?

"You're Simon?"

"Aye."

"How old are you?"

"Thirty."

"Exactly how is that possible?"

"Time travel."

What did she expect him to say? Falling through a

rabbit hole and waking in the Land of Oz didn't hold a candle to this conversation.

"Time travel."

Simon folded his roped-with-muscle arms across his chest. His lips didn't crack into a chiding smile. He was serious.

"Two years ago, your time, my mother and I were whisked back in time, just as you were today. We found happiness there and decided to stay."

"Decided?"

He nodded. "Yes."

She took another drink. Damn glass wasn't full enough so she poured more wine. "If you decided to stay, how is it I found you in 2011?"

"You didn't. You found me in 1596."

Whisky. There had to be at least half a bottle somewhere. Helen shifted back to her cupboard and opened it wide. There it was. A few years ago, she'd had a boyfriend who liked Canadian whisky. *Thank God.*

The eyes of the man who called himself Simon followed her around the kitchen as she found a clean glass. Glancing at him, she went ahead and grabbed a second glass. After pouring the amber liquid, she handed him a drink, which he took with a nod.

Still he said nothing. It was as if he was giving her time to digest everything. Only offering answers to the questions she asked.

1596. "I guess that answers the questions about the men in costumes swinging their swords."

In a strange way, the time travel explanation sat easier on her mind than Simon being a thirty-year-old kilted man. Scratch that, naked man. She was about to ask what happened to his clothes, but didn't think she'd like his answer.

The whisky burned the back of her throat.

"If you decided to stay back in time, why are you here now?"

Simon narrowed his eyes. "That is a very good question, lass. One only you hold the answer to."

"I don't have any answers. I didn't think time travel was possible until today."

"So you believe me?"

Helen barked out a laugh. "Sure. Why not? This is all probably some crazy dream, and I'll wake up tomorrow in Scotland with a hangover."

"I understand why you'd wish that. But tomorrow you'll wake here in California. The hangover is a possibility if you continue to drink the rest of that bottle."

Licking her lips, Helen felt some of the sizzling buzz generated by Simon's presence start to numb. The threat of a hangover didn't deter her from lifting the glass to her lips again. A hangover sounded better than dealing with time travel sober.

"You think I'm the reason you're here?"

"You were searching for me, right?"

"I was."

"Then you *are* the reason I'm here. What you and I need to discover is how you shifted time so I can return to my family."

His family? Was he married? Did he have children of his own?

He finished his drink and set his glass to the side.

"I'm not sure I can help you."

"No need to worry about it tonight. We'll think more clearly in the morning."

In the morning? Did he think he was going to sleep in her apartment? She didn't even know this guy.

"Listen, I don't know if it's a good idea for you to stay here."

"You're safe with me." Simon walked around the couch and propped up one of the throw pillows for him to use.

"I don't even know you."

"That is changing with every minute. Besides, if you have no idea how you shifted time, there's no way for you to stop it from happening again. Facing those Highland warriors again, alone, might not have such a pleasant outcome."

Helen grimaced and finished the contents of her glass.

"I'll find you an extra blanket."

* * * *

A mild headache greeted Helen in the early morning hours. When she rolled over in her own bed, not the one costing her over a hundred dollars a day in Scotland, she couldn't deny the events of the previous day.

If the wound on her leg hadn't reminded her of medieval men and their massive broadswords, the huge doorstop of a man lying on her living room couch did. With a few words of warning not to answer the door, Helen slipped out of her apartment to find some clothes for Simon.

His naked chest was a distraction. And for all she knew, he was a married man. *Off limits*. Not that she should be thinking about whether or not he had a main squeeze back in a castle somewhere—not considering the craziness her life had turned into during the past forty-eight hours. Still, she wondered.

****

A pair of sweats, an extra large t-shirt, and a pair of shoes later, Helen arrived back in her apartment to find Simon dipping into some of the junk food in her pantry.

"Here." She thrust the clothes toward him. "I should ask you why you ended up naked, but my mind can't take a whole lot more."

A strange smile inched over his lips. His brow lifted in what Helen thought was admiration.

Simon snagged a potato chip and tossed it in his mouth before turning toward her bathroom. "I'll change."

They continued to talk through the thin walls of her apartment. "Any theories yet as to how I ended up in the sixteenth century?" She asked questions to avoid thinking of him dressing.

"The magic must have been very powerful for you to

41

have traveled without any aid."

"Magic?"

"What else do you think powers time travel?"

Helen fluffed the pillow on the couch and went around tidying the room, a nervous habit she developed since childhood. "I don't know, a fairy Godmother," she whispered to herself.

"What was that, lass?"

"Nothing. I just don't believe in magic."

"Now you're lying to yourself."

Simon stepped from the bathroom in the ridiculous clothes. They didn't suit him at all. The size of the shirt was a complete miss. It stretched across his chest and highlighted every muscle beneath. *Not bad, too small, but not bad.*

The baggy pants were too big. A shopping trip including his participation, would be necessary. Even so, he'd turn plenty of heads dressed the way he was.

"You're calling me a liar?"

"I said you're lying to yourself. You believe in magic, or at the very least, power beyond the average person's mind. You traveled all the way to Scotland because of a *feeling.*" Simon picked up the bag of chips and tucked his frame into a chair.

"That's not magic, it's intuition."

He glanced at a chip in his hand and waved it in the air. "I've missed these."

The silly grin reached all the way to his eyes, reminding her of the picture she had of him as a kid. "You really are him."

She slid down on the couch and stared.

"I am," he said around the chip as it made its way into his mouth. "Magic is very real, Helen. Not many people believe it exists because most people can't access it."

"But I can?"

He nodded. "It's in your heritage."

"I wouldn't know squat about my heritage. I'm an orphan."

Simon stopped chewing and placed his hand over hers. "I'm sorry."

Her hand heated under his, and she quickly pulled away. "It's nothing new. Nothing to be sorry about."

"Family is most important where I'm from."

Focus, Helen. The man needs to get back to his wife. "I'll bet yours is missing you already."

"Painfully, I'm sure."

"And I'm responsible for you being separated from them. I'm sorry."

Simon waved his hand in the air. "I'm not holding you responsible. But I do think you hold the key to my return. Tell me every detail that led you to Scotland."

She settled into the couch and explained what she could. "A few months ago I came across a pair of candlesticks at the auction house I work for. I'm a photographer," she explained. "Something about them...."

Oh, boy, she wanted to say "called to me" but didn't want to sound like a crack pot "I wanted to know more about them." That sounded better.

"And?"

"Apparently, your mother was involved with their original sale. The paperwork regarding the transaction had her name all over it. It was then I learned of your disappearance."

"And my mother's."

"Yeah, but it was you I felt a need to find."

Simon leaned forward, staring into her eyes. His eyes were soft eyes when he was relaxed, but she remembered how they'd turned hard during battle.

"Anyway. I told a friend of mine about what I'd discovered, and it was her that led me to the book."

"The book?"

"The one with your picture in it, a picture of you as an adult wearing a kilt. At least, I think it's you."

"Where is this book?"

"In my backpack tied to your horse."

Simon blinked a few times and looked away. "That's

43

good."

"Good? Thousands of dollars worth of camera equipment, and the book that probably has the answers to how we get you home, are stuck in your century, and we're here. How is that good?"

"Kong will return to the Keep, and my family will find your pack. They'll know I'm safe. 'Tis a good thing. They may even be able to travel here and help me return."

Helen's jaw dropped. "They can do that?"

"It's not been tried in some time, but aye, they can."

"Then we don't have to do anything. We can just wait for them to come and get you."

"I don't think so, lass."

"But you said—"

"I know what I said, but consider this. You had a compelling need to find me and you did. You defied everything I know of time travel to do so. My family may be able to come and get me, as you say, but until we know exactly how you traveled and are able to prevent you from doing it again, 'tis best I stay by your side to keep you safe. There are immense powers at work here."

Helen unfolded from the couch and started to pace. "Keep me safe? Why would you think I'm not safe?"

"What do you think would have occurred had I not been in the woods when those men happened upon us?"

She shuddered with the thought of being left alone with six men who didn't seem as if they'd seen a woman's bare legs before.

"It was probably a fluke...my traveling through time." Yet even as the words left her mouth, she knew better.

"Do you really believe that?"

"No. It sounded good though."

Simon laughed. The sound was rich and full of humor. For the first time in two days, Helen smiled.

"Tell me where you found this book you speak of. Maybe we'll find answers there."

Chapter Six

"Where is she?" Philip's brother Malcolm barked into the institutional style black, corded phone connected to his side of the glass.

"Scotland."

"Why is she there?"

He'd expected Malcolm's questions, but not his anger. "Following a lead."

One of the prison guards glanced Philip's way and narrowed his eyes.

"Calm down, Mal."

"I don't understand why you're not with her. She's my ticket out of here." Malcolm had been in the state penitentiary for over a year. There wasn't an attorney alive that could get him acquitted of the crime he'd been caught committing red-handed.

With Helen out of the country, Philip would be able to search her apartment and gather more information. He couldn't exactly explain that to his brother while cops surrounded them. "I'll be joining my *girlfriend*," he said for the sake of the cops, "In a few days. Maybe we'll be able to find more evidence that proves you're not guilty."

Malcolm took the hint and lowered his voice. "You shouldn't let her out of your sight. She's good for you."

Right. But trailing beside her all the way to Scotland would look questionable. He was her employer, after all. As much as he'd tried to engage the woman in a relationship, she hadn't budged. Maybe subtle had been the wrong approach. If Philip was sleeping with her, he'd know more about her inner thoughts.

He already had a plan to explain why he'd followed her to Scotland. First, he needed to check out her apartment.

"I'll see you in a week."

Malcolm frowned beneath his beard. "A week is like a year in here."

Yeah, well, next time keep your fucking hands to yourself. Philip tried his best to push the thought into his brother's head. Useless. Philip's little parlor trick worked on everyone he knew except his brother and Helen.

This was why Philip knew Helen was part of his solution to freeing his brother.

She held the power, only she didn't know it.

* * * *

The ride to Mrs. Dawson's home brought back many memories. The landscape sped past the open windows on the car. Everything looked bigger. Busier. People drove with cell phones to their ears completely disregarding everyone around them.

Anxiety prickled his skin when he and Helen walked through a department store to purchase a few things. People stared. As men eyed the woman at his side, Simon inched closer to make certain the men doing the staring knew she and Simon were together.

Simon wasn't the scrawny preteen boy he'd been in this century. Scotland and the MacCoinnich family had made him into the man he was now. This century would never have grown him as big. He knew the power of his body, of his mind. He took comfort in his Druid gifts. They were always there, even when he wasn't using them. He may not have his broadsword strapped to his hip, but he could protect Helen.

Protect.

That single word ripped through his mind when he witnessed her standing before his family's enemies with only a dagger to protect herself. When the energy of a time traveling vortex began engulfing her, Simon didn't hesitate and jumped in.

The Ancients had their way of placing the people in his family directly in harm's way, but always for the greater good.

Helen Adams needed his protection and he was honor-bound to deliver it.

The task wasn't difficult when his charge was as stunning as she was. Simon caught her staring at him several times. He'd catch a surge of desire bouncing off the lass, but she'd pull it back nearly as soon as she released it. Why?

Why did she deny her obvious attraction?

"You're staring at me."

He turned his torso toward her and continued his perusal.

Her hand twitched on the steering wheel.

"Didn't your mother tell you it was impolite to stare?" Her cheeks started to grow a rosy color.

"Aye."

"Then why are you doing it?"

"You're a bonny lass."

Her cheeks were full red now.

She opened her mouth to say something, and then closed it. Her lips turned down and her jaw tightened.

"'Twas a compliment. Meant to bring a smile to your lips, not a frown."

"You're flirting with me." She sounded surprised.

"I am."

Helen took her eyes from the road and shot a dagger from her eyes.

"The problem with that is?"

"Won't your *wife* have an issue with it?"

"My wife?" he laughed. "Did I marry when I wasn't looking?"

Helen's knuckles turned white on the wheel, her gaze moved to the road. Now the blush had returned but it was marred with embarrassment.

"I-I assumed when you talked about getting back to your family...I thought...."

Simon leaned forward and placed a hand over hers.

The spark he'd felt the first time they'd touched, rekindled, leapt, and ignited with the contact. Helen jumped, assuring him she'd felt the same ember. Perhaps the Ancients were bestowing Helen upon him and there wasn't evil lurking.

"I'm not married, love. Far from it."

"Oh."

"The family I talk about is the clan MacCoinnich. My mother's husband, my father by choice, is from a large family. All of us live in MacCoinnich Keep. We live, laugh, fight, and love each other."

"All of you live in the same house?"

He laughed again. "We call it a Keep. 'Tis the size of a castle."

"Oh."

Helen held her questions as they drove the rest of the way in silence.

Mrs. Dawson's modest home was behind gates and in a more remote part of the county. Helen announced herself to whoever answered the call and the gates opened.

"How do you know Mrs. Dawson?"

"Her husband was a collector of antiques. She'd commissioned us to sell a few things over the years. She and I hit it off."

Helen parked the car, and the two of them walked the short path to the front door.

Mrs. Dawson greeted them herself. The older woman had to be in her eighties. The cane in her hand helped her stand to a maximum height of maybe five-foot-three. A pair of kind eyes sparkled when they landed on Helen.

"I thought you were in Scotland," Mrs. Dawson said.

Helen leaned down and kissed the woman's cheek and pulled her into an affectionate hug. "I was."

"But you've only been gone two days."

Helen slid Simon a glance. "It's a strange story."

Mrs. Dawson turned her attention his way. A corner of her mouth lifted, and she shifted her eyes back to

Helen. "Who's the hottie?"

Helen's face instantly blushed and Simon laughed. He hadn't expected the older woman's delightful words.

"He's a…. You're not going to believe—"

Simon stepped up and bent slightly at the waist. "The hottie," he said winking, "is very pleased to make your acquaintance." He reached for Mrs. Dawson's free hand and lifted her fingers to his lips.

"I like your hottie." Mrs. Dawson placed the hand he'd kissed against her chest and smiled.

"He's not *my* hottie," Helen said.

"Well I like him anyway. Where are my manners? Come in. Come in. No need to stand on the porch."

Helen stood at Mrs. Dawson's right, and Simon offered her a hand on her left.

"Let's go to the day room. Have you eaten?"

"We ate before we left."

"How about coffee, then? I think Mavis made some chocolate chip cookies yesterday."

Chocolate wasn't something Simon ran across often in the sixteenth century and he wasn't about to pass up an opportunity to taste it now. "That would be wonderful."

Helen frowned. "But not necessary. We don't want to impose."

"You're never an imposition, Helen. You know better than that. Mavis?" Mrs. Dawson called out to the empty hall.

The woman Simon assumed was Mavis stepped into view. "Yes, Mrs. Dawson?"

"Please bring a pot of coffee and your delicious cookies for my guests."

Mavis nodded and disappeared as Mrs. Dawson led them into her day room.

Once seated, Mrs. Dawson asked. "Tell me what I'm not going to believe."

Helen ran her hands over her thighs and her spine stiffened.

"'Tis best to just say it," Simon suggested. He

49

already knew Helen trusted Mrs. Dawson and intended to tell her the truth.

After meeting the woman, he understood a little more about the bond these two had formed. Helen told him Mrs. Dawson and her late husband weren't able to have children of their own. Mrs. Dawson treated Helen like a granddaughter. And Helen loved her for it. The woman was the closest thing to family Helen had.

"Okay, here it goes. But keep an open mind."

"Don't I always, dear?"

Helen smiled. "This is...Simon McAllister."

A slow, methodical shift of the old woman's chin and her eyes met his. Her stare pinned him down. She said nothing while considering Helen's words.

The clock on the mantel above the fireplace ticked.

Helen held her breath.

Simon waited.

A small ache touched the back of his head. Instead of fighting the ache, he took a deep breath and opened his thoughts. Mrs. Dawson might not be asking one question with her lips, but she was searching for the truth with her mind. Simon felt her inside his head.

Druids had a way of reading other people's intent. He couldn't help wondering if the act was subconscious or intentional.

Mrs. Dawson was Druid.

No wonder she and Helen 'hit it off'. They were kindred spirits.

Did Mrs. Dawson know of her gift? Or had she walked through life oblivious of her heritage?

"Aren't you going to say something?" Helen asked.

Mrs. Dawson lifted a hand, quieting Helen.

Mavis stepped into the room and filled the table in front of them with the refreshments. Mrs. Dawson thanked her and asked her to close the door behind her.

"When did you leave Scotland, Helen?" Mrs. Dawson didn't move her eyes from his as she spoke.

"Yesterday."

"If you left Scotland yesterday, and you are Simon

McAllister." She pointed a finger at his chest. "Then every question I have is going to have a magical answer and not a logical one." Mrs. Dawson finally turned toward Helen. "Start at the beginning and don't leave a thing out."

"You believe in magic?" Helen asked.

"There's a lot about me you don't yet know. Now from the beginning."

Helen blew out a sigh and started to talk.

Simon relaxed into the sofa after swiping two cookies from the plate.

* * * *

The events of the past two days rolled off Helen's tongue in a steady stream of words. Mrs. Dawson kindly folded her hands in her lap and listened. Not once did she scoff or raise an eyebrow in disbelief.

Simon devoured the plate of cookies and didn't offer one syllable while Helen told her tale.

"I still have a hard time believing magic is real. But you can't argue with living proof." Helen pointed at Simon.

He awarded her with a wink and heat surged to her face. They really didn't have room in all this for flirtation. So what if he wasn't married. He still lived in a completely different time. A time he wanted to return to. Not that he didn't appear completely comfortable sprawled on Mrs. Dawson's sofa sipping coffee as if he had nothing better to do. There was nothing about his demeanor screaming anxiety. He didn't even seem prepared to defend what Helen was telling Mrs. Dawson.

"I think Mrs. Dawson believes in magic, lass."

After a half an hour he finally spoke. His tone was a little condescending, and his assumption of Mrs. Dawson's beliefs niggled at Helen's nerves.

Simon didn't know Mrs. Dawson. Did he?

"We've been here for less than an hour and suddenly you're the authority on Mrs. Dawson's emotions?"

Simon sat forward. "Aye."

Talk about arrogant. Before Helen could protest, Simon directed his next words to Mrs. Dawson. "This lovely woman believes in magic because she's experienced it herself. Haven't you?"

"There have been a few things Mr. Dawson and I have seen."

"What? Why didn't you tell me?"

"I didn't want to scare you, dear. When an old woman starts talking about magic, men in white coats tend to arrive late at night and take her away."

"I would never have done that."

"Maybe not you, but others." Mrs. Dawson leaned forward and patted Helen's hand. Her weathered, old hand held on as she continued. "The night we found the book, don't you remember the wind kicking up inside the house?"

"A window blew open."

Mrs. Dawson actually rolled her eyes and patted Helen's hand again. "Go look at my windows."

Helen's gaze shifted to the wall of windows lining the room.

"Go."

At the window, Helen touched the modern locks on the double paned glass. "Are the windows in the study the same?"

"Mr. Dawson insisted on replacing everyone in the house to cut our electric bill."

"Then one must have been opened that night."

"Helen, I'm an old woman. I wear sweaters when it's 90 degrees. Do you really think I'd leave a window open?"

Helen glanced beyond the glass to the beautiful garden outside. Mrs. Dawson's long-stemmed variegated roses were starting to bloom and a deep orange hummingbird stopped at her feeder for a snack. "So what caused the window to open?"

"I'm not certain. My guess is Simon could answer that question."

Turning on her heel, Helen met Simon's gaze. He smiled with one corner of his mouth.

"Well?"

"Magic, lass. There are forces at work here driving the events of the past days. Our lives are intertwined, somehow, and it will be up to us to determine why."

"I thought we were just trying to figure out how to get you home."

"That, too. There is a reason I'm here. A reason you were looking for me to begin with."

"I was curious about how a child could disappear without a trace."

"'Tis more than that."

"Nope, that was it," she lied. She didn't care for how Simon assumed he knew everything going on inside her head. Didn't want him thinking he *could* get inside her head.

"Are you sure?"

"Yep." Helen looked away.

Mrs. Dawson placed her hands on the edge of her chair and started pulling herself to her feet.

Simon jumped to his and assisted her. "Allow me."

Mrs. Dawson took his arm and didn't let go. "If there are any answers here, they'll be in the study. Mr. Dawson collected tomes of work regarding folklore and magic. We were fascinated by the unknown."

Helen could only watch as Simon listened intently to Mrs. Dawson. Trailing behind the two of them, she was awarded with Simon's broad back, narrow waist, and perfect ass. An ass she'd seen completely...along with his other fine attributes. He might be arrogant, but as Mrs. Dawson intuitively stated, he was a *hottie*.

Once inside Mr. Dawson's study, Helen was once again captivated by the sheer enormity of the room.

The architecture here was filled with floor to ceiling bookshelves, overflowing with books dating back hundreds of years. Thick plush carpets divided the dark mahogany floors. The fireplace filled one wall. Candles stood on top of large decorative spindles making it possible for a reader to finish a novel if the electricity failed. Deep leather chairs dotted the room, adding to the masculine pulse of the space.

Even with the floor to ceiling windows allowing in natural light, the room felt dark. Mr. Dawson collected books and artifacts from libraries throughout Europe and Scotland.

"If there is any hope of finding answers in a book, it will be in here," Mrs. Dawson announced.

Once Mrs. Dawson was safely deposited in a comfortable chair, Simon stepped up to the first bookcase and ran his hand along the spines stacked on it.

"How did you find the book you lost, lass?"

The sheer number of books made the task of finding a clue overwhelming.

"One night Mrs. Dawson and I were talking about those candlesticks, and I decided to see if there was any reference to them in here. As I started picking through the books, I kept thinking of the picture I had of you as a child."

"Then the book found her," Mrs. Dawson added.

"Ahh, I see." Simon removed a book from the shelf and carefully opened it for inspection. He sighed and replaced it. "This may take more years than I'd care to spend in this century."

"It is a mountain of books. My husband never could open every one, let alone read them."

Helen watched as Simon touched a few more. "Do you have any idea what you're looking for?"

"Of course."

So cocky.

"What?"

"Answers."

Helen grunted. He was winging it.

Mrs. Dawson laughed. "I'll tell Mavis to prepare dinner. I think you'll both be here for a while."

Simon quickly came to the woman's side to help her stand. "Would you mind helping me with something first?" he asked.

"Of course."

Poor Mrs. Dawson was already putty in this man's hands. His Scottish accent and easy charm probably opened many doors.

Once Mrs. Dawson was on her feet, Simon stepped around her and closed the study door.

Helen mutely stood and watched him walk around the room, rearranging several unlit candles.

"What are you doing?"

"You'll see. There's no guarantee this will work, but it's worth trying."

"What's worth trying?"

Simon apparently finished what he was doing and stepped up to Helen and Mrs. Dawson. "I told you most people don't believe in magic because they can't tap into it."

"Right." Where was he going with this?

"I'm not one of those people."

Before Helen could utter her next question, Simon waved his hand in the air and the wicks to the candles lit. Flames topped every candle in the room.

No wonder the man had a cocky air about him. He had a right. Helen stared in fascination at the flickering flames. "How did you…? Never mind,"

Simon smiled and reached both his hands out. "Take hold of each other," he directed.

Although she felt silly standing in a small circle holding hands, Helen didn't break away. Curiosity over what would happen next ruled her every breath.

Simon's hand grew warm in hers. When he started to speak, it felt as if it were on fire.

"In this day and in this hour, we call upon the Ancients' power."

Helen's hair brushed against her shoulders as a warm breeze drifted around the room. With wide eyes, Mrs. Dawson's lips split into a huge grin.

"My windows are closed," she said, laughing. "And it's cold outside."

Helen slid a glance to the window anyway.

"Deliver the books to help us see, what will be our destiny. If the Ancients will it so, give us a sign so we will know."

The singsong rhyme drifted from Simon's mouth and lifted high. Helen wasn't sure what was supposed to happen, if anything. But when books flew off the shelves and stacked themselves on Mr. Dawson's desk, all she could do was clutch Simon's hand and gasp.

The wind died down and the candles flickered out.

On the old desk sat several piles of books, five to ten deep.

"How did you...?"

Simon sought her gaze and said. "I'm a Druid, love. As are you and Mrs. Dawson."

"Druid?"

"Aye. I'll explain while we're doing our homework. Seems the Ancients aren't in a hurry for us to find the answers."

"You realize I have no idea what you're talking about, right?"

Mrs. Dawson laughed and let go of her hand. "I'll have Mavis prepare dinner."

Chapter Seven

Three hours later, they were no closer to finding an answer than when they'd called the Ancients for help.

Simon had explained his heritage, what he believed was Helen's and Mrs. Dawson's heritage, too, although he knew Helen doubted his words. In fact, as the day had drawn on, she'd become more and more distant.

Mrs. Dawson retired for the evening, suggesting they stay as long as they desired. She'd even had her helper prepare rooms for them to use if they chose to stay the night.

At Helen's suggestion, they'd piled the books into categories. Only those categories were vaguely similar. There were books on myths, folklore, and magic. There were many directed at Celtic lore while others spoke of ancient witches.

The Ancients may have narrowed their search, but the common thread eluded them.

"This is useless." Helen closed the book in her hand with frustration.

"The answers are here."

"Just because a bunch of books fly off the shelf, doesn't mean they have the answers."

Simon sat back and watched Helen's temper surface. "You've seen books fly off the shelf before, then?"

"Don't be a smartass."

"The answer is here, love, trust me."

Helen pushed out of her chair. "Trust you? I don't even know you. And why do you insist on calling me love or lass? I'm neither."

Where had this angry outburst come from?

"I don't mean any harm by using these endearments. They're meant to put you at ease."

"Yeah, well, they're not working. Besides, I think you should actually know someone before you start using endearments. It's kinda like a man in a black van hanging outside an elementary school saying, 'Come here, darling little girl, and pet my puppy.'"

She paced the room while she spoke.

Her words penetrated his mind and tightened his jaw. "I'm not an evil man hiding behind a small animal."

"I don't know what kind of man you are. Sure, we've been on some kind of cosmic rollercoaster together, but I don't know you from Adam." Her voice was elevating; her pace became more frantic. She reminded him of a caged animal needing to run.

"What has you upset, lo—" Simon stopped his words, not wanting to push her further.

"You know, when you shoot flames from your fingertips, you might give a little warning next time. That's some startling crap. Mrs. Dawson's not a young girl. She could have had a heart attack when these books started flying around."

Ahh, so that was the problem. The lass was worried about her friend.

Simon stood and walked to her side. "Mrs. Dawson is a strong woman."

Instead of backing away, she placed her hands on her hips and glared. "You're so arrogant. You've been in my life for what? Ten minutes? Mrs. Dawson ended up in the hospital last fall with angina. Her heart can't take a whole lot of stress. Your little stunt today could have killed her."

A trickle of guilt slid over his skin. Mrs. Dawson may be stronger than Helen believed, but she was elderly, and he'd do well to remember that.

"I'm deeply sorry for causing you worry, lass."

Her chin shot up and surprise lit her eyes. "Good. You should be."

Simon stepped closer and felt the heat of her skin. She smelled of the strawberry shampoo she used in her hair. Helen's hands slid from her hips and fell to the side.

"'Tis time we clear up a few things in your lovely head about me."

He stepped closer, and Helen, the wise girl, took a step back until her bottom met the edge of the desk. She reached behind her to steady herself and keep from falling.

Like a predatory cat cornering his prey, Simon towered over Helen, watching her body twitch and her eyes travel over his.

"Really?" Her voice wavered. After clearing her throat, she asked. "Like what?"

Simon licked his lips and glanced at hers. "I'm not evil."

"Uhm...." Her eyes never left his mouth while he spoke.

"And I'd never lure a child into my presence."

Simon leaned into her, their thighs touched and Helen's breathing started to quicken. He placed one hand on the table beside her, leaving her very little room to escape should she want to. From the hunger in her gaze, and the heat of her body, he didn't believe she would.

"A woman, however, might tempt me to entice her attention."

"I-I didn't mean to suggest you're some kind of pervert."

"Yet your words said exactly that. Perhaps I should show you my desire lies in the company of women and not girls."

Helen opened her mouth to respond, shut it, and froze.

Simon focused on her pert little nose and soft rosy lips. A firm set of breasts brushed against his chest with every quick breath Helen took. He wasn't sure who was breathing faster, him or her.

Her mouth opened again, and Simon moved in to make his claim.

In the next instant, a leg wound around his and a firm palm pushed him squarely against his sternum.

He hit the floor with a thunk, scrambling his brain and his aroused lower body parts.

"What the H. E. double L. do you think you're doing?"

"It's called a kiss, love, or hasn't anyone from this time introduced you to them?" With as much dignity as he could muster from the floor, Simon lifted his taut chin in her direction.

"I know what kissing is. Don't be absurd." The blush rising up her neck spoke of innocence. An innocence Simon didn't think Helen could possibly know. Then again, perhaps he was wrong about her.

Maybe the tough act was just that…an *A.C.T.*

Simon shook his head. Thinking of *K.I.S.S.I.N.G.* her was making him *C.R.A.Z.Y.*

He froze. Why was he spelling things out in his mind? He didn't care for spelling tests when he was in school, he certainly didn't think of how to spell words now.

Helen must have rattled more than his pride.

H.E.L.E.N.

Without ceremony, Simon shoved himself from the floor.

"What is it?" she asked, backing away like a frightened child.

Innocent. Her body language screamed it. And he'd nearly destroyed the trust they were building with a simple seduction. He wanted to reach out to her now and offer comfort, but he didn't think she'd welcome his touch.

"The books," he said, backing away. Best to give her some space.

Confusion raced over her brow.

He scrambled to the front of the table and gathered the books they'd already examined. He positioned them next to each other on the table.

"What are you doing?"

"The answer is here."

She stood beside him now, farther away than she'd been all day.

Looking over his shoulder, she asked, "Where?"

Focus, Simon. "Each book has a different title. Each title starts with a different letter." He found the book he'd passed several times without so much as a glance. *Hence Forth.* "This starts with an H." Simon placed it at the top left of the table and removed the other books to make room for others. He shifted through several books before he found the one he sought. *Enlightening.*

"E."

Both of their hands fell on the next novel, *Living.*

Helen pulled her hand away.

"These book titles are an acronym?"

"Aye. All this time we've looked for what's inside, but what we see on the outside is what we wanted."

They spelled out Helen's name and stopped. Several more books were stacked up on the table. They sat back and studied the books that spelled out her name.

"I think you're onto something," she told him.

They managed Helen's name but then faltered. There were plenty of books left over with many different outcomes for an acronym.

"Let's write down the first word of the books and I'll find a program that will calculate possible word combinations." Helen scribbled the names of each of the books onto a piece of paper as they spoke.

"You mean a computer program?" It had been years since he'd thought of a computer.

"Yeah."

"I'd forgotten how useful they were." They were easy to live without, in sixteenth century Scotland.

"You really have been living in the dark ages, haven't you?"

Simon shook his head. "Actually, the dark ages of Scotland were long before the turn of the century—the tenth century—or so I'm told. I do believe the time in which I live in Scotland will be remembered as the Renaissance period."

"The word Renaissance makes it sound romantic. The guys trying to take me out with a sword ruined a perfectly good image in my brain."

"The strong survive. If one isn't strong, they must be wise enough to avoid conflict and keep quiet to avoid detection." Simon moved to the couch while they talked, giving her as much space as she needed.

Helen wrote the names of the books down and pushed the papers aside. "How do the women protect themselves?"

"Their men protect them."

"What if they don't have a man to protect them?"

"Even the widows have the protection of Laird Ian. No one is abandoned when in need of our assistance."

"Is that why you helped me out? Because you'll help anyone on your grandfather's land?"

"I'd like to think I'm an honorable man. Leaving a lone maiden scared and out of place would have damned me to a thousand years in hell. I'd have not been able to live with myself had I turned my back on you."

Did she really believe he'd have left her alone if given the choice? Simon couldn't help but wonder why she had such a low opinion of her worth. Or maybe she carried a low opinion of others.

"Maiden?"

"It doesn't matter," he said, cutting her off. "The men trespassing on our land wouldn't have offered their protection."

"They looked like they wanted to kill me."

"Killing you would have been merciful."

She shivered. "That's a pleasant thought."

"Consider it a warning. If you managed to travel back to my time without me, you must stay in hiding until you can get word to my family. They will offer you protection."

Helen's hands were restless in her lap. The

conversation might be uncomfortable, but it could save her life. "I'd have to trust someone to get a message to your family."

"A wise person listens and studies who they approach before doing so."

"Like you did with me?"

"You left me little choice. But had I stumbled upon you, I would have watched long before introducing myself."

Helen hid a yawn behind her hand. "I don't plan on returning to the sixteenth century, so your warnings really aren't needed."

"You chose to travel there before?"

"Well, no."

"Then heed my words, Helen. I can't be with you every moment of your day. Unless you want me by your side day *and* night."

Helen's head shot up, her eyes grew wide. "Ahh."

"Calm yourself, lass. I'm only kidding."

She wiggled a finger in his direction. "Men."

Simon laughed, knowing he'd given her a chance to regain some of her earlier composure.

"I'm going to bed," she announced. "Alone."

"Sleep well."

Simon watched her turn to leave the room. When she reached the door, he called out. "Helen?"

"Yeah?"

"It might be wise to leave your door open in the night. In case something were to happen."

With a nod, Helen left the room.

Simon waited until he heard her footsteps travel up the stairway and into the room Mrs. Dawson encouraged her to use. His was one, not far down the hall, but he didn't intend to use it.

He glanced at the books one last time before turning off the lights. By the time he passed Helen's room, her light was off but her door was open a few inches.

After pulling back the covers on his bed, Simon stepped to the bathroom adjoining his guest room and removed his clothes.

Helen might not want Simon McAllister in her bed, but he wasn't about to leave her alone. They were no closer to finding out how she traveled in time, and there was no guarantee it wouldn't happen again.

No, Simon, in one form or another, would be by her side to protect her.

Standing in front of the mirror, Simon closed his eyes and allowed the shift. He pictured himself shrinking, the hair on his back sprouting. Everything in his body turned to flexible, expanding in some places, contracting in others. He reached for the floor and held in the haunting cry of pain.

* * * *

Helen punched her pillow with a fist and attempted to find a comfortable position. After her day, she was having a hard time falling asleep.

Talk about a confusing night.

Talk about a confusing man.

Simon McAllister or MacCoinnich, whichever name he wanted to use for the day, riddled her mind with questions and unease. Every hour he seemed to deliver one more compelling puzzle for her brain to decipher.

First was the undeniable fact that he'd traveled through time. Was a veteran of the sport in fact. The first time he'd ripped away time and space and traveled to the sixteenth century Scotland was because his mother wanted to prove his aunt was healthy and happily married to a Highland warrior. The second time was to return home so he could finish his first year in junior high school.

Things were sketchy from there. Simon told Helen he and his mother were forced back to the sixteenth century because of an evil woman who threatened all of Scotland. He didn't elaborate about how or why. He simply said it took some time for the family to figure out how to destroy her.

Destroy had been his word. So Simon had killed, or at the very least been a party to another human's death.

Then again, how could she think he was anything but a medieval killer? The way he'd gone after the men in the forest suggested bloodshed wasn't new to him.

Now that she reconsidered the events she'd witnessed, how had Simon escaped the men in the forest? There had been six of them. Only two caught up with her.

What was up with the Druid thing? The man literally shot flames from his fingers. A part of her, an adolescent part, was in awe of his ability. He'd made a flippant comment about how all Druids were capable of the task, even her, with practice.

Yeah, right!

She'd had a hard time mastering the fine art of snapping her fingers. Flinging fire across the room was not on her list of talents.

The thought of warm flames brought heat to her cheeks and reminded her of their near kiss. The fullness of his lips close to hers.

Electricity to the tune of a zillion volts simply didn't compare. She hadn't really expected it. Really didn't expect to have shoved him on his ass. Call it a twitch, instinct even. She'd been well practiced at keeping men away. Thanks to the foster homes and would-be father figures early in her life, Helen's trust in men didn't come quickly. She'd learned that men eager to catch her attention usually disappointed her. There had been very few she wanted close.

Simon sorely tempted her.

Helen wanted to believe he was honorable. But he was a man. A masculine, sexy chunk of the opposite sex who didn't compare to any man she'd had the privilege of knowing.

I'm never going to get to sleep with all this chatter in my head!

Helen battered her pillow again and attempted to clear her mind of all things Simon.

She'd just closed her eyes when a soft mewing noise forced them open. Small furry paws pounced up on the foot of her bed and reflective eyes regarded her with caution.

"I didn't know Mrs. Dawson had a cat." Helen said to her feline companion. The large midnight black cat tilted its head to the side, taking cautious steps her way as if waiting for an invitation to curl up.

"Who are you?" Helen asked the cat while reaching over to pet the beautiful coat.

The cat rubbed its face into her palm and purred. "You're certainly friendly."

Helen scratched the cat behind the ears. "Are you a Tom or a Tammy?" She looked and smiled. "Hi, Tom. I'm sure that's not your name, but it will have to do. I don't usually sleep with strangers...." Her words drifted while the cat took up residence at her side. He circled a couple of times before making himself comfortable.

"Well, okay then."

The cat licked his paws and settled his head against her hip. He watched her intently, stared actually.

At least the cat had forced Helen's thoughts to something other than the man sleeping in the next room. Helen stroked the cat's back until he purred and his eyes drifted close.

For what it was worth, the cat offered some comfort and within minutes, Helen was in a world of dreams. Dreams of Highland kilt-wearing men who seduced women like they'd gone to school to learn the art.

Chapter Eight

The next morning the cat was gone. By the time Helen showered and left her room, thoughts of her furry bedfellow disappeared, and Simon refilled every corner of her brain.

It was damn unnerving. Men weren't to be trusted, even a Druid man with a hero complex. A serious sword swinging, damsel in distress saving, follow me I know what I'm doing, hero complex. His disturbing words about being uncertain if she'd vanish out of her comfortable world and find herself thrust into his at any moment, gave her nightmares. Life-size nightmares where Simon didn't reach her in time, and the two smelly medieval men latched on to her in the overbearing way men did to weak women.

But she wasn't a weak woman. Not anymore.

Knowledge gave her control and control gave her power.

They were missing a piece of vital information about how she'd managed to get to the sixteenth century, and Helen was hell-bent on finding out what it was.

In the kitchen, Simon sat with a steaming cup of coffee, his eyes half open. "You look like how I feel," Helen said as she crossed over to the pot and poured herself some much-needed caffeine.

"Sleep here is difficult."

"It has to be more comfortable than what you're used to."

"What makes you think that?"

Helen sat across the table from him and sipped her

coffee.

"I'd think without electricity it would be either too hot or too cold. I doubt you have duel-pained windows and insulation."

He nodded. "You have a point there. Yet each room has its own fireplace for warmth. In the hotter months, we keep the windows open to catch the breeze. It isn't as bad as you may think."

"That's what people say who live back east. Cold is cold and hot is hot. No way around it."

"Aye. You're right on that count. But the noise here is suffocating. 'Tis difficult to clear my head."

Helen narrowed her eyes and noticed the strain setting into his temples, stress she hadn't seen the day before. "Mrs. Dawson's house is quieter than my apartment."

"It's deafening."

"How can you say that?"

Simon reached over and carefully covered one of her hands with his. "Close your eyes."

His warm thumb stroked her index finger and sent a swift current up her arm. "Please," he said.

Helen lowered her eyes lids. "What are we doing?"

"Shh, just listen."

She didn't hear anything. Not even a television in another room, or an ambulance screaming outside. As she started to shake her head, Simon held onto her hand tighter.

"Do you hear the refrigerator?"

"Of course, but it isn't loud."

"Not loud, but there. The hum and click of it going on and off. I hear the furnace running, the clock in the hall ticking, the coffeemaker percolating, and there is some kind of machine running outside."

"It's a lawnmower," she told him, hearing it now for the first time.

"A dog is barking and an airplane is flying overhead." His hand squeezed hers again as he added, "Even the mice in the attic are scratching inside the walls."

"You hear the mice?" Her eyes sprung open.

A strange look of guilt passed over his face. "My point is it's noisy. Electricity and technology are noisy."

Helen removed her hand from under his. "Small price to pay for conveniences if you ask me."

"Spoken by someone who's never awakened to quiet mornings where only the sun interrupts their sleep, where alarm clocks are unheard of, and the smoke drifting away from a cook's fire generates the only pollution in the air. I've lived in both worlds, Helen, and this one is loud and suffocating." His voice sounded full of longing, and his gaze drifted beyond her out the kitchen window.

"We'll find a way to get you home," she assured him. "We will."

An hour later, they'd packed the books into boxes and loaded them into the trunk of her car. Mrs. Dawson tried to encourage them to stay longer, but Helen didn't want to impose. Besides, she needed the use of her computer back at her apartment. Mrs. Dawson's ancient computer was a dinosaur, and she didn't have access to the Internet, rendering it useless for their purpose.

After she parked her car in the secured garage, Simon removed two of the boxes to carry, insisting she leave the other one for him to retrieve.

"I can carry the box."

"But you don't have to. I'm here."

She moved to grab the box anyway. "I'm used to taking care of myself."

"You've provided for me ever since I arrived, I need to do something useful."

Helen knew it was a trick to get his way, but what the hell. She didn't feel like lugging the box anyway. "Fine."

Simon smiled and followed her into the building. She held the door open for him and led him up the stairs. The complex had an elevator, but Helen seldom used it.

"I need to call the hotel in Scotland and tell them to send my stuff back. How am I going to explain my sudden departure?"

"Tell them you had a family emergency."

Not that she had a family, but the hotel didn't know that. "And the car I left in the field?"

"You can tell them it broke down."

"Yeah, I guess."

If carrying thirty pounds of books up three flights of stairs was tiring, Simon didn't say. His muscular arms hardly strained under the weight. His sword was probably heavier, she guessed.

Drawing her eyes away from Simon's beefy arms, she opened the door to the third level of the complex, took two steps into the hall, and froze. Philip, her boss, was exiting her apartment.

Simon collided into her back, and Helen quickly turned and pushed him back into the stairwell.

"What is it?"

"Shh!" *What the hell is he doing coming out of my apartment?* How had he gotten in? Her mind raced and her heartbeat skipped. She needed to poke her head through the door to see more but was afraid he'd see her. He knew she was supposed to be out of town, so he wasn't there for a social call. Not that he'd ever been to her home.

Helen grabbed the boxes from Simon and dropped them to the ground. "Quick, look down the hall."

Simon stiffened beside her, but did as she asked without question.

"What do you see?"

Simon retreated from the hall. "A man with short brown hair walking the other way."

Helen pushed past Simon and peeked for herself. Philip slipped around the corner and the chime from the elevator rang.

"What is amiss, lass?"

"That man came from my apartment."

Simon's spine straightened, his eyes narrowed.

Helen leaped over the boxes and grasped the handle on the door.

A large hand covered hers and stopped her. "Not this time." Simon shoved in front of her. "Stay here."

Fine, he could go in front, but she wasn't cowering in a stairwell. Helen walked behind him.

Simon scowled but didn't argue when she glared at him with renewed resolve.

At the door to her apartment, he twisted the handle.

Finding it locked, he opened his palm for the key. Luckily, Helen kept a spare at Mrs. Dawson's home, or she'd be breaking into her own place, covering up whatever damage Philip might have done.

She kept glancing around to make sure Philip didn't double back.

The hall was clear.

Simon unlocked the door and stepped inside. She followed, stuck to his back. Her apartment looked like it did before they'd left the previous day. She wasn't sure what she expected. The thought of Philip ransacking her place for a few bucks would have made her laugh if not for the fact that he had been in her home without her permission. The question was still, why?

For a big man, Simon moved with slow grace as he ducked into every corner of her apartment, making sure they were alone.

"Empty," he finally said.

She released a breath. "What was he doing here?"

"Who was he?"

"My boss, Philip."

"The man you work for?"

Helen turned a full circle, searching for anything out of place. "That's usually what the title of boss means."

Simon stepped to the window and peaked through the curtain. "Do you see him?"

"No."

"He could have parked out back."

Simon darted around her and out the door. "Where are you going?"

"Your car."

The books!

Helen followed Simon as far as the stairwell. "He'll recognize me."

"Go back to your apartment and lock the door."

Nodding, Helen grabbed the heavy boxes and hustled to disappear into the quiet of her home. She dropped the boxes and double keyed the lock.

* * * *

Simon reached the door to the parking garage and swung it open. The hinges squeaked in protest with the force of his arm and the sound echoed in the cavernous parking lot. Glancing side to side, he walked in the direction of Helen's car.

The man who'd left her apartment stepped into the garage and scanned the cars.

Simon watched from behind a concrete pole until he noticed the other man walk toward Helen's car. Without pause, Simon made his way in the same direction, determined to divert the intruder.

Like anyone trying to escape notice, the man saw Simon and twisted his face away.

Simon kept walking toward the car. The intruder made a show of patting his pockets as if searching for keys, and then turned and walked away.

To make certain he left, Simon followed him.

Outside the parking lot, Simon leaned against the building and waited. Helen's boss glanced over his shoulder once before jogging across the street to a dark car. He jumped in and drove off.

Satisfied he wasn't returning, Simon retrieved the books and returned to Helen's apartment.

****

"Oh my God, what took you so long? Did you see him? Did he see you?" She spat out questions faster than he could answer them. Helen grabbed for the box and tossed it on the couch as if it were in her way of getting his attention.

"Calm yourself, lass."

"Calm myself? Calm myself! Are you kidding me? My boss, who knows I'm out of town by the way, just committed a crime by breaking and entering into my home, and you're asking me to calm myself?"

"'Tis easier to think with a clear head."

"Yeah, well, mine ain't clear, kilt boy, mine is full of whys, what ifs, and how comes. Not to mention a heavy dose of 'that sonofabitch'."

Simon took her hand and led her to the kitchen. "Why don't you make some coffee, or tea."

"You're thirsty?"

No, he was trying to calm her down. Giving her a task was the only way he knew to do it.

"Please."

Helen grunted and swung away. As she stomped around the kitchen preparing coffee, Simon eased his way over to the front door and inspected the lock. There didn't seem to be any forced entry. "What is your boss's name?"

"Philip Lyons."

Mr. Lyons knew how to pick a lock. *Wonder where he acquired that skill?* "Are you sure he doesn't have a key?"

"Positive."

Simon walked around the room, attempting to catch the man's scent. If Helen knew about Simon's other skills, he'd have shifted into a wolf and heightened his senses. Glancing her way, he noticed how she shoved the coffee grounds into the maker, agitated. This probably wasn't the best time to reveal his many talents. He was able to distinguish the smell of the man's soap, or maybe it was cologne. Either way, the scent didn't belong to Helen.

"Where are you going?"

"Checking to see if anything looks out of place."

Helen finished her task all too soon and stepped to his side.

73

Philip's scent was stronger in Helen's room, especially around her dresser drawers. "Do you keep valuables in here?" he asked reaching for the first drawer to pull open.

Helen's hand stopped him. "No, just my underwear."

And from the tug of her hand, she didn't want him searching farther. A corner of his mouth lifted, and Helen seemed to forget about the drama of having her boss in her home, long enough to blush.

"You search here. I'll look in the bathroom."

Helen nodded and waited for him to turn his back before pulling the drawer open.

Simon looked around the bathroom. He could smell the other man but couldn't tell where he lingered.

"I don't see anything missing."

They searched the entire place and found nothing. Why would a man search a woman's apartment and take nothing? A sick thought penetrated Simon's mind. "Is it possible your boss has feelings for you?"

"Feelings? What do you mean?"

"Care for you? Has Philip ever shown interest in you as a woman?"

She opened her mouth to deliver what Simon thought was going to be an instant denial, than snapped it shut. "Eweh, are you thinking that he wants—?"

"He does desire you."

"No, I mean in a sick way?" She shook her head and her face grew pale. "I'm good at picking out perverts, and Philip didn't strike me as one."

Simon met her troubled gaze. "But he was here when he knew you weren't, searching through your things."

"We don't know if he was in my things."

Yes, Simon did. He could smell him nearly everywhere. "I see this two ways. He was either here for some sort of perversion..."

Helen cringed.

"...or he was searching for something and didn't find

it. I don't like either option."

"I don't accept either option," Helen denied.

"Do you have another?"

She paused, and glanced at the ceiling. "There has to be something we're missing."

"How well do you know him?"

"Better than most, I guess. He seems to do okay for himself. Single. Doesn't date much that I've seen."

"Do you know where he lives?"

Helen nodded. "He had a Christmas party last year."

Simon stood and nodded toward the door. "Let's go."

"Where?"

"Know your enemy and you will determine what motivates him."

"Philip isn't my enemy," she denied. Then after a few seconds, the strange stoic smile she'd been wearing fell.

"Today he crossed the line. Today he became your enemy." Simon grabbed her hand. "C'mon."

Chapter Nine

The trip to Philip's house was a waste of time. He wasn't there. She'd racked her brain trying to figure out what he'd been looking for. She didn't have anything he'd need. The whole thing stunk.

"He thinks you're in Scotland?"

"Yeah." Helen and Simon were sitting in her car across the street from Philip's empty house.

"Are you supposed to check in with him while you're gone?"

"I told him I would in a few days. Nothing's scheduled."

"Then a call is in order. He might say something in your conversation that enlightens us to his reasons for his deception."

Could she do that? Talk casually to a man who'd violated her privacy only hours before? "I don't know."

Simon shrugged. "Or I could talk with him." Simon clenched his hands into fists.

"Back off, he-man. Clocking my boss probably won't give us any answers either."

"But I like *clocking* my enemies. To tell you the truth, I miss it."

Helen couldn't help but let her eyes wander to his well-formed biceps. *I'll bet you do.* "I'll call first. If we run into him breaking in again, I'll help you pound him. But let's try this with a little less violence."

Back in her apartment, Helen used a call blocking number and dialed the office. Lisa, the secretary, answered on the second ring.

"It's Helen," she offered as casually as she could. "Is

Philip in?"

"Hey, Helen, how's Scotland?"

Helen glanced around the walls of her apartment. "Beautiful. You should come sometime."

"It's on my bucket list. How about the guys? Any of them wearing kilts?"

Licking her lips, Helen glanced at Simon and remembered the way his legs grasped hold of his horse's back and the way his thighs flexed under his plaid. At the time, she hadn't thought of much other than getting away from the maniacs attacking them, but now with the threat behind them—as in 500 years behind them— it was easy to picture Simon in a kilt. "Yeah."

"Ohhh, that sounds like an awfully breathy 'yeah', Helen. Who is he?"

"Who is who?"

"He? The kilt wearing he?"

Helen shook her head out of the fog and closed her eyes. "No one. Is Philip there or not?"

"Wow, talk about sensitive."

"Lisa?"

"No, Philip already left. He should be there tomorrow."

Already left? Tomorrow? "What are you talking about?"

"Philip. He's on his way to Scotland. Didn't he tell you?"

None of this made sense. "Must have slipped his mind."

Lisa paused. "Is he surprising you? Hey, you two aren't—"

"No!"

Simon's gaze jolted toward her with the outburst.

"No. Philip and I aren't anything." And because she had nothing to hide with her confusion, Helen added. "I don't have a clue as to why he's coming. Did he say anything to you?"

"Nothing more than the usual."

Deciding there wasn't any more information to gain,

Helen ended the call.

"Philip is en route to Scotland."

"To join you?"

"We didn't discuss him going."

Simon rubbed the side of his face and the small amount of facial hair he had on his chin and lip. Funny, Helen hadn't thought much of the goatee until Simon stroked his fingers over it. "He may think whatever he searched for here is there with you."

"With me? My camera? My clothes?"

"There must be something."

Helen ran her hand on the back of her neck and rubbed the ache. Her hand caught on her necklace and she found herself playing with the pendent.

The same necklace worn by the woman in the book.

"Wait." Her fingertips buzzed and popped with discovery.

"What is it, lass?"

Helen glanced at her chest. She reached behind her neck and attempted to undo the clasp on the necklace. It wouldn't give. "Help me with this."

Simon stepped behind her, his body close enough to hers she could feel the heat off his frame. His breath brushed over the nape of her neck as his fingers played with the chain.

"I don't see a latch."

Helen tugged her hair in her hands to give him a better view. "It's a screw thingy."

Simon tugged on the chain.

"Don't break it."

"I'm not. There isn't a latch."

Helen reached around her neck and felt around. All she touched was a chain. She wiggled the pendent until she could see the back.

Nothing. It was as if someone placed the necklace around her neck and welded it together.

It suddenly felt like a noose, something that had to come off.

She grasped two ends and pulled.

"You'll break it that way."

"I don't care. There was a clasp and now it's gone." Helen didn't like the fear lodged in the back of her throat. She pulled harder. All she gained for her effort as a nicked finger. "Dammit."

Simon covered her hand with his, stopping her frantic tugging. "What has you so worried, love?"

"This darn necklace." She tugged again. "It started this whole." Pull. "Damn." Tug. "Thing!"

Nothing. It wouldn't budge.

Simon grasped her hands in his and held them tight.

Helen tried to pull back, but he didn't let go. He stepped closer and captured her gaze. His stare dove deep inside her mind until all she noticed was his amazing blue eyes. Thoughts of the necklace faded.

God he was gorgeous. He had this cocky little smirk with a hint of a dimple showing over his right cheek. He screamed control. Even in the most impossible conditions, Simon held a quiet calm Helen never felt, telling her everything was fine.

Well, it wasn't fine. Far from fine!

He stood so close she could smell the masculine scent of his skin mixed with a musk that drifted with him all the way from the sixteenth century.

It unnerved her. Made her itch in places she didn't want to.

Somewhere Simon McAllister stopped being a teenage kid and became this kilted hunk of a man who scrambled every nerve in her body and then some.

A man whose fingers grazed over hers and made her loosen her grip on the necklace around her neck.

A man who stepped even farther into her personal space than she'd thought she wanted.

A man who dropped her hands, spread his own over the nape of her neck, and held her in waiting.

Helen's heart knocked hard against her ribs, pounded even harder as Simon dipped his head closer and brushed his full, soft lips against hers.

She gasped with the kind of sound born in soap operas and melodramas. She didn't mean to, it just happened. With the noise, she moved closer and felt her tingling body melt into his.

The closed mouth kiss only stayed that way for a minute, probably less, and then Helen felt Simon tilt her head even farther back and her lips opened at his command.

Simon was everywhere, instantly. His body, from knees to head, leaned into her. His tongue swam into the cavern of her mouth as if being welcomed home after a long journey. The sweet taste of his lips on hers forced thoughts of necklaces and time travel far, far away.

Helen unclenched her fingers, which had grabbed handfuls of his shirt, and spread them wide over his firm chest. It was then she realized just how hard he was—everywhere.

She stiffened and Simon retreated.

"I'm sorry." The words escaped her lips before she could filter them.

"Sorry? Love, you have no reason to be sorry." Although Simon was no longer kissing her, he hadn't stepped out of her arms.

A hot rush of heat fanned over her face. God, what was wrong with her? A desirable man held her in his arms, kissing her in an extremely sensual manner, and she froze and pushed him away. Memories of her last foster dad swam in her head. Simon was nothing like him so why was she so locked up? She opened her mouth to offer an excuse.

I don't think about you that way. But she did! Had thought of nothing but him since they'd met.

You're not my type. What was her type? Lord, if it wasn't a strong, built, in control man, then what was?

I'm not ready. Okay, she could work with this.

"I'm not ready to be kissing you. I know there's this crazy chemistry going on here, but I'm not ready." Oh, no, did she have to mention their chemistry?

Simon lifted her chin and stared deeply into her

eyes. "I never had the opportunity to take chemistry."

Helen chuckled and felt the tension of the moment pass. "It was boring. You didn't miss much."

"Mayhap you'll instruct me on what I've missed."

She smiled. "Mayhap." Oh, boy...who says *mayhap*? Sixteenth century men from Scotland, that's who.

Simon stepped away, but not far. "Tell me about the necklace."

Right! The necklace that wouldn't come free of her neck. "I found it in a pawn shop. It isn't valuable. I checked."

Simon was swinging the pendent around her neck and taking a closer look. His fingers were warm on her skin...comfortable.

"What is this stone in the middle?"

"I've no idea. A rock, maybe? The metal encasing it is old. I had it radiocarbon dated."

"Carbon dated?"

"Sorry. I guess chemistry has its purpose. When we try to date an antique that isn't easily placed in a specific time, carbon dating is a process used to determine the year it's made. Any material that has the compound of carbon can be dated back over 60,000 years. Carbon really refers to skin, bone, teeth. Metals are different, more difficult to date. They use a radiocarbon dating system, but it isn't as accurate as dating completely carbon based products. In this case, I asked the lab to use uranium dating. There are traces of lead in the chain. And surprisingly, carbon was found, too."

"What is the source of the carbon?"

"Human tissue. Which is kind of gross when you think of it. My guess is the person who made it scraped their skin, bled on it, or something."

Simon's thumb traced the stone, his expression shifted.

"When did it date back to, Helen?"

The serious tone in his voice removed all the lingering hormones swimming in her body.

"The dating wasn't exact."

"When?"

"Early seventeenth century. Maybe before."

"You said this necklace started it all. What did you mean by that?"

Helen stood back and Simon's hand dropped to his side. "After I found the necklace I came across the candlesticks. Then your picture. Then the book."

"The book?"

"The one with your picture. I told you about the woman in it."

Simon sent her a questioning look. "You told me of the woman, but not the necklace."

"I didn't? I thought for sure I did." Could she have forgotten that detail? "The woman in the book was wearing this necklace. Or one exactly like it."

Simon's jaw dropped. "'Tis a very important detail."

"I thought I told you."

"You didn't, I assure you." He moved over to the books piled into the boxes by the door. One at a time, he removed the books and arraigned them in the middle of the floor.

"Did you think of something?"

"Aye."

He moved the books using the acronym method they'd come up with the night before.

H.E.L.E.N. Soon Simon moved the books and found the word "necklace."

"Helen necklace," she whispered. She found a massive tome titled "Sorcerer" and made her name possessive. "Helen's necklace."

There were eight books left. T.E.K.H.I.E.S.Y.

"His? These? Tie?"

"Tie Helen's necklace?" Simon said aloud.

Kneeling beside him, Helen moved books around.

"We need a verb."

"Impossible. Sainthood. Is. Helen's necklace is."

Simon shoved the books back and forth as a thought struck. When he was done, they both smiled.

"Helen's necklace is the key."

"I believe we found what we were looking for."

The weight of the pendent on her neck felt heavy and warm. "You think the necklace moved me in time?"

"If not, then what?"

She tugged on it, wanting it off. If it moved her though time once, it could do it again.

"Get if off." She batted it with her hands, pulled and attempted to break it free. But the chain was thick and unrelenting. She'd loved the heavy chain the first time she put it on. Not anymore.

"Calm down." Simon attempted to grab her hands, but she moved away.

"It needs to come off."

"Relax, Helen."

"Relax? Easy for you to say. The thing isn't fused to you."

"If the Ancients wanted it anywhere but around your neck, you'd be able to remove it easily. Don't fight with it."

Simon and his Ancients, those spiritual beings he credited for everything that happened. She didn't lend much belief in spirits.

Helen stopped pulling and walked briskly to the junk drawer in her kitchen. There she found a pair of pliers and moved them to the chain.

"Halt!" Simon yelled his voice stopped her instantly. "You may be destroying my only chance to return home."

The pliers fell from her hand, hit the counter, and then tumbled to the floor. He was right. Her own insecurities and fears were making her rush to action. "I'm sorry. You're right." Her hands shook with the force of her fear.

"We'll figure out what makes the necklace work. Together."

"But what if I wake up in your time and you're here?"

"You won't." Simon's hands rested on her shoulders.

She wanted to believe him but didn't know what to believe anymore. "You don't know that."

"I'll not leave your side."

"But—"

"Shhh."

Not leave her side? Her body tightened in a ball of pressure. What the hell was wrong with her?

* * * *

Amber palmed one of the small stones and rubbed her thumb along its smooth surface. "I know you've done this for a reason," she voiced to whatever, whoever might be listening. The Ancients only appeared in dire times. This obviously wasn't one of them. Simon might be missing from this century, but Amber no longer felt the forbearing weight of loss she did when he'd first stepped out of this time. She guessed the lack of acute pain was due to Lizzy's emotions calming. Bearing the weight of other peoples' emotions, experiencing their joy, pain, and sorrow, became more oppressive with each passing year.

This was her Druid gift.

Lately it knifed her like a curse.

Her burden was shared with her parents. Her father, Ian, encouraged her to find a husband, someone of her own to love and start a family. Each suitor Amber turned away, unable to bear their touch or experience their lingering pain.

Lora's premonitions had faded as she aged, giving Amber hope that hers would diminish, too.

Through the years, the pain of the family faded enough to bear their direct contact. But even that became increasingly difficult. Simon was a part of that family. Although they didn't share any blood relation, he was a brother to her. She missed him.

A knock on her chamber door sounded, followed by her mother's voice. "'Tis me."

"Come in."

Lora's skirts swished along the floor as she crossed the room. She wore grace and elegance as others would wear a scarf. Her mother's long dark hair was bundled into a snood at her neck; the lace matched the deep umber color of her dress.

"Are you still studying the stones?"

Amber returned her eyes to the table on which the smaller stones lay. "Aye. The Ancients are trying to tell us something."

Lora lifted one of the stones and rolled it in her hand. "Agreed. And I think I may know what they're suggesting."

"You've had a premonition?"

She shook her head. "More feeling than anything predetermined."

"Don't leave me waiting."

Lora lifted the stone to Amber's chest and tilted her head to the side in thought. "When I close my eyes I see a necklace. Nothing ornate, or made with any precious metal. A simple design any of the villagers might fashion."

Amber lifted her palm to her mother. The stone fell into it. "A necklace? As a way of disguising it?"

"Mayhap. Remember Simon's suggestion years ago about hiding the larger stones in plain sight. He said something about a pet rock."

Amber laughed. "Lizzy's endless explanation of a pet rock lasted for weeks. But yes, I remember."

Lora sat on the edge of the bed and folded her hands in her lap. "I thought of Simon, as a child, talking about pet rocks. Now these small pieces of the sacred stones may very well be lost if left unattended. Placed in a piece of jewelry, or in the handle of a knife, they wouldn't disappear without notice."

"I think you're right. I'll ask Cian to take me to the village tomorrow so we might obtain materials to achieve your goal." Making jewelry wouldn't bring Simon back, but the task might empty her mind and help guide her to the answers she sought.

Chapter Ten

"They're sending my things." Helen hung up the phone and turned Simon's way.

How had he seen the necklace around her neck and not thought of home? Clearly, there was a simple design of Celtic knots inlaid around the stone. Maybe because he was used to seeing such designs, he didn't pay any attention to Helen's. But he should have noticed it before now.

"What will happen when your boss arrives and doesn't find you there?"

"I really don't care. I obviously can't trust him."

"You must let him believe he came here undetected. 'Tis the only way we can determine what he sought."

"Are you suggesting we wait for him to do it again?"

"It may not come to that." The distress covering Helen's face forced Simon to keep his thoughts to himself. Something about Philip Lyons felt dark. If Amber were by Simon's side, she could better determine the man's motivations.

"He's going to be more than pissed when he gets to Scotland and I'm not there."

Simon rubbed the stubble on his chin. "When your enemy is angered, they act irrational."

"Oh, joy!" Helen said without amusement.

"It will take at least two days before he returns."

"That doesn't seem like a lot of time."

"We've more than enough time to penetrate his home as he did yours and learn more about him."

Helen's jaw dropped open, her eyes grew wide. "Break into his house?"

"We aren't going to steal anything, lass. We're only going to look around."

Helen ran a hand through her hair. "It's still illegal."

"You can stay here. I'll go alone." The task would be easier solo anyway.

"And risk jumping in time by myself? I don't think so."

He didn't want that either. "Does he live with anyone?"

"Not that I know of."

"A housekeeper?"

Helen shrugged.

"Then we'll go after dark."

"Oh, man." Helen rubbed her palms over her jean-clad thighs.

He could tell Helen was going to be a bundle of nerves until their task was done. Best to get her mind off their coming adventure. He held out a hand to her and stood. "Come."

Her gaze slid from his hand to his face. "Where to?"

Simon wiggled his fingers, coaxing her. "'Tis been a long time since I've been in this century. I think I'd like a walk through the zoo and maybe a little Chinese food."

"Chinese food? You're thinking of food at a time like this?"

He laughed. "A body needs fuel no matter the time. C'mon."

Relenting, Helen placed her small hand in his and allowed him to help her to her feet.

* * * *

The aroma drifting from the bag of takeout filled the interior of Helen's car. He didn't remember the food he liked, so he had Helen order for them. It was after two when they arrived at the zoo. Helen wouldn't understand his desire for this trip, not until she understood the extent of his Druid gifts. For Simon, it was a long denied outing. His ability to understand an animal's motivation and desire, to communicate with them, had come to him after he left this century. In Scotland, the domestic animals and an occasional wild fox or bird were his only animal friends. In a zoo, the possibilities were endless.

As a child, he remembered standing beside the ape exhibit wondering if the huge animals were as bored as they looked. Or were they constantly searching for an escape route, a way to free themselves from their pens?

Helen paid the admission and led the way. "My life is upside down, and I'm walking around the zoo."

"What better place to clear your head?"

She rolled her eyes. "Chinese kind of sucks cold. We should eat before *clearing our minds*."

They passed the paper containers back and forth. The bite of the spicy chicken made his eyes water but the flavor exploded on his tongue. "Amazing."

"It's pretty good," she said while scooping a forkful of chow mien into her mouth.

"You've no idea how blessed you are." He shook his head. "Spices are rare and expensive where I'm from."

"You're from here."

"You know what I mean."

"So, what do you eat?"

"Roasted meats, boiled vegetables...stew. What we can grow or hunt. Though there has been more trade from Europe in the past few years."

Helen waved her fork at him. "You eat organic. Which isn't a bad thing."

"Organic?"

"It's the buzz word of the new millennium. This is tasty." She picked up the container and snagged another bite. "But it's horrible for your body. MSG, saturated fats, concentrated sugars."

Simon stared into his box, shrugged his shoulders, and took another bite. "I'm not at risk of dying from overindulging. Not in the short time I'll be here."

"Your confidence about finding a way home astounds me."

A small child in a stroller waved at him from a few

feet away. Simon winked and wiggled his fingers in the lad's direction.

"We've already found the key. The rest is easy."

In all reality, Simon was reasonably sure he could travel home at that very moment. However, leaving Helen wasn't something he was ready to do. For the brief moment he held her in his arms, laid claim to her lips, something inside him stirred that he'd not felt before. The passion inside her was wound on a tight leash, and Simon wanted to be the one to unfurl it. He also had to consider Philip Lyons and his deception. Why had the man broken into Helen's home? Why was he traveling half way around the world to "surprise" her? Simon had too many questions to leave this century now.

He watched, fascinated as Helen made silly faces at the child in the stroller. Her animated features made the child laugh and had his own laughter bubbling to the surface. Instead, he smiled. He had too many reasons to stay. At least for now.

"If the rest were easy, you'd be home already," said Helen.

Simon didn't counter her comment. Instead, he finished the remainder of the fried rice

"So why the zoo?" Helen asked as they were winding their way around the exhibits.

How much was she ready to hear? Simon inched closer and lowered his voice. "Every Druid has at least one special gift."

"More than fire from your fingertips?"

"Aye, much more."

They stopped in front of the snow leopard. The huge cat couldn't be bothered to lift his head to see who walked by. It napped in the afternoon sun, ignoring everyone.

"What kind of *gifts*?"

"Gifts from nature. Organic, you might say."

"So what? You can make plants grow?" She was laughing at him, obviously not believing a thing he said.

"That is my Aunt Tara's gift."

"Yeah, right!"

He shrugged. "She's always complaining it isn't explosive enough."

"Explosive?"

If Helen couldn't imagine Tara helping the soil warm with her fingers, than she couldn't fathom his mother hovering above the ground, or his father causing said ground to shake.

"My grandfather...step-grandfather, has the ability to call rain and lightening with a mere thought."

As Helen opened her mouth to protest, Simon continued. "My grandmother predicts the future. Sometimes, long before it happens, other times moments before it occurs."

Helen's smile started to fall, her steps slowed.

"My cousin, Cian, heals wounds with his hands. My cousin Amber feels the emotions of others. Her I worry about. She bears everyone's sorrow and joy."

Helen's smile fell. Mayhap the words expelled from his mouth or the tone of them made her pause, but she did. She appeared to consider what he'd said.

"I'm told that our gifts are stronger than most. We believe it's because we've been called upon to stop a great evil from destroying us...from destroying many."

His thoughts drifted to his childhood, to the witch who kidnapped him. The one who taught him that the boogieman was alive and real, living inside an ancient woman with powers beyond imagination.

He shook thoughts of Grainna aside. She was dead. No need to think of her now.

Then again, she was the reason he'd landed in the sixteenth century and why his mother had married Finlay. Simon would give her credit if the thought didn't leave him physically ill.

"My God, you're serious." Helen had stopped walking and so had he.

"Aye."

"So, what's your special gift?"

Simon opened his mouth, but before he could utter a word, a woman's scream pierced the air with a shrill that caused every nerve in Simon's body to stand on alert.

He pivoted, and saw a woman leaning over the railing of a gorilla exhibit a few yards away. "My baby!" she cried.

Simon didn't pause, he ran toward the woman who was attempting to hoist herself over a rail. When he reached her side, he noticed a toddler, a child no more than three, sitting in a bush, deep inside a ditch of the exhibit.

Pushing the mother aside, Simon leapt over the rail and jumped twenty feet to the ground. The sounds of the crowd gathering hardly registered as his mind opened to the animals around him.

A male, the alpha, bounded forward to see who the intruders were. A female, less dominant, but even more intrigued, darted down the ditch and came within feet of the crying child.

The female heard the cry and tilted her head. A rush of instinct filled Simon's body. He couldn't tell if it was his or the gorillas, but he knew it as the same.

Help.

The gorilla moved closer to the child and the noise around Simon wailed. He thought he heard his name, but he didn't respond.

Help the baby.

The thought filtered in his head like a mantra.

Above him, the 400-pound male watched and stood tall, making sure Simon saw him and knew he was the master of this space. Simon kept his head low and moved closer to the crying child.

"Mommy!" he cried. The child's arms reached above his head, big tears ran down his plump cheeks.

"It's okay, lad. You're okay."

"Mommy."

The female gorilla scrambled toward the child.

Simon moved forward slowly.

"Help him," he heard above his head.

The female eyed Simon as he inched closer and barked a warning.

The child hiccupped and started to calm. Simon was the same distance to the child as the gorilla. The chocolate eyes of the animal caught his and held. The gorilla's weathered hand reached toward the child and stroked his cheek.

The mother of the child screamed.

With as much power as Simon had, he asked the female not to move.

The gorilla shifted her eyes above her, then back to Simon. Then moved her arm to her side and sat.

Once realizing he had control, Simon scooped the struggling child in his arms and held tight.

In the back of his mind, Simon felt the massive male move forward. Curiosity about what was taking place swam over him.

"Alex!"

Simon backed away from the female and stood. The steep barrier that kept the gorillas in their pen would make it difficult for Simon to escape.

The sound of a smashing door made him jump. The gorillas shifted their gaze to a far wall. The thought of food and routine filled Simon's mind.

Go, he suggested to the animals. Within seconds, the gorillas lumbered toward their keepers, awaiting their unexpected meal.

Keeping the toddler pinned to his side, Simon climbed up into the gorilla encampment.

While the apes were distracted, Simon moved along the outer fence to a door. A pair of zookeepers waved him forward and ushered him into safety.

The toddler clung to him, but his cries had muffled to whimpers.

When the mother burst around the corner, Simon handed the child over.

"Alex. Oh, my baby."

"You have a brave young lad," Simon told the

mother. "You didn't even shy away when the gorilla tried to help, did you?" he asked the child.

"Thank you." The mother fell on Simon and hugged him. "Thank you."

"Best keep a watchful eye on this one." Simon warned her.

The mother smoothed a hand over her child's face and sat down to assess her son's body.

Simon felt a hand on his arm and he turned to find Helen's deep, penetrating gaze. "Let me guess."

He narrowed his eyes.

"You have a thing for animals?"

* * * *

Helen was still shaking when they left the zoo an hour later. The gorilla encounter had lasted only a handful of minutes, but the time stretched out in slow motion. The young mother's scream played repeatedly inside Helen's head, followed closely by the image of Simon leaping over the railing to the child below. When the charging gazillion-pound ape skidded to a stop next to the child, Helen nearly lost her lunch.

Who the hell willingly jumps into a wild animal's cage? Okay, so what if the ape hadn't charged him, still, who in their right mind stands up to an ape?

When chaos erupted around her, it was obvious the people who'd been there thought the same way.

Simon approached the child and the ape with calculated ease. He'd kept complete eye contact with the gorilla while gathering the child in his arms. Beside Helen, the child's mother alternately would cry out one moment and bite her tongue the next to keep from screaming.

And all the while, Simon didn't react to anything going on above him. A small miracle, since a fair amount of dopey-eyed females batted their eyelashes at him when he returned the child to his mother and walked away. People took pictures. Video cameras angled in his direction. His stunt in the gorilla cage would be viral by dinner.

Helen's hands shook when she placed her key in the ignition and started the car.

"Are you well, lass?" Simon asked.

She killed the engine and twisted in her seat toward him. "No. No, I'm not. It's been a crazy-ass couple of days and that stunt topped off my wack-o-meter."

"Wack-o-meter?"

"Yeah, and stop smirking like you don't understand what I'm getting at. What the hell was that, Simon? Something tells me that if any other person had dropped into that pen, those apes would have had them for lunch."

"The female only wanted to help the child. The male wanted to protect the female. They aren't all that different from our own species."

Helen tossed a hand up in the air. "And how the hell do you know that?" Her voice rose, her blood pressure with it.

"Animals are my gift."

"Yeah, I gathered that, Einstein. But how? What did you do, talk to them or something?"

When Simon didn't deny her crazy statement Helen shut her eyes tight. "No way."

"I don't talk to them, not the way you mean, but I do understand what's going on inside their heads. Those gorillas are used to people. They were surprised by the child's presence inside their space, but they didn't feel the child was a threat. Not like me. I could have easily been a threat. So I used my link to suggest that I wasn't there to harm them and they responded."

Helen sucked in her lower lip. "This is crazy."

"I know. Imagine how I felt the first time I realized I could climb inside an animal's mind. With some effort I can take over the animal's actions."

Helen's knuckles turned white as they gripped the steering wheel. "Are you saying you could make an animal attack or retreat?"

When he didn't say anything, she glanced over and saw her answer in the depths of his gaze.

"Oh, God."

"There's more," he said.

She thrust her hand out, palm up. "Stop. I'm not ready for more. Okay. I'm not ready."

Her head already spun to the point of pain. It would take her months to sort out everything Simon was telling her, maybe even years. Her entire world was imploding around her and all she could do was watch and roll with it. It reminded her of her early days in foster care and orphanages. Every day was a new drama, a new obstacle to overcome. There was no consistency in her life, and everyone but Helen had the control.

She hated it then. She loathed it now.

Taking back some control, Helen started the car again and pulled out of the parking lot. They had a couple of hours to kill before they broke into Philip's home, and Helen could use a little liquid courage.

She drove to the nearest bar, jumped out of the car, and didn't watch to see if Simon followed her or not.

Chapter Eleven

The dim interior of the bar provided a blanket over the chaos of the day. Helen had tucked herself along a far wall and was already sipping something from a glass. A couple of heads turned Simon's way as he walked into the room. A woman behind the bar slid an appreciative gaze up and down the length of Simon's frame and let a half smile spread over her lips. As attractive as the lass was, he didn't have a second thought for her as he made his way to Helen's side.

Helen didn't lift her eyes from her drink as he rested his arms on the table in front of them.

A waitress started toward the table, but Simon waved her off. The lady took the hint and moved to another group of patrons who were watching one of the many sets of televisions hanging from the walls of the establishment.

"They have pills for crazy," Helen said over her glass. "Pills to make the crazy one feel more grounded, to feel more like they're sane."

"You're not crazy, lass."

She voiced a short humorless laugh and brought her glass to her lips. "Sanity is being able to judge and reason sensibly. I'm not falling into that category. Against all sensibility, not to mention everything I've ever been taught in life, I'm starting to believe everything you've been telling me since we met." She took another swig from her glass and squinted her eyes as the amber liquid went down. "And you just jumped into a cage with wild gorillas. That's not sane, Simon! Not sane at all."

"Would a mother not jump into the ocean to save her child even if she couldn't swim?"

"You weren't that child's mother."

"But I was the only one who could help. The boy needed someone to look out for him."

"Who elected you?"

Ahh, now Simon started to see the stress ease from her eyes. Her anger stemmed from her concern for *his* well-being.

"Are you afraid of cats?"

"What? Cats?" She narrowed her eyes to his.

"Kittens? If you were to see a child reaching to pull the tail of a cat, would you not try and stop him before he's scratched or bitten?"

"Kittens are harmless," she argued. "Gorillas, not so much. I've watched enough Animal Planet to know they can take out a man, even one as big as you, without much effort."

Simon sat taller. Her unrealized stroke to his ego warmed his insides and brought a smile to his lips. "The risk of jumping in with those animals was no greater than you driving your car on the freeway." He covered her hand with his and squeezed. "Once you know all of my talents, you'll understand better."

"Really?" She tilted the glass to her lips and drained it. "Lay it on me, Simon. What else is there?"

Her brave front was a mask, one he didn't want to rip off in a room full of strangers. Besides, it wasn't as if he could prove his ability to shift into an animal here in a public place.

"Perhaps this isn't the best time to explain."

She shook her head. "Of course not. Now that I'm ready, you're not. Story of my life." Helen raised her hand to the waitress, and pointed to her glass.

Someone at the bar raised his voice. "That crazy son of a bitch!"

"Would you look at that?"

Simon glanced at the television then turned toward Helen. Helen's eyes grew wide and she grabbed his forearm. Above the noise in the bar, Simon heard the words hero and zoo and his body froze.

Helen's mouth hung open, her attention riveted to the television. When he looked, Simon saw himself on an amateur video. He sat poised on the balls of his feet in a gorilla enclosure having a stare-off with a wild animal.

"Can you believe this guy?" the waitress asked as she sat Helen's drink on the table.

Simon reached for the glass and drained the contents in one swallow.

His image plastered in the media would bring unwanted stares and scrutiny, something Simon desperately wanted to avoid with his brief time in this century. Breaking into Philip Lyons home, or spying on the man would be near impossible if strangers could identify him.

"Holy cow, that's you!"

A couple of patrons shifted in their chairs with the server's outburst.

Helen's fingers dug into Simon's arm.

"Time to go." Simon helped Helen to her feet as she reached for her purse and tossed a few bills on the table.

"That is you, isn't it?"

Simon shook his head. "You wouldn't catch me in a cage with a gorilla," he denied. "The guy just looks like me."

No less than eight sets of eyes watched them as they left the bar.

* * * *

"It looks like the two of you have been busy," Mrs. Dawson greeted them when they arrived at her home an hour later.

"You saw the news?"

"You're quite the celebrity, Simon. What on earth possessed you to confront that beast?"

Helen watched as Simon leaned over and kissed Mrs. Dawson's cheek. "Saving small children is one of my many talents," he joked.

Mrs. Dawson blushed and patted her hand on his chest. "He's good with kids and animals, Helen. You

98

know what they say about that, don't you?"

"No, but I'm sure you're going to tell me." Helen had been spinning in circles since leaving the bar. Their plans to sneak into Philip's home were on hold. "Too dangerous," Simon had said earlier when he suggested they return to Mrs. Dawson's where they could explore their options without as many neighbors watching.

"He's a keeper. Men who are good with kids and animals are a rare find."

As if! Simon wasn't a stray Helen could keep. And he wouldn't be around forever, so the whole 'keeping' theme was moot.

Not that she was considering keeping anything. Getting her life back to normal...now that had a nice ring to it.

Normal. What would that look like? Philip couldn't be trusted, and the pendent around her neck might whisk her away to unknown times. The only way *normal* would occur again is if Helen escorted Simon back to his time, returned, then found another job where her boss didn't break into her apartment. Then things could be *normal.*

Helen ignored Simon's eyes as she placed a small suitcase by the stairs. "I'll go get the books," she said turning toward the door.

"I'll do that," Simon said.

Fine! Let the macho, muscle bound guy do the heavy lifting. Hell, he was probably having withdrawal not carrying around his big sword and whacking off people's heads with it.

Helen took Mrs. Dawson's arm to help keep her steady as they walked into the library.

"Are you okay, dear?"

Helen forced a smile to her lips. "I'm fine. It's been a crazy few days."

"An exciting few days I'm sure. I've not felt this alive in years."

The sparkle behind Mrs. Dawson's brown eyes spread to the crow's-feet beside them.

"Excitement is fine, danger...not so much."

Mrs. Dawson took a seat and pulled Helen down beside her. "Danger? Who said anything about danger?"

"Simon and I spied my boss sneaking out of my apartment."

Mrs. Dawson's smile faded. "What was your boss doing there?"

"I haven't a clue. He broke in but didn't take anything. Not that he'd need any of my things."

"Did you confront him?"

Helen shook her head. "Simon thinks we need to watch him to see what he's up to. Now that Simon's mug is plastered all over channels four, five, and seven, hiding behind bushes and not getting noticed isn't doable."

Simon returned to the room with boxes of books and set them on a table. "That means we need to find someone else to help determine what the man's motivation is."

"But who?" Helen asked. "Mrs. Dawson's a little too old for breaking and entering. No offense."

Mrs. Dawson winked. "I'm afraid you're right about that. Though I'd have loved to try it if I were a few years younger."

The woman's enthusiasm made Helen smile.

"We can use your help by having a sanctuary in your home," Simon said.

"Helen is always welcome here. And you, too."

"Much thanks, lass. But I have to ask you to extend that welcome to others in my family."

Helen twisted in her chair. "Who?"

"We need an extra set of eyes and talents I don't possess."

"Any family of yours is welcome here, Simon," Mrs. Dawson said.

"You don't have to do that," Helen told her and offered a glare to Simon. The last thing she wanted was to bring any danger to Mrs. Dawson's doorstep.

"You worry too much," Mrs. Dawson said. "This

home is lonely. When Mr. Dawson passed away, I considered selling it and moving to a smaller, more manageable place, but something kept me from calling the realtor."

"I thought you said you felt closer to your husband here and wouldn't have the same memories in a new home."

"That's true, hon, but now I think there's more to it than that. Things happen for a reason and perhaps my keeping this big house wasn't only for me, but for others." Mrs. Dawson smiled at Simon as she spoke.

"My family will compensate you."

She waved a hand in the air. "When will I meet the others?"

"When we return."

Helen's head shot up. "Return? Have you figured out how to leave?"

When Simon responded with only a smile, Helen's entire body broke out in gooseflesh. *He had.* Her kilt wearing, animal talking, fire starting, druid, gorilla-man had figured out how to move them back in time. Which meant Helen was about to experience medieval Scotland for a second time. *Oh, joy. The first was so much fun. Why not do it again?*

* * * *

"Why do we have to leave tonight? Isn't tomorrow soon enough?"

Simon gathered Helen's hands in his and forced her to look at him. "We're told to never attempt to be in two places in one time. The sooner we return here with Amber and Cian, the easier it will be to spy on Philip. By morning, he'll know you're not in the hotel in Scotland and will either be returning here or searching for you there. You've left a trail for him in Scotland, one he'll probably search."

Simon had directed Helen to call the hotel back and forward all her calls to another hotel deeper in the Highlands. Depending on how determined Philip was, he'd follow the path they'd left and deter him for a few days. Keeping him there felt safer than him searching for Helen in Los Angeles. And Mrs. Dawson didn't need danger on her doorstep without Simon there to protect her.

"But tomorrow is only a few hours away."

He could see the fear in her eyes. "I'll protect you, lass."

"But—"

Simon placed a finger over her lips. "My solution to move us back may not work." It would work, but he wasn't going to tell her that. Simon's mother Lizzy had drilled into him how she and Fin had returned to the sixteenth century with only one stone. The words of her chant drifted in his head like the lyrics to the birthday song.

"You don't think it will work?"

He didn't answer.

"Oh, God."

"I'd go if I wasn't needed here to make my spare bedrooms presentable." Mrs. Dawson stood by the back door of the house as she spoke.

The old were always more adventurous than the young. People would argue the opposite, but Simon had seen enough in his short life to argue the point. Life was too short. Taking risks was the only way to really live.

Simon loved risk.

Helen would too if he could find a way to calm her down.

He grasped her hand and pulled her out the back door of Mrs. Dawson's home. On the back porch, Simon leaned over and kissed Mrs. Dawson's cheek. "We'll call you when we're back. I've left my dirk in the room you've allowed me to use, this will guide the way for my family to come without me if they need to."

Mrs. Dawson nodded and Simon kissed her cheek again.

He stood back as Helen pulled the older woman into her arms. "I'm doing the right thing, right?"

"Oh, dear, you've the best tour guide with you. I'm

jealous. Make sure you bring him back in a kilt."

Helen chuckled. "I love you."

"I love you, too, dear."

The foliage surrounding Mrs. Dawson's backyard and the mile of distance of her nearest neighbor gave Simon the privacy he needed.

Helen's hand shook in his as he led her away from the house. Lizzy had spoken of the power of Druid blood and how it aided her return. Helen wouldn't like what Simon was about to do. "I need your hand."

Helen lifted her left hand and he removed a small knife he'd retrieved from Mrs. Dawson's kitchen.

"What's that for?"

"We only need a few drops." He lifted the blade to her finger and she tugged away.

"I don't like this."

"You need to trust me."

She sucked in her lower lip and thrust her hand to his again. He made a small cut in her finger and did the same to his. After tucking the knife in his pocket, he gathered both their hands and squeezed small drops of blood in a circle around them.

Once he completed the small circle, he willed fire to leap from his fingers and catch into a ring. Helen pushed closer to his frame, the heat of her skin met his. Her breath caught and her breasts pushed against the fabric of her shirt. With his non-bleeding hand, Simon pulled her softly into his embrace. "Trust me."

Something flickered in her eyes and Simon placed her bleeding finger and his, to the pendant on her neck. Then he began to speak. "In this night and in this hour, we ask the Ancients for this power. Send us now across the sea, to be back with my family. If the Ancients will it so, send us now and let us go."

A familiar rumble of the earth jolted beneath them and fear raced through Helen's body.

Simon did the only thing he could think of to distract her.

He leaned forward and melted his lips to hers.

103

Chapter Twelve

The world exploded around her. Unlike the last time Simon had kissed her, this time felt safe, rational, and more grounded than the falling earth. The palm of his hand flattened against hers as their bodies plunged into time. The soft dance of his lips parted hers until his tongue explored deeper. The rush of noise around them grew as it had before but all Helen could hear was the pounding of her own heart and the rushing of blood through her veins.

The long, firm length of Simon's hardened body pressed so close she couldn't move a finger without touching him somewhere. He was delicious, smooth, and infinitely more experienced at kissing and distraction than Helen ever thought she'd be.

She felt his thigh push between hers and her hips surged forward with a will of their own. A deep coil of desire produced a moan against Simon's lips.

The world quieted around them, and Helen's body felt as if it were wrapped in a warm, soft cloud. Simon's hand lifted from her neck to her cheek. He broke away from her lips, and Helen slowly opened her eyes to find him staring. She moved to lift her arm but found it wedged between Simon and something. She tugged again and turned her head. Helen's face met with a soft pillow.

They had landed in a bed, with Simon's knee wedged intimately between her legs.

"Are you okay?" he asked, his voice low and deep in his chest.

She glanced beyond his shoulder, ignoring their

tangled limbs, and noticed the cold stone walls and high ceilings. The bed was nothing like she'd slept in before. Massive wood posts framed a mattress of some sort. Across the room was an empty, dark fireplace and sitting chair arranged in front of it.

"Where are we?"

He smiled and pulled in a deep full breath as if he was tasting fresh air for the first time in years. "Home," he sighed.

"Scotland?"

"Aye."

Another rumble sounded behind the wooden door and Simon's body stiffened.

The door crashed open and several people stormed the room all at once.

Helen would have bounded from the bed had Simon not been holding her. She only managed to untangle their limbs before a beautiful blonde woman dressed in an ornate rust colored gown ran toward the bed. "Simon."

Simon stood up, drawing Helen with him. "I take it you missed me."

Helen stepped away as the woman threw her arms around Simon. "You scared the crap out of me."

"Did you think I wouldn't return, Mom?"

More family filled the room, each of them glanced Helen's way but swiftly returned their attention to Simon.

Helen took a moment to soak in the massive amount of people. *My God, he said his family was large, but this makes the Waltons look like 'orphans'.* The men were massive, all over six feet tall and thick as steel. The women might not be as large, but their presence wasn't a timid shadow behind the men. And beautiful, they were all stunning in their own way. Even the children who sneaked around the adults were pretty.

No wonder Simon was anxious to return. Who wouldn't love the support of a family this large?

"You must be Helen." The oldest woman in the room

acknowledged her first.

"How do you know my name?"

"Your pack..." The woman glanced at the woman who must be Lizzy.

"Backpack," Lizzy said.

"Your backpack arrived without you."

"Oh."

"Helen," Simon called from over several heads. He lifted a hand to her, on autopilot; she moved to his side and welcomed the comfort of his familiar presence. With a hand to the small of her back, Simon started the introductions. "As you may have guessed, this is my mother Elizabeth and my father Finlay."

Helen accepted a smile from Lizzy and Fin stepped forward and took her hand in his. He kissed the back of it and winked at her when her face flushed.

"The Laird of this clan, Ian and his wife Lora. Grandparents of my heart."

"'Tis good to see you home, lad." Ian didn't bother kissing her hand, he pulled her into a hug that compressed all the air from her lungs. When he released her, he left his hands on her arms and squeezed. "Many thanks for bringing him home, lass. Our house is yours."

"Ah, thanks."

"Welcome," Lora said.

"Duncan and Tara, my aunt and uncle."

Duncan kissed her hand.

"There isn't a test on the names, feel free to ask," Tara suggested.

"I'll have to do that."

"You might remember Todd, the missing cop?" Todd waved and skipped the hand kissing. His face was vaguely familiar. "And his wife Myra. Again, an aunt and an uncle."

Myra was very pregnant as she greeted Helen from across the room. Helen waved with a short "Hi."

"Amber." Simon pointed out.

Amber waved.

"And Cian." Cian was slightly larger than Simon,

but the tight edge of his jaw had Helen swallowing hard.

"Don't forget us," one of the children said.

Small arms lifted to Simon. He quickly picked up the child and offered a tickle with a smile. "This is Aislin, Myra and Todd's youngest child. Over there is her big brother Jake. Selma, Kyle, and Tavish are my sister and brothers." Selma was a beautiful teenage girl and her brothers not far behind in age. "Briac, Fiona, and Ian belong to Duncan and Tara."

Tara spoke up again. "There really isn't a test. In fact, kids?" The children turned to Tara. "Be sure and tell Miss Adams your name when you speak with her to help her remember."

A chorus of "Yes, Aunt Tara" and "Yes, Mom," followed.

"Please call me Helen."

"We have the easy part. 'Tis you who will stumble over names for weeks." This came from one of the boys, his name already forgotten. "I'm Kyle," he reminded her.

"Thanks, but I don't think I'll be staying here for weeks."

Kyle titled his head to the side and furrowed his brow. "Yes, you will."

The convicted tone of the child would have been comical if it wasn't for the fact that all the people surrounding her had one skill or another. Telekinesis, premonitions, reading people's minds...heck, Simon's father could cause an earthquake and his grandfather could charge lightning from the sky. So to hear a ten-year-old tell her she wasn't going anywhere made her squirm. Did he know something she didn't?

Simon must have sensed her unease. He moved closer and placed a hand on her waist again. "Helen and I have some unfinished business to take care of at her home."

That caught the attention of the adults. The children appeared unaffected.

"What kind of business?" Fin, earthquake man, and Simon's step dad said. The names might not be too difficult to remember if Helen could match them with their Druid power.

Simon glanced at the kids and raised his brow.

Lizzy stepped forward. "My guess is we have a lot to discuss. Let's get Helen dressed, and we'll continue this over dinner."

Dressed? Helen glanced down at her jeans and t-shirt then at all the women in the room. Lord, when was the last time she even wore a dress?

"How did you manage to travel, Simon? None of the stones were missing."

"Helen's necklace."

Simon glanced down at Helen's neck, and his smile slid from his face.

"What?"

"Don't panic."

Oh, God, nothing good ever came from those words. "What?"

"What necklace, Uncle Simon?"

Helen lowered her eyes to her chest.

It was gone. Her necklace, her ticket home, was gone.

* * * *

All the color in Helen's face washed away in the space of one breath. She pushed passed him and jumped back onto his bed, tearing the coverings away in an attempt to find her time-traveling necklace.

"It's got to be here."

Lizzy narrowed her gaze.

"She has a necklace that opens the portal of time," Simon explained. "It's how we got here."

"It's not here," Helen cried franticly.

Simon reached over and placed a hand on Helen's shoulder. "'Tis okay, lass, we'll find it."

Tara motioned the kids out of the room.

"How am I going to get home?"

"We have other stones to move you."

"You do? Oh, yeah...you do." Helen nodded now, her eyes still wide with uncertainty. The fact that Helen allowed his arm to stay around her waist as he helped her off the bed and onto her feet was a testament to how unbalanced she felt.

"What does it look like?" Lizzy walked around the bed and looked at the floor.

"The pendant is made of a plain rock, the chain and setting has Coltic knots wound together."

Amber, who had moved around the bed with his Mom, stopped Liz from kneeling to search for the missing necklace.

"Was the stone this big?" Amber raised her hand and circled her forefinger with her thumb.

"Aye," Simon told her.

"The necklace isn't lost, it doesn't exist yet."

"Excuse me?" Helen asked.

"After Simon went to your time, five of the sacred stones multiplied leaving large and small stones beside them. I've only recently started creating pieces of jewelry to disguise them. 'Tis safe to conclude from your return that after the smaller stones have been generated both cannot be present in the same time. Hence, your necklace simply vanished once you returned."

"But I came and went before and nothing happened."

"The small stones weren't born yet," Lizzy said. "When Fin and I returned with one stone from the future many years ago, that stone disappeared."

Helen shook her head. "I don't get it."

"Not to worry, lass," Ian said. "All you need do is assist Amber in creating the necklace, and you'll be able to return home with as much ease as you've traveled here today."

"But we need to get back right away, don't we?" Helen glanced up at Simon.

"We've all the time in the world. When we return we'll do so within minutes of our leaving. We are talking time travel, love. As long as we don't try to return to a time when we are already there, everything will work out."

Helen barked a tiny laugh. "I wouldn't want to disappear while staring at myself from across the room."

"Exactly. Now why don't you go with my mother and the others, and I'll meet you back downstairs when you're ready."

Simon could see a slight hesitation before Helen nodded and allowed herself to be led from the room.

"'Tis good you're home," Fin said again.

"'Tis good to *be* home."

"Change, son, and we'll see you downstairs."

Simon glanced at the blue jeans fitting snuggly against his skin before nodding.

* * * *

Every inch of Helen's skin buzzed. Amber escorted her to her room where she proceeded to remove a couple of gowns for Helen's inspection. "You and I look to be similar in size," Amber said, holding up yards of material in the shape of a dress.

"Why can't I just wear this? It isn't like you guys don't know where I come from."

"Our family understands, but the others have no idea."

"The others?"

"The servants, my father's men."

So far, Helen had only seen the multitude of MacCoinnichs. The thought of employees running around this ancient stone Keep hadn't occurred to her. "I didn't think of that."

"'Tis very important to keep where and when you're from away from the others. We don't call attention upon ourselves as Druids. Perhaps Simon has already told you, but in these times to be called out as a witch would mean death."

Helen swallowed. "I don't shoot fire from my hands like Simon. I shouldn't have any problems."

Amber placed a dark umber gown on her bed and returned the other to a trunk. "I'll teach you."

"Teach me what?" Helen sat and toed off her shoes.

"To shoot fire from your hands."

"I don't think so. I've gone my whole life without that talent, no need to start it now."

"You make it sound as if you're old."

Helen felt old. Like she'd lived a hundred years in her small handful. All the family members who surrounded Simon on their arrival made her remember all the years she'd gone without. Still went without. Mrs. Dawson was the closest to family she had and she was thousands of miles and hundreds of years away.

Amber placed a hand on her arm and flinched. "I'm sorry."

"I'm not offended."

"For your loss. I've always had my family and can't imagine what it must have been like to have grown up alone. It must have been difficult."

Helen opened her mouth to question how Amber knew so much, and then remembered Simon telling her about Amber's empathic gift. "Life isn't fair. In fact, it sucks most of the time." Wanting to change the subject, Helen tugged her t-shirt from her shoulders. "So how do I get into this thing?"

Twenty minutes later, Amber escorted her down a dark hall and to a set of massive stairs. MacCoinnich Keep was huge. Stone walls reached high overhead. Wall sconces with candles burned as they walked down the stairs. Everywhere Helen looked was another impressive antique. Though it wasn't antique at present. She fingered a tapestry hanging on the wall for warmth. "The latest in modern medieval," she whispered.

"My mother's actually."

Helen stopped and pulled away to take in the needle and thread art. "Your mother made this...by hand?"

"We don't have machines, nor electricity to run them."

"That's amazing. The hours she must have put into it."

"Years. Nearly a decade, actually."

"Wow." And it was *wow*. Who did this kind of thing?

"There you two are." Simon walked into the room and paused.

As his gaze travel down Helen's frame, hers did the same to his. He'd transformed into a Scottish Highlander with a long kilt. The shirt he wore tapered at his waist, his broad shoulders emphasized by the clothing on his back. He was even more gorgeous in a kilt.

The way his heated gaze raked over her body in the dress Amber provided gave Helen's heart a little kick.

Helen sucked in her lower lip and returned her eyes to his. He wore a tiny smile and mischief danced behind it.

"Amazing," he whispered as he reached her side and placed her hand in the crook of his arm. Electricity zinged from the contact. He offered the other to Amber and walked them both into what Helen thought was a dining room.

She had little time to consider the man who traveled back and forth in time with her as Simon's extended family surrounded them both.

"Sit over here," Tara, or maybe it was Myra, who spoke. Placing the names with faces would take some time she figured.

Thankfully, Simon sat beside her and addressed everyone around them by name. All the children sat at the far end of the table and waited patiently for the meal to begin.

Ian, the Laird of the MacCoinnich clan started the small feast once the servants filled the room.

Helen sat in awe of the amount of people streaming from a kitchen. Some eyed her with curiosity, but none said anything directly. Perhaps they were used to strangers 'popping up' out of nowhere and kept their thoughts to themselves.

"'Tis good to see ye home, Lord Simon." One of the servants braved.

"'Tis good to be home, Maggie," he said with a wink.

Once the servants left the room, Lora said, "I've had a room prepared for you adjacent from Amber's."

Was that an inconvenience? Was she putting someone out? "Thank you."

"There are many empty rooms," Simon told her. "Once the children started coming, expansion on the Keep became necessary."

"Filled with love and laughter, right children?" Lora asked.

"Aye, Nana."

Helen helped pass trays loaded with cooked meats, bread, and vegetables around the table.

"Do you have family, lass?" The question came from Ian.

"No, not really." She moved along a tray of beef after taking a small sliver for herself.

"No family?" one of the kids asked.

"I'm an orphan." The words were spoken on autopilot, but the entire family paused. "It's okay. I've been that way my whole life. No big deal."

"I'm sorry," Fin, *earthquake man* said.

"Don't be. I'm used to it.

"No sisters, brothers?"

Helen shook her head.

"Who raised you?"

The food started to flow around the table again, but ears were intent on her answers. "Foster parents...life. I have Mrs. Dawson," she said defensively. Helen wasn't completely alone.

"Mrs. Dawson is like us," Simon said, as if the words meant she were part of a cult or religion. "She has a large, private estate where we will return."

Ian scanned behind Simon. When the room was void of anyone but family, he said, "Tell us what happened."

Helen nibbled on her meal as Simon explained what transpired since he'd left.

As his story unfolded, and the watchful eyes of his family sat in acceptance of every strange happening,

Helen was reminded of how alone she'd been all her life. What would it have been like to have a family who accepted your word as gospel simply because they believed in you? All her life, she had to prove herself to anyone and everyone who crossed her path. With the MacCoinnichs, life didn't roll that way.

As the adults spoke, the children attended to each other, the oldest helping the youngest with an occasional direction from an adult. Laird Ian listened, as did most of the men without so much as a creased brow or exclamation.

The women watched her.

The crazy thing was, when a servant stepped into the room the MacCoinnich's skipped into casual conversation. "How is the meal? How high can Ian lift his sword?" The answers were given, and then as soon as they were alone, the chat shifted to the subject of Helen and Simon's travel in time. The well practiced art of deception. Funny, Helen always thought deceit had a nasty connotation to the meaning. This family didn't seem to have any bad vibes to speak of.

Yet, the entire meal was surreal.

Simon relayed the past few days, and Helen only offered answers to the questions he couldn't answer.

Myra, who looked an awful lot like Amber, helped the children from the table and resumed what Helen thought were bedtime rituals. The adults moved to the massive hall and gathered around the hearth.

"What do you plan now?"

"We need to go back and determine what Philip was searching for."

"He could be a petty thief," Todd said. "Though, I doubt it."

"I doubt it, too. He left with nothing and acted like a man with a secret."

"Could he be Druid?" Amber asked.

"I didn't get close enough to tell."

Helen shrugged. "Don't look at me. I didn't know anything about Druids until last week."

Lizzy laughed. "A few of us know the feeling. Crazy, isn't it?"

"Nuts."

"You'll get used to it."

"If he is Druid, there is no telling what he's capable of."

Helen glanced at Tora. "What do you mean?"

"Not all of us use our gifts for good." For the first time that night, Cian spoke. During the entire meal, he'd only listened, his eyes occasionally drifting toward her. Because he chose that moment to speak, and because of the words he used, a cold dart of uncertainty traveled over her body.

"What do you mean? You think he might want to hurt me?"

"Mayhap."

Simon swung his head toward Cian, he eyes narrowed. "We shouldn't speculate."

"No, you need to investigate," Todd said.

"Exactly. This is why we need to return. We'd like to go back with reinforcements."

Simon watched the head of the house and waited for Ian to nod.

"Amber can help determine Philip's intentions."

Ian's jaw tightened. But before he could say a thing, Simon added. "And Cian and I can escort Amber and Helen."

Chapter Thirteen

After hardly sleeping the night before, Helen shoved aside the plush blankets on the softest bed she'd every lay and moved to the hearth to stoke the smoldering logs. The room was small compared to the one Simon slept in, but larger than the one in her apartment in California. The solitude of the past few hours helped ground her thoughts. For the first time in her life, she was surrounded by a loving family who thought of each other first, then thought of the world second. They accepted her as if they knew she was coming, and as if she'd play a vital part in their lives.

Throughout the previous evening, she was assured they'd help her find a way home. The only guarantees Helen had in her life were the ones she made happen so to trust in the Clan MacCoinnich was a huge step. She'd put aside her worry about being trapped in time and bask in the world unfolding in front of her.

She'd always appreciated art in its many forms. The tapestries, paintings, candelabras, and furnishings were all pieces of art that would sell in the thousands if not millions. Everything she saw had a practical use—well most of it. Tapestries and rugs kept the walls and floors warm. Still the cold from outside seeped into the rooms and reminded you there wasn't any central heating system to ward off the chill.

The paintings were the only snapshots in time. Something Tara had encouraged the family to commission. Ian and Lora's portrait dominated the main hall. Duncan and Tara along with Myra and Todd, Fin and Lizzy all had their portraits along the galley at the top of the stairs. Helen wondered where the paintings were in her century. She'd not seen them before, or she'd have remembered them. Maybe a private collector or a distant relative kept them hidden. She made a mental note to search them out when she returned home.

Helen poured water into a basin and washed away some of the sleep from her eyes.

Amber had told her to prepare for a solid day of learning the ways of Scotland in the sixteenth century. "Open your eyes and ears, but say little unless to me or the family. Best not to call attention to yourself."

Impossible. Already the maids eyed her with cautious unease.

A soft knock on the door pulled Helen out of her thoughts.

"Come in."

Amber glided into the room with two maids at her heels. "Good morning to you, Helen. I hope you slept well."

"I did," she lied.

"This is Lita and her sister Anabel. Both work wonders with a needle and thread and will help us tailor a few things for you to wear."

The maids actually dipped into short curtseys before unloading their hands of the yards of material they carried.

Helen started to protest, but a stern look from Amber had her shutting her mouth before uttering a syllable. Open your eyes, close your mouth. *I guess the lessons begin now.*

Amber crossed to the window and opened the heavy blinds. The milky dawn of Scotland didn't stop the glare of light from pouring into the room.

Within an hour Lita and Anabel had all the measurements they needed and were busy hand stitching clothing for Helen to wear. At home, Helen's wardrobe consisted of clothing made in China or Taiwan. To have something not only tailored to her, but handmade, was truly jaw-dropping.

Once the maids left the room, Amber opened the conversation about her near future. "It took time for Lizzy and Tara to accommodate to the clothing we wear here. As I'm sure I'll have to adjust when I travel with you." As she spoke, a shadow of excitement washed over her face.

"Do Tara and Lizzy ever wear clothes from the future?"

"At times, though not often any more. And never in front of nonfamily members."

Amber helped her into the second dress set aside for her the day before. As they spoke, Amber pulled on the corded fastening on the back of the gown. Helen wouldn't look at a zipper again in the same way. Little connecting metal teeth did wonders to fashion.

"I don't think I could wear this every day."

Amber laughed.

"You've heard that before, haven't you?"

"Lizzy complained the most and still refuses a corset more often than not."

"You'll understand her frustration when you come home with us."

"Aye, you have the right of it."

Why was it Amber was resolved to shoot hundreds of years into the future without showing a nerve?

"Tell me, what is your strength?"

Helen moved to a chair and pulled a brush through her hair. Amber followed her and took the brush from her hand to finish the task. Helen didn't have girlfriends and seldom had another person brush her hair outside of a salon. This quiet moment caught her in her chest. "I'm a photographer."

Amber waved a hand in the air. "Not your job, though the thought of women working as anything but maids and merchants still baffles me, but your Druid strength?"

"Oh, that. I'm not sure how to explain it."

Amber dropped the brush and proceeded to pull

strands of hair together in a small intricate braid, pulling only small amounts of hair as she went. Out of a pocket in the fold of her dress, she produced a copper color ribbon and wove it into Helen's hair. "Try."

"When I'm searching for something, or someone, I feel, *eh,* energy I guess you might call it. Kind of like dogs knowing where something is by scent."

Amber kept weaving, her hands steady. "Can you control it?"

"I'm not sure what there is to control. The feeling is there or it isn't."

"Does it overwhelm you?"

"Only when I find what I'm looking for. The air feels thick, like humidity on a hot day."

Amber's fingers stilled. "But it vanished quickly?"

"Yeah."

Helen heard Amber swallow and before she turned her head. A brief unease shifted in Amber's gaze and she went back to Helen's hair. "Now that you know your gift is a skill much like stitching a skirt, or weaving hair, it grows with practice."

"I wouldn't have a clue how to practice."

Amber finished her task and laid her hands on Helen's shoulders. "My family can help."

"Getting me home is a priority, not sharpening my Druid skills."

"That is where you're wrong. You're here for a reason. 'Tis important to learn all you can before returning."

"You sound like some divine intervention happened. I stumbled on the necklace by accident and ended up here searching for a lost child."

"But you found a man, a warrior worthy of your attention."

Helen met Amber's gaze and felt her cheeks flush. "Simon's easy on the eyes, but we come from two different worlds."

"You come from the exact same world."

Okay, maybe they did. Still, his life was clearly in

the sixteenth century while hers wasn't. "He's kissed me, but that's all."

Amber smiled and said nothing. Helen remembered that Amber's empathic gift gave her the advantage in their conversation.

"I'm not relationship material. Hell, I don't even date."

One brow on Amber's face lifted.

Helen pushed from the chair afraid of what Amber might see if she chose to dig deeper into her mind. "I don't know what you guys eat for breakfast around here, but I'm starving." Maybe changing the subject would help.

Before she reached the door to the room, Amber laid a hand on her arm. "Somewhere deep inside you've been hurt. I won't pry, but if you ever want to talk, I'm here."

An instant surge of tears filled Helen's eyes. For a non-emotional woman, the feeling left her disjointed and bare. "I don't know what you're talking about."

Amber dropped her hand and her eyes. "As you wish."

"I wish for food."

As they made their way down the same massive staircase, the sound of men's voices shouted from the hall below.

"They attack from the North and the East, the village is directly in their path."

Amber held her arm out to stop Helen's descent. They leaned over the banister and listened. From the sound of the voices, and the sheer number of men gathered below, Helen thought an entire army had assembled in the Keep.

"What's going on?" she whispered to Amber who glanced over the rail with white knuckles.

"An attack, I think."

Attack? "You mean here?"

"Close enough to drive my father's men inside."

Her father's men. As in, his army. Dozens of fierce warriors all with fierce swords and unnamed weapons kept filling the room. Some walked around Ian, Simon, Fin, Duncan, Cian, and Todd and warmed themselves by the fire as if they had walked into their own home. Worry crept into Helen's thoughts. "I don't understand."

Amber placed a hand on Helen's and winced as if burned. After pulling her hand away, she said. "Don't fret. My father is a very powerful Laird with many men in his service. We'll be fine."

The sound of several small feet tapped behind them. Helen turned to see many of the MacCoinnich children gathered. "What's happened?" one of them asked.

"I don't know."

"Shh!" Briac, the oldest of the children scolded. "Listen."

"Trevor and his party met with trouble past the moor. 'Twas only a band of scouts and easily deterred."

"There are others?" Ian asked.

"Aye, many."

"And growing."

"'Tis as if they lay in wait, for their numbers to increase."

Even from the balcony Helen could see the tension in Ian's shoulders, could see Simon clenching his fists.

Something was terribly wrong.

* * * *

There was a large sitting room on the same floor as the bedrooms in the main wing of the Keep. Amber explained that its use was mainly a room for the children to play. Several chairs were brought in and many of the children's things were removed to accommodate the MacCoinnich family.

The main hall of the Keep was littered with warriors. Some rolled out bedding while others fell asleep against walls. A steady stream of people filled the home and the surrounding courtyard and garrison.

Apparently a village nearby was threatened and Ian ordered its occupants to the safety of the castle.

Helen observed everything as an outsider. History unfolded before her eyes as she watched a Highland clan prepare for attack. There were high towers in the Keep where some men stood guard. The elderly from the village were given rooms inside while the majority of villagers sheltered in tents throughout the yard. Helen couldn't go anywhere without running into someone. That alone astonished her considering how huge the MacCoinnich Keep was. Only a day before the place appeared massive. Now it felt cramped. Not to mention some of the Scottish accents were terribly thick, and the words used so foreign, that she couldn't understand what people were saying.

Simon hadn't made a direct appearance all day. Tara and Lora kept the family aware of what happened below through their wacky ability to speak to their spouses with their minds. Maids hustled in providing food but quickly scurried out to meet the needs of the gathering men below.

Amber retreated to her room and Helen now sat with Liz, Simon's mother, who might be older but certainly didn't resemble anyone used to what was happening around them.

"How are you holding up?" Liz asked.

Helen thought before answering the question. Threats were coming from all sides. There wasn't any room that she knew of to escape. But then again, maybe Liz knew something Helen didn't. "How are *you* holding up?" Best way to answer a question when you're not sure of all the possible answers was to ask a question of one's own.

"I'm scared shitless."

The expletive made Helen smile. Simon's mother might be dressed medieval style but she spoke completely twenty-first century when cornered. "Me, too."

"We'll be okay."

"How can you be sure?"

Liz glanced over at Tara and Myra who were consoling the children. "We've been against worse."

"Back home one man is following me and I thought

it was the end of the world. Seems there's a whole army out there coming down on us. I'm not sure what is worse."

Liz nodded. "Magical is much harder to deal with than physical."

"Am I supposed to know what that means?"

"No, I guess you don't." Liz took a deep breath and continued. "There are enemies approaching with swords and cannons, arrows and fire. But these are physical. There are very definite ways of defeating them—"

"Or losing to them and ending up lying in a pool of blood."

Liz shot a look at the kids but Helen was careful with the tone of her voice.

"Ya, well," Liz continued. "There are ways to physically defeat your enemy. When you're dealing with magic the sky is the limit in possible outcomes."

"You're talking fire balls and moving objects with your mind. Not that I get any of that, but okay, I see where there might be an element of surprise. Still, eventually you'll know what's coming if you observe."

"Fire balls and telekinesis is the least of what we've seen."

Helen ignored the edge in Liz's voice. "I forgot premonition and empathy." There were other things Simon had said his family was capable of, but Helen hadn't heard much of his unbelievable splatter.

"You really have very little idea what we're capable of."

"I'm held up in a medieval castle while some crazy war is being strategized below. Seems to me like we're hiding and waiting for others to determine our future. I'm not sure how stoking a fire or making a clock fly across the room is going to help anything."

Liz's blue eyes caught Helen's. A flicker of surprise shuttered behind her gaze before a knowing smile spread over her lips. Maybe fate took a hand when Tara walked their way and she interrupted. "Simon is on his way back. We should know more soon."

Helen's back stiffened. "Back? Where's he been?" The thought of him out among their enemies made her heart beat a little faster.

Tara glanced at Liz. After a nod she continued. "Scouting."

One answer.

Not one she liked.

"Alone?"

The question didn't raise any alarm with the women. Both of them nodded.

Helen's heart skipped a beat. "You let your son go out alone when an army is trying to beat the walls of the ton of bricks down?" Her voice rose and several anxious faces turned her way.

"He won't be seen."

How could Tara be so sure one man on a lone horse wouldn't be seen? Suddenly the need to see Simon in one solid masculine piece overwhelmed all other needs. Helen stood and ran her suddenly damp palms along the confining dress she wore.

"You don't know, do you?"

"Know what? That it's crazy to send one man by himself to scout an army? I know *that's* crazy." Helen headed for the door. A Keep full of medieval men be damned. She wanted to know Simon was healthy and wasn't going to let anyone stand in her way in seeing it with her own eyes. Then she might have a word or two with *Laird Ian*. Who the hell sends a solo man to do the job of a small army? Helen may have skipped a class or two in history, but even she knew that wasn't a very successful strategic plan.

She made it past the door and a few steps down the hall before Liz caught up with her. "You're going the wrong way."

Helen stopped and turned toward Simon's mother. "I want to see that he's not coming back half-dead."

"And you think I'm all kinds of terrible for not running with you."

"Well, yeah, I do."

124

Liz held out a thick piece of plaid and thrust the material into Helen's arms. "He'll need this and you'll find him at the highest peak." Liz shifted against a stone wall and pointed down a dark hall. "Go up these stairs and turn left. You'll find a spiral of stairs that branch off to several floors. Don't stop until you're at the very last door. Once you're passed through there, an even darker hall will lead you to three more doors. Open the second one and wait."

Dark halls and doors? What did this have to do with Simon?

"I love my son, Helen. Maybe after you speak with him, you'll have a better grasp of what's happening around you. You have to trust us in order to work with us. The sooner that happens, the better."

Helen glanced beyond Liz and down the dark passage.

"Here's a candle."

Great, like the small stub of a candle would help. What if she got lost?

Though Helen didn't remember Simon saying anything about his mother reading minds beyond his, the strangest words came out of Liz's mouth. "And if the candle goes out, cowboy up and try something new. Look at any sconce on the wall, get good and pissed, scared or any damn thing. Think of a firecracker on the Fourth of July and watch that sucker light your way."

Helen felt her brow crease. The noise from the hall below grew louder.

"I know you're scared right now. I know you don't understand what you've gotten into. But the sooner you're up to speed, the easier it will be for everyone."

Cian bounded up the steps behind them and stopped when he saw them speaking. "Excuse me."

"It's okay, we're done here." Liz stood back giving Helen room to walk beyond her.

"I'm fetching Simon."

"It's okay, Helen's all over it. Aren't you, Helen?" There was a challenge in Liz's voice.

"Up the stairs and turn left?"

Liz nodded.

Fine. "Fine," she repeated aloud.

Helen turned and placed one foot in front of the other. Once the casting of light Liz held in her hand was behind her, Helen started toward the stairwell.

"You know she's unaware of what she'll find, right?" Cian's question to Liz made Helen hesitate.

"The sooner she learns the truth, the better."

"I'll tell my father to expect a delay. But he won't wait long."

Helen took another step.

"Reality has a way of jump starting the brain, Cian. Tell your Dad to take a chill-pill. Helen needs this and Simon shouldn't have kept her in the dark this long."

"An army of men wait his word."

"And a few minutes isn't going to change a damn thing. Check on Amber. See if she's okay, and then take your time going back to Ian. It won't feel that long."

The last word Helen heard was Cian saying "Women!" Then, because she wasn't going to ask for an explanation, she bounded up the stairs repeating Liz's directions in her mind. All the while praying the stupid candle wouldn't die.

Chapter Fourteen

Through the eyes of a falcon, Simon swooped behind a tree and silently slid past the guard posted on the western turret of the Keep. Not that a knight would consider a falcon a threat, but Simon didn't need to call any attention to any animal form he might take. He enjoyed the final blast of air that ran along his wingspan as he dove for the dark window that served as his refuge.

Before his talons could reach the floor, he willed his form to shift. Familiar pain popped every vertebra into place, skin stretched and feathers retreated. No matter how liberating it felt to sprout wings and soar above everyone and everything, having arms, legs, and an appetite for human food always welcomed him more.

Shaking his body from head to foot, Simon stood from a crouched position and took a deep breath.

A shuddering breath filled the room.

He wasn't alone.

The sky had grown dark and the moon hadn't yet risen. Without a candle, it was hard to see who welcomed him. He thought he heard the rustling of skirts. "Mom?" he asked, hoping it wasn't she. Something about being a full-grown man standing in front of his mother naked was just wrong.

"Oh, God."

Not his mom.

He could feel Helen's panic long before he saw her face. A kilt skidded to the floor at his feet, and he heard Helen's back as she hit the door.

"Helen."

She turned and ran her hands along the wall, searching for the handle of the door. Simon grabbed the plaid, shifted it over his hips, and caught the door before she could open it.

"Wait."

"Let me go."

Simon kept a firm hand on the door and attempted to surround Helen with the other to calm her down.

She ducked below his arm and fled to the far side of the small room. "Get away from me." Her voice shook. The shock of seeing him shift must have been horrific. Why was she waiting for him anyway? Who sent her?

"Helen, it's okay."

"Okay?" she hissed. "Y-you just... Oh, God."

She moved again in the dark, shadows played on the walls from the torches lit outside. He willed a sconce on the wall to light with only a thought, and soon a warm glow lit up one very distressed Helen. Her beautiful blue eyes were owl-wide, her body rigid and poised to run. She shifted back and forth between her feet, and her fists clutched the fabric of her dress.

"How did you know to come here?"

"Your mom sent me."

He'd have to have a word with her. And not a pleasant one. This wasn't the way he wanted to reveal his gift to Helen.

"What's going on, Simon?"

"I should have told you on my own."

"Told me what? That you're not human?"

"I am human," he said lowering his voice and glancing to the open window beyond her back.

She took the hint and lowered her voice. Her clipped whisper no less effective in displaying her anger. "You *flew* in here. That isn't human in my book."

Simon raised his hands and turned them over a couple of times. "Does this not look human to you?"

A quick glance to his arms and her eyes darted back to his face. "I thought you were an animal whisperer. You didn't say you became them."

"Would you have believed me if I'd said I did?" He took a step closer.

She leapt back. "I don't know what to believe any more." Her hands were clearly shaking.

Dammit! His mother had some serious explaining to do.

"I discovered my gift shortly after we came here. I never asked for it, but I'm not ashamed of it either." Which was true, though he wished he could erase the past few minutes from Helen's mind and tell her when he felt she was more ready to accept it.

"S-so, what are you? A bird-man?"

He shook his head. "A falcon is convenient. I'm able to scout without detection."

Her face softened a small margin. "They told me you were scouting alone. It sounded like a suicide mission."

"Hardly. Only the family knows what I can do. Certainly, our enemy is clueless. My safety, all of our safety, depends on secrecy."

"Good. I guess." Her fingers flexed and her brow creased. "You're okay, then?"

"I'm fine, 'tis you I worry about, lass."

Helen started to pace, which Simon took as a good sign. Every time she paced she was working a puzzle out in her mind. "Birds? Only birds?"

A lie by omission waited on his lips, but to keep up the disguise now was pointless. "And other forms."

She stopped. "What other forms?"

"A wolf."

"Like the one in the woods that first day."

"Aye. That was me."

She started the restless walk, again. "The gorillas?"

"No, but I've not tried. I've taken the form of a shark. Damn uncomfortable breathing underwater."

She stopped her intrepid pacing and let out a tiny, forced laugh. Her body started to tremble as the stress of the past days clearly caught up with her. Helen buried her face in her hands as she tilted toward the floor.

Simon caught her before she fell, enveloping her in his arms.

Shaking, she buried her head into his bare chest. Simon soothed her cries and offered words of comfort. She'd been through too much. Holding her while she cried was becoming routine. Not that he minded her in his arms, but he'd prefer it be on better terms. The floral feminine scent of her filled his over-enhanced olfactory senses, the ones he had whenever he took on an animal form. A faint scent of lavender he knew the women put in the soap had him pulling in a deep, refreshing breath.

Helen's palms flattened out over his chest and started a slow inspection. Maybe she was determining if any feathers remained. A simple slide of her fingers over his nipples made them pebble, brought his cock to attention.

He needed to stop her assessment of his frame or he'd end up taking advantage of her fragile state. Grasping her hands, he held her still until she moved away enough to look deep into his eyes. Desire leapt up his spine as she tilted her lips to his and lifted on her toes.

A whisper of a kiss met his lips, willingly given by a woman he'd desired from first glance, and he was powerless against it. Dropping her hands, Simon pulled her tiny waist close to him and slanted his lips over hers. They were hot, moist, and open to explore. This wasn't a stolen kiss, or one born of shock, it was delicious and giving, fulfilling on levels beyond sensation. Want quickly morphed into need as she willingly pressed her body closer. The firm swell of her breasts met his chest and Simon lifted his hand to touch even more of her offering. Her breath caught as the first swipe of his thumb made her breast pebble.

Helen kissed him harder and ran her hands down his bare back. She stopped at his waist and moved back up, her nails dug in.

He lingered over her mouth, tasting every inch until

they were both breathless and in need of air. In the back of his mind, Simon knew he needed to stop this seduction but his body had different plans. A tender spot on Helen's neck pulsed and Simon nibbled and licked his way lower. He tugged away the loose bodice of her dress, and explored the creamy expanse of the top of her breast. He half expected her to push him away, was elated when she arched back giving him room to take more. The deep rose of her nipple slipped free of her gown and Simon covered it with his mouth. He smiled over her breast as her knees gave way, nearly pulling them both to the floor.

The floor.

He needed to end this or he'd end up taking her on a damp, stone floor. He drew her nipple between his teeth and licked its end one last time before reluctantly releasing it and pulling back.

God she was beautiful. Her lids half closed, her lips opened in invitation. But now wasn't the time.

Soon.

"W-why did you stop?"

"I care too much for your comfort to take you here in this dingy room."

He tucked her breast away but kept her close. If he'd learned one thing about the woman in his arms it was that she ran away whenever they stopped holding each other. Simon didn't want her running.

Like clockwork, she tugged back, but he didn't let her go. Instead, he dipped his lips to hers for a promising kiss. When she relaxed, he released her lips again.

"You're making me crazy, Simon."

He smiled. "Someone is bound to come looking for us. A war rages, or have you forgotten?"

She sighed and dropped back to her flat feet. "Your family catching us kissing *once* is enough for one lifetime."

"Aye. Makes it difficult to face my mother without a childish blush."

"Right."

"Mayhap when things calm we can explore each other further."

The blush he spoke of, now filled her cheeks. "I'd like that."

Simon kissed her forehead and took her palm in his. When he opened the door, they noticed Cian leaning against the outer hall, a smirk played on his lips.

* * * *

Helen hadn't seen Simon for three days. Three long, nerve-racking days and sleepless nights. While he scanned the Highlands as a falcon, spying on his enemies, the MacCoinnichs rearranged their home to accommodate the growing number of knights flowing in. Laird Ian had many allies and few enemies, which meant the Keep exploded with bodies. The more people who entered, the farther Amber receded into herself. They attempted to begin work on reconstructing the necklace but gave up after only a few hours. Although Helen had only known the woman for a few days, she worried about her health. Each day she grew more pale and said very little.

When she found a moment alone with Myra, Helen asked what she could do. "What's wrong?"

"'Tis her gift. Her empathy for others reaches beyond those she touches. The weight and worries of the impending battle is on everyone's minds."

"And Amber feels everyone's anxiety?"

"Grief, sorrow, hate—she feels it all. 'Tis worse in the past ten years or so. She's careful not to touch others, but she doesn't need her hands to channel her gift."

"Can't she turn it off?"

Myra shifted a long strand of her coal-black hair over her shoulder. "Nay."

"What about creating a buffer? Something to quiet the empathy she feels for others?"

"Like placing your head under a pillow to dull the noise?"

"Yeah. You guys have told me some fanciful stories about how you've read other peoples' minds or kept the noise inside a room so no one would learn the truth about you. There has to be something we can do."

Lora returned to the room with Tara and Lizzy. Most of the kids were already asleep in the two rooms set aside for them, boys in one, girls in the other. The women would take turns watching over the children since the men were often unavailable. Only when the kids were down for the night did the news of the day spill for Helen to hear.

"Selma, Briac, come here children," Lora told the oldest.

Once the teenage kids were at her side, she graced them with a smile. "I need you to watch over the others so I might have a word in private with your aunts."

Briac, who clearly felt he was too old to be cast aside as a child puffed his chest out. Tara stopped her son before he said a word. "Your father asks that you keep your sword at your side in your task, son."

Briac's mouth quickly shut and he stood taller. He reached a hand out to his sword perched against the wall by the fireplace. The broadsword flew into his palm safely.

Helen swallowed. She's seen Myra open a door with her mind when her hands were full, but she'd never witnessed one of the kids do something so powerful. Ya kinda had to have a little respect for a teen with a sword, an attitude, and the ability to knock you on your ass with a thought.

"They'll be safe with me." He sauntered out the door and to the boys' room.

"What about me?" Selma asked Lizzy.

Lizzy reached for her daughter and smiled. "Myra and I'll be in there soon. We don't expect trouble tonight."

The girl nodded and kissed her mother before following Briac from the room.

Alone, Helen asked. "So, what was that all about?"

"Briac needs to know he's helping or he'll seek trouble. Cian was exactly that way as a teen. Best he stays with the others. His training isn't complete to stand on the field with the men."

"He's just a kid."

"At sixteen, men are often placed in battle here."

"That's too young."

"Mayhap," Lora said.

"What news do you bring?"

The five of them moved closer to the fire and made themselves comfortable. "We've learned one of the clan names who fight against us."

Helen wouldn't know any clan names, so the answer wasn't one she had any anxiety in hearing, but the other women in the room jumped at the news. "Who?"

"McNeil."

Tara and Lizzy shrugged their shoulders. Myra pitched her brows together in thought. "Do I know that name?"

"I hardly know it," Lora said. "Been many years since their name was whispered here. Long before our search for Grainna."

That name Helen knew. All of the MacCoinnichs spoke of the evil Druid witch who sought to destroy every last MacCoinnich. She lost, thankfully, but not without cost.

"Why do they attack?"

"We do not know. To fortify this region with their own men? 'Tis hard to say."

"So what, whoever has the biggest knife wins the house?" Helen tried to grasp why men fought in this time.

"In years past this happened more often. Seems with the shift in power in both Scotland and England this land and others that surround us have become worth the risk to take over."

Helen wished more than ever that she'd paid attention to her European history. Staying in school was hardly possible where she grew up. She dropped out and later earned her GED as an adult. Even took a few semesters at a community college. European art she knew something about. If a piece was forged during a particularly turbulent time the piece would be more valuable, but outside of those dates, she was clueless of the political climate.

Lizzy shook her head. "I don't get it. There isn't any talk about a war in this region on the books."

"The books, what books?"

"When we sent Myra forward in time I asked her to bring a few things back with her. History books were on the list." Tara leaned forward as she spoke. "Not that we planned on changing history, but we thought it would help to keep the stones safe if we kept them out of war zones."

"Not to mention a little self preservation," Lizzy added.

"We'd not abandon MacCoinnich Keep even if we came under attack," said Lora.

"But we wouldn't risk a total wipeout of the family by lying in wait for a bomb, either." Lizzy didn't believe in going down with a sinking ship. There was comfort in knowing someone in the house was willing to retreat if the fight was useless. Helen had survived a rather lousy childhood and didn't desire a bloody death in the sixteenth century.

"We've been fighting off small bands of men for nearly a year. There are several known mercenaries we've brought down, which proves whoever is behind the attack doesn't have a strong loyal following."

"Then how are they organizing such a grand scale attack? Seems to me all those beefy guys downstairs could easily overpower small search parties." Helen tried to imagine a small rebel attack on an army. There had to be something she was missing. "How do the McNeil's inspire this fight?"

"That is the question. One I hope Lizzy might be able to find an answer to in her books."

Helen turned to Lizzy. "I take it you're the resident

historian?"

"Because I loved school so much." She rolled her eyes.

Helen laughed.

"I'll look up the name, see what I can find. It would help to know exactly where the family is now."

"I'll show you on your maps when we retire."

"Simon should be back by tomorrow with more news."

Helen had heard he was off again, but did her best to curb her worry for his safety. "Tomorrow? I thought he was back every night."

"He needed to go further to see how far away the enemy is staged. We've already spread our men beyond the eastern flank of the enemy." Lora explained Ian's strategy.

"He'll be back." Lizzy covered Helen's hand with hers.

"It's the waiting that sucks," said Helen.

"I'd much rather be out there kicking ass."

"But exposing our gifts would bring more than the McNeil's. All of Scotland and most of England would join the fight to rid the region of witches."

Lora glanced around the room. "Where's Amber?"

"Sequestered in her room," Myra told her mother.

"I should have guessed."

"She's not well. If I didn't know what plagued her, I'd worry about an illness." Tara walked over to the fire and placed another piece of wood on top of the flames.

"Helen and I were discussing Amber's plight. Helen thought maybe there was some type of blanket we could place over her to dull the onslaught of empathy."

"A magical one?" Lizzy asked.

"I guess," Helen said. "Not that I have a clue how to achieve it, but it seems like you guys might." Helen pointed to a ratty cord draped over the handle on the door. Myra explained that the cord kept their conversations and noise within the room silent to anyone on the outside of the door. It was something

Myra and Lizzy had come up with years ago to avoid the servants discovering the MacCoinnich secrets. The cord was kept handy, but only used when private matters needed discussing. "The cord you did your MoJo on works. Why not do the same to something else for Amber?"

The women quietly pondered Helen's words.

"I like the way you think," Lizzy said.

"That might work."

"We have to try. There's no telling how long this battle will continue. I hate to see Amber suffering." Myra glanced at Helen with hope in her eyes.

"Constructing a circle with the Keep full of knights is risky," Lora said.

"More risky than losing Amber?"

Lora shook her head. "Nay."

"Then talk to Ian while we plan our next move. It will do us good to be doing something to help someone. Besides, if Amber were needed now to use her gift to detect a spy among us, she wouldn't be able to." Leave it to Lizzy to cut everything down to the basics. No wonder Simon had grown up so well adjusted even in the mist of time travel and magic.

"I'll be back." Lora stood to leave.

"So, what's all this about a circle?" Helen glanced between the three women and waited their answer.

Chapter Fifteen

Helen sat on the floor in a circle with Myra, Liz, and Tara. Lit candles surrounded them and in the center of all of it was a plain brown cloak. The goal was simple. Light the candles, join hands and therefore forces, and draw upon their individual power before forcing it into the cloak. Liz was apparently the Druid of the hour. She had the knack to come up with rhymes or spells, or whatever the heck they called them, that worked.

Unable to leave her own chamber without enduring physical pain, Amber remained in her room. Joining hands, even with family, was too much for her senses to bear. She filled their thoughts even though she wasn't with them.

"We need to hurry," Tara said, glancing toward the door guarded by Cian. Outside Duncan watched and planned to divert any people who might be wandering around the Keep.

Lizzy presented her hand to Helen, which she took. "I'm not sure what I'm supposed to do."

"Just listen to my words and believe them. Concentrate on the cloak."

"And don't let go," Myra added with a slight edge in her voice.

"Even when we start to levitate."

Levitate? Helen felt her eyes grow wide. Liz squeezed her hand.

"Sorry, forgot to tell you about that. Whenever we do this, our gifts merge to some extent. Since I'm the flyer in the family, you guys come along for the ride." Liz spoke as if she was talking about a trip to the supermarket.

"What do you mean by ride?" Helen asked.

"We just hover. Nothing too drastic."

Myra placed a protective hand on her protruding belly. "It's not dangerous or I'd be sitting this one out. Besides, Lizzy has more control over the hover thing. We only levitate a few inches now."

Tara laughed. "We soared to a couple of feet at times in the beginning. The drop sucked."

Helen's hands grew damp. Even with the casual tone in the conversation, her anxiety about what was happening peeked. "Dropped?"

"We don't fall any more. Lizzy controls our descent." Tara smiled at her sister when she spoke.

"Oh." They sounded so breezy about all this. Helen's pulse tapped too fast, her breathing raced.

"If you're done tutoring Helen, you might want to move along," Cian suggested without a hint of a smile on his face. "Everyone waits."

Scolded for their chatting, Helen shifted her focus to the cloak lying in the center of their circle.

"Ready?" Lizzy asked.

A chorus of yeses was her answer. Helen watched the others and attempted to mimic their actions, all the while hoping her presence wasn't going to muck up the operation.

Lizzy lifted her voice and squeezed Helen's hand. "We cast our circle by candle light and seek great help for our sister's plight. Her gift has weakened her mortal self and all we ask is for the Ancient's help."

As Lizzy's singsong voice lifted, so did their bodies. Sure enough, all four of them levitated slowly from the floor. Strange, her body didn't feel a loss of gravity, or even the missing floor beneath her, but her dress now hung below her bent knees as did the others in the circle. The flames of the candles spiked like some special effect on a movie screen. Something in the air felt electric and the hair on Helen's arms stood on end. It was hard to concentrate on Lizzy's words with the strange sensations rolling over Helen's skin, but she tried. Helen stared at the cloak and repeated Lizzy's words in her head. She added the words, for Amber, and did her level best to ignore the fact that she was floating above the ground.

"Give her peace and tranquility when wrapped inside the cloth you see. If the Ancients will it so, give us a sign so we will know."

They all held their breath and waited. Just when Helen didn't think she'd see anything of importance the air in the center of the circle warmed and blew her hair behind her shoulders. Like any time in the past when her own gift led her to what she wanted to find, her skin tingled and a deep sense of knowing she'd find what she looked for settled over her.

As the air swirled and heated, the cloak drifted from the floor and stretched itself out taut. A blast of light spun with the heat, streaking amber and silver flecks that looked a lot like pixie dust Helen had seen in animated films. *Sonofabitch this is gonna work.* No sooner did the thought leave her head the cloak drifted slowly to the floor and settled between them.

"Wow," she whispered.

"In this day and in this hour, we thank the Ancient's for our power." Lizzy tilted her head to the side and with slow measured movement, Helen felt her backside touch the floor. The flames on the candles made a small snapping noise and all blew out at the same time. The light cast by the fire was the only glow in the room.

Lizzy let go of Helen's hand and patted her knee. "You did well."

"I didn't do anything."

"Yeah, I think you did." Tara stood and helped Myra from the floor. "We've been doing this for a while and I don't ever remember feeling my skin sizzle as much."

"Oh, aye, I felt it, too." Myra rubbed her bottom as she spoke.

"We all add to the circle. We can do some things

solo, but together we're just better. Don't know why, we just are."

The door behind them clicked as Cian left the room without saying a word.

"What's up with him lately?" Tara asked.

"Wish I knew," Myra said.

"Is he acting odd?" Helen thought it was his stoic personality and not a new behavior. He seldom smiled or even acknowledged her presence, let alone tried to talk. He only really said something when it was important. No chitchat from that one. He embodied the textbook Highland warrior image.

"He isn't himself."

Tara moved the candles around the room while Lizzy picked up the cloak. "Whatever's eating at him is getting worse. I wish he'd talk to someone. He used to open up to Simon."

Lizzy folded the cloak over her arm. "He needs a girlfriend to knock him out of his funk."

Helen smiled. "Is there such a thing these days? From what I see, people are either married or flirting." She'd seen a fair number of sideway glances and raised eyebrows from the huge men downstairs but nothing else.

"There isn't a club scene or a movie to go to if that's what you mean, but courting in this time isn't a whole lot different than in the twenty-first century," Tara said.

"We don't call it courting."

"And casual sex isn't all that acceptable here either," Lizzy explained. "But that doesn't mean it doesn't happen. With all the extra girls running around, you'd think Cian would find someone to hook up with, even if it's temporary."

Helen shrugged her shoulders and said, "Privacy is at a premium around here. Kinda hard to find a secluded place for a quiet thought let alone an intimate moment."

The words no sooner left her mouth, then she realized what she'd said. And to whom she'd said them.

Heat filled her cheeks, and she was certain they turned a deep shade of scarlet. Holy cow, she'd just told Simon's mother about her desire to steal a few minutes alone with Simon. Talk about awkward.

"And on that note," Tara chuckled. "Let's get this to Amber and see if it works."

Lizzy lent her a smile as they left the room. The woman really was a gem. Too bad she and the rest of his clan lived so far in the past. They'd be a lot of fun to hang out with in the future. A future Helen was having a hard time picturing going back to as they walked down the long candle lit hall connecting the bedrooms, or chambers, as the maids called them.

Myra knocked softly on Amber's door before they walked in. More pale than Helen had seen her, Amber sat by the small fire burning in the hearth with a wan smile as they approached.

"We have something for you to try." Lizzy unfolded the cloak from her arm for Amber to see.

Amber glanced at each of their faces. "You're all so hopeful."

"We think it's going to work."

"If flashing lights and a breeze coming out of nowhere is any indicator, something happened." Helen sat on the edge of the bed as she spoke.

"Try it on," Myra said.

Amber lifted herself out of the chair much like a woman three times her age. "Even if it doesn't, thank you all for trying."

"If it doesn't, we'll go back and try again."

Amber turned away and presented her back to Lizzy.

Lizzy shook out the garment and hesitated for a moment before placing it over Amber's shoulders.

Amber drew in a deep cleansing breath and blew it out with a sigh. Her frame started to tremble and Lizzy placed her hands on Amber's arms. "Are you okay?"

"Aye." When Amber turned around the tired lines that had etched her face since Helen had met her started to fade. A tear ran down her cheek. "Aye." She took a step and nearly fell.

Helen shot to her feet.

Lizzy caught her and Myra rushed forward. Tara reached Amber first. "What's wrong?"

"Something didn't work."

"Nay, I'm fine." They assisted Amber back into the chair. "'Tis like the weight of Scotland has lifted is all. I'm a wee bit dizzy."

"Do you want to take it off?" Lizzy asked.

Amber pulled the edges of the cloak further around her. "Nay. 'Tis working. The images from the minds below are fading, slowly...but they *are* fading."

"It worked. Thank God it worked," Myra latched onto Amber's arm and smiled when Amber didn't pull away in pain.

Helen watched the sisters fuss over Amber. One offered her water while the other placed another log on the fire. *Such a loving family.*

Not *her* family.

This was a family Helen was destined to leave. Temporary, like everything in her life had always been.

"I'll go find Simon and let him know what's happening."

Lizzy spared her a glance as she left the room. The others hardly realized when she left.

Outside the chamber door, the hall was relatively quiet. A low rumbling of voices drifted from below. Somewhere in the past hour, her head started to pound, and now the pain edged toward migraine status.

Helen tugged out the binding from her hair and let it loose, removing some of the pressure. A couple of aspirin would be helpful, but she doubted there was anything like that available. She pushed away from the door in search of Simon.

More than one set of eyes followed her as she entered the main hall. Men clustered in groups. Some sat before the fire to keep warm while others dozed on blankets. It was strange seeing so many men in one place. Helen knew the men protected the Keep in shifts. Most likely those who slept had kept long hours during the day while the rest of them found their rest.

The kitchens never seemed to cool. It wasn't yet dinnertime and a large group of people were outside in the courtyard. Helen ignored their stares the best she could as she searched the room for a familiar face. Seeing none, she pivoted in the direction of Ian's study.

Shadows played on the wall of the dimly lit hall en route to Ian's study. Helen knew instantly that someone followed her.

"What a bonny lass ye are. Where've the MacCoinnichs been hiding ye I wonder?"

Helen turned and nearly ran into the huge chest of the man behind her. He must have been six four on a bad day, his body sheer steel. A body that hadn't seen fresh water in a very long time. She took a step back to let the man know he was way too far into her personal space. The warrior's hard features were covered by a short beard and a scar that ran down the left side of his face.

"I'm looking for Laird Ian," she told him. Best to name-drop the biggest one of the house to avoid any unwanted attention. The way this man's eyes rounded over the curves of her body made her skin itch.

"Are ye a MacCoinnich?"

"No," she answered without thought.

"Ye're dressed too fine to be a servant." Scarface stepped forward and touched the edges of her hair.

Helen stepped back and felt the wall on her back.

"I'm not a servant, and I'm not interested." Even with a castle full of warriors, Helen felt more vulnerable than she did walking in Hollywood after midnight without a friend.

"Yet ye speak like a woman."

What the hell was that supposed to mean?

He reached for her hair again and she batted his hand away. "What part of *not interested* did you misunderstand?"

"Feisty. I like that in a woman." As the man reached for her again, Helen lifted her hands to push him away. Her hands never made contact.

Scarface flew across the hall in a blur of movement.

Simon stood between Helen and her unwanted admirer with a set jaw and a hand resting on his sword. "Is this man bothering you, Helen lass?"

She wasn't sure how to answer the question. Tension in the hall filled every crack as both men squared off on each other. Simon looked like he wanted to kill the guy. Fighting when a war simmered outside their doors seemed ridiculous.

"I didn't know she was yours, Lord Simon."

Lord Simon? What is that all about?

"Now ye know."

Scarface relaxed his stance and tilted his head toward Helen. "My apologies, my lady."

"Yeah, okay."

Scarface turned and left.

"So, I'm yours, am I?"

Simon removed his hand from his weapon and pivoted her way. "'Tis best they all believe you're under my protection."

"And I don't have a say in this?"

Simon's brow pitched together. "Do you want the attention of Geer, or any of the others?"

"That's not the point." Her voice hitched higher as the energy from the confrontation with Geer started to seep from her pores.

"It is while you're here." And apparently that was the end of the discussion. At least according to Simon. "What are you doing down here anyway?"

"I was looking for you. Amber is...." Helen glanced beyond Simon to the empty hall. "It worked. She's doing better."

He nodded. "I'll tell the others."

"Fine."

Neither of them moved.

"You should return above stairs. 'Tis safer. Next

time bring another woman with you."

"I need an escort?"

"For now."

"This is crazy," she said as she brushed passed him, pissed at the inequality of the times. She wasn't a women's libber, but an escort? Please!

She made it to the opening of the main hall when Simon's voice stopped her.

"Helen," he all but barked.

"What?" She turned, ran into his big, yummy chest. She tried to push him away but his arm snuck around her waist and captured her close. He kissed her firmly and all too quickly, and then set her aside. "Tell Amber to be well. I'll tell the others."

Someone nearby chuckled, and Helen realized they had a large and attentive audience. Good God, Simon had marked his territory right there in front of an army.

"Of all the stupid, crazy—"

He kissed her again and shut her up.

This time when he released her, his hands spun her around and he patted her ass. "Go, lass. You're distracting me."

She spun on him and gave him a hard shove. "You'll pay for that." Then she marched up the stairs, leaving behind the laughter and boasting of men.

Chapter Sixteen

Simon watched the sway of her ass as she stormed up the stairs. She was pissed, but she'd get over it. He knew his testosterone-charged display would push her twenty-first century buttons, but it couldn't be helped. There would be many more Geers before they could safely return to her time, her world. Best they all know now she was *not available*.

And she wasn't.

He didn't dwell on the thought longer than thirty seconds before he found Todd and Ian huddled over a map in the study.

They offered him only a glance before returning to the map. "If I were hiding out I'd want shelter, water, and food. Only two places we've not looked meet those needs. Here and here."

"Sounds like you have my night planned," Simon said as he walked into the room.

"Only if you're ready. You've had a long day."

He'd flown over fifty miles in three days. He was exhausted.

Still, his family needed him, and he wasn't about to let them down. "I'll eat and rest. I'll be ready."

Ian nodded and patted his back. "Don't overextend. You're of no use to anyone ill...or worse."

"I'll be fine." Simon ignored the look between Ian and Todd and added, "Speaking of ill, the women's plan worked. Amber is feeling better apparently."

"You've seen her?"

"No. Helen came down to tell me."

Ian sunk into his chair and lowered his head.

147

"Thank, God."

Just watching Ian melt into his seat brought to light how grave Amber's health had been. Simon kicked himself for not paying more attention. He knew when the Keep filled with people her gift plagued her unless she kept above stairs where she could put some barrier between her and all the emotions swimming below.

Still, he didn't realize the impact on Ian. The man held the weight of a huge family, a village, and a crush of knights on his shoulders, but concern for his youngest daughter brought him down. Simon knew if Amber were married, settled, Ian wouldn't have all those parental emotions tearing at his heart. But Amber's gift had become her curse.

When she and Simon were younger, after the fall of Grainna, she started to feel the changes in her abilities. At that time, Simon spent many hours with her, talking, contemplating life. As the years took their toll on Amber, she became more distant. Suitors offered their attention, but she couldn't stand their touch.

There was nothing the family could do. They'd tried to block her gifts. They'd asked the Ancients to show pity and take back some of her empathic abilities—all of them, if they could—to offer her peace.

Nothing happened.

Now, with Helen's suggestion, a different tactic was taken, and Amber was afforded some relief.

The Ancients had a plan. Who knows, perhaps the Ancients were Angels of God working with him to keep his precious world from falling apart because of human nature.

"This can wait, Papa." Simon used his childhood title for Ian, a title the older man adored when Simon used it. "Let's visit Amber while the powers hold."

Ian's glossy eyes met Simon's. "Aye. You're right, lad. Winning a war means little if I can't help my own child."

Simon knew Ian didn't completely believe that. He'd fight to the death for the villagers, their children.

Todd rolled up the map and placed it under his arm before following them out the door.

By the time they'd made it to Amber's room, Duncan, Fin, and Lora had arrived. Helen sat beside Amber and barely acknowledged Simon's presence in the room.

"Da!" she said and held out her arms.

The room stilled as Ian embraced his daughter for the first time in years. The room went silent. Tears flowed down several cheeks, some of the men blinked watery eyes.

Simon choked on a breath and swallowed hard.

"'Tis better. So much better."

"She's been dizzy, Ian. Let her sit," Lora told her husband.

Ian shot a concerned glance at his wife and helped his daughter back to her chair. "Dizzy?"

"A little," she confessed.

"Even that is easing," Myra told him.

"Is the gift gone?"

Amber shook her head. "Not gone. Darkened. When I touch you," she placed a hand aside her father's cheek. "I know you're concerned, relieved, but the emotion doesn't choke me. I don't feel everyone in the room at once, and nothing below."

Tara kissed her husband on the cheek. "I'll talk to the children, let them know they can visit later."

Duncan placed a hand around her waist. "I'll go with you."

"We should leave, too," Todd announced. "I'm glad you're feeling better, Amber."

"Thank you."

Everyone but Simon, Helen, Ian, and Lora left Amber's side. Lora sat holding her daughter's hand, and Helen flanked her other side.

"There is light behind your smile again," Lora said.

"I fear I'll have to bathe in this cloak. Still, 'tis better than the weight of everyone's emotions."

Simon knelt beside Amber. "It might be possible to

149

find other suitable clothing to help."

"This will work for now." She snuggled into the garment as if it were a blanket on the coldest day of the year. Amber hid a yawn behind her hand. "I could sleep for days."

Ian nodded in Simon's direction. "Then we'll leave you to it. Simon, you should find your rest now, too. You've a long night ahead of you."

"What is happening?" Amber had been kept from most of the activities of the Keep in an effort to help her condition.

"Nothing for you to worry about. Simon will scout again tonight is all."

"Didn't you just get back?" Helen asked.

"A few hours ago. I'm fine." But he was tired and knew a few hours sleep would help him later.

Helen narrowed her eyes, unconvinced.

"Go, sleep. I'll have food sent to your chamber," Lora directed. "And you, my husband, when was the last time food met your lips?"

Ian winked at his wife. "I could eat."

"Out with both of you. Helen, would you mind staying with Amber a while?"

"I'm not a child," Amber told Lora.

"I know, but you're *my* child and I worry. We've no idea what to expect with this." Lora fingered the edges of the cloak. "Until we do, you should have company."

Amber lowered her head and accepted her mother's sound advice.

Simon left the room with his adopted grandparents, all the while feeling the weight of Helen's stare on his back.

* * * *

Perched mid branch with nothing but the moon as light, Simon listened to the murmurs of the men below. Most, like any war party, spoke of their conquests, their desire to see the enemy fall. What puzzled Simon was the disdain these men had for the MacCoinnich family. From what Simon could tell, none of them had ever had any contact with Ian's family or with Simon's family. Still, they talked of capturing them to abuse and torture. That too was odd. Why?

"We remove all obstacles and take the women."

"Aye, they're a prize to hold."

Helen.

They were after the women?

There was a leader somewhere in the throng of these men, and Simon was determined to find out the man's name. The name McNeil hadn't been used once.

Something wasn't adding up. A siege didn't often result in hostages.

Simon flew through the trees, keeping his falcon self hidden from any eyes below. The word *prize* and phrase *take the women* were echoed throughout. The flat tone of their voices bothered Simon even more than their words.

He waited for over an hour, watching, listening. No clear leader manifested. However, one name was uttered. Malcolm.

Simon didn't know the name, nor the man behind it.

Men shifted into comfortable positions under the stars to sleep while others took watch. Simon soared into the night breeze for the long journey home.

God's teeth, he was tired. He'd spent more time in falcon form than human. He was half-tempted to hunt for a wild rabbit, something he avoided when he shifted. But shifting always made him famished. Not to mention tired. And since Helen had entered his life, horny.

Helen. Just thinking her name sped up the beat of his heart. Human or bird. He supposed he owed her an apology for embarrassing her in front of the men. But with him away from the Keep as much as he was, he didn't like the thought of the others hitting on her. Simon wasn't a Viking, wasn't about to toss her over his shoulder and claim her as his, but being a warrior in the Highlands had a few advantages over being a mere man of the twenty-first century.

He knew she watched him in the courtyard when he

sparred with the other men. Felt her eyes as he walked across the room. And her taste, sweet lord he could live with it forever. Under all her spirit there was an innocence he didn't expect. She'd lived the exact opposite of his life. Alone and without a family to bring her up when she was low, or take her down when she needed to learn a lesson. The MacCoinnichs had been a blessing to him and his mother. Fin and Lizzy's love and commitment to each other was something Simon wanted for himself.

Was Helen for him? So what if she lived in the future. He had too at one point in his life. Who knew, maybe she'd choose to stay in the past? Or maybe a higher power intended a different plan for them altogether.

If there was one thing in life Simon knew, it was that tomorrow could hold his unexpected future. A future with magic, family, even death. He remembered his days in Mr. Price's algebra class wondering if he'd ever use the crap they taught him. Wondering if he'd ever make it through junior high school without getting his ass kicked or kissing a girl. And then his Aunt Tara disappeared, and his mom lost it.

Okay, maybe lost it wasn't quite the way it all happened. But she poured every minute she wasn't working into searching for Tara. Then Myra appeared from nowhere talking about time travel and magic. Simon reflected back on how he thought his mom had hooked up with a bunch of quacks. In amongst the craziness that followed, Simon found one resounding theme.

Family.

How he'd craved a normal family as a child. How he wanted a father who gave a rat's-ass about his well-being. Fin fell into his mother's arms, and Simon's entire life changed.

So yeah, tomorrow might be the first day of the rest of his life. He was a living testament to that cliché.

Simon caught the first flickering light of the Keep

just as a few drops of rain started falling from the sky. He bent his beaked-head toward the fresh scent and willed his massive wings to hold on a little longer.

Dawn broke and from the distance he could see the activity of Ian's men beginning their day's preparations. A crow announced the end of the night or the beginning of the day, however you looked at it.

The closer to the Keep he flew, the more tired he became. Simon was ready for bed. Needed a few hours sleep before reporting to Ian. He was beyond taxed.

On the highest turret, he found the open shutter and aimed directly home.

As his falcon talons reached for the floor, Simon pictured human feet touching the cold, stone surface. His entire body reached toward his human form with one long, electrifying snap. Every muscle stretched, every bone crushed and elongated into a man.

It hurt like hell.

Before his feet touched the floor, he knew this morph would be like none other. He'd pushed himself too far and his body was going to let him know how pissed it was. When this had happened one time before, he'd fallen into a deep sleep and lost hours of his life.

Simon willed the shift to complete, knowing it would be better to be found as a naked man in the Keep than a wounded falcon.

His last viable thought as he hit the ground was *Who left the blankets on the floor?*

* * * *

Helen no sooner lifted her head from the pillow before Simon, in all his naked splendor, fell into a heap at her feet. His elbow met with her cheek with a sound crack. She reached her hands out and barely managed to keep his head from splitting open on the stone below.

"Simon?"

Nothing. She didn't hear a thing.

Her heart leaped inside the small cavity of her chest, and she scrambled onto the balls of her feet. She ran her hands over his arms and chest. "Simon?" her voice rose in a rushed whisper. "Please, answer me."

Still he didn't move, didn't utter a sound. Helen pushed her ear to his chest and held her breath.

His heart beat in a rapid tattoo, slowing with every deep even breath he managed. Unable to stop herself, she collapsed on him. *Alive. He's alive.*

Once she caught her breath, she moved far enough away to watch the steady rise and fall of his chest. He was exhausted. On some level, she knew being tired was his only illness. She grasped onto the pillow and bedding she'd dragged up to the turret while waiting for his return. After placing his head on the padding, she tucked one of the two blankets under and over his body. Unable to stop herself, she took her time making sure he wasn't injured. His body was lean, strong, and completely lethal. Even asleep, his masculine vitality that ruled her brain and her libido since she met him, shone through. She wanted to run her hand over his six-pack abs and narrow waist, but to do so while he slept felt like a violation, even though she doubted he'd mind.

She diverted her gaze away from his sex and covered him completely. Glancing at the door, Helen pushed away the thought of leaving to find him clothes.

When he awoke would be soon enough. She decided to lay beside him. After closing the shutters and some of the draft coming from the Scotland dawn, Helen lifted the second blanket and covered them both. She made use of his arm to lay her head on and curled up into his warmth.

She took in a deep breath, inhaling his rain-scented skin, and tasted a strong dose of pine. His scent changed constantly, she decided. This cologne was born of the falcon.

How did it feel to fly? To soar above the treetops and see what no man has ever witnessed?

And what of the wolf? The form he took that very first day? She remembered a wildness about his scent then. A fierceness hiding behind his eyes. Did he ever lose himself to the animal?

How would it feel to be pursued and cornered by the beast and then made love to by the man?

Helen shifted next to him as warmth flooded her belly and her nipples hardened beneath the long sleeping gown she'd been given to wear.

With a will of their own, her fingers fanned over the expanse of his chest and rested above his heart.

Simon moaned in his sleep, his hand moved to hers and held it there. He didn't wake, but managed to pull her closer to his side.

Forcing her mind to clear, Helen touched her lips to his chest and closed her eyes. Safe. Even with a war raging, warriors fighting, she felt safe in his arms.

Chapter Seventeen

Warm mist caught him as he flew into the pristinely white clouds. The wind kept him afloat with little to no effort. The cloud caught him and smelled of strawberries as it held him close and brought him slowly down to earth.

It felt good to sleep, to awake feeling rested and whole.

And warm.

And not alone.

Even before he opened his eyes, Simon knew Helen was curled up beside him, one of her legs resting intimately over his. Deep, even breaths blew hot air over his exposed chest and his eager body responded.

A lock of her shiny brown hair drifted over her eyes, her heart shaped lips were opened enough to breathe. She was beautiful, and the way she wrapped around his body in sleep gave her an endearing look of vulnerability. Simon would bet his sword she wouldn't enjoy the title of 'vulnerable'. She worked so hard to prove she wasn't, but he'd seen her at her weakest. Each tear he had witnessed her shed was one too many. As always, the overwhelming need to protect her gave him reason to wake every morning.

He draped the arm she slept on around her shoulders and melded his body more firmly against hers. Helen sighed in her sleep, her knee lifted, and brushed against his expanding erection.

Simon bit back a moan and failed miserably. He growled. A sound from deep within his soul escaped.

Helen tilted her chin up, even in her sleep, inviting.

A better man would have let her open her eyes.

Simon didn't. He bent his head and captured her lips, soft and warm and sweet like the nectar of an overripe fruit. Helen nestled closer and let out a tiny moan of her own. The mewling cat-like noise drifted from her lips and inflamed Simon even more. When her lips started to move over his, and her breathing sped up, he knew she woke.

She hesitated briefly, making him wonder if the innocent woman he'd known when they first met would appear. Instead, Helen climbed up further on his chest until her tongue met with his. The nerves in his body gave off tiny sparks of joy with every touch of her hand, every noise of pleasure she uttered. Whatever demons she'd combated before, Simon had obviously managed to vanquish them. The woman kissing him was a confident woman who knew what she wanted.

His woman.

Simon ran a hand down her waist and captured her backside in his palm. She squirmed over him, her hips dancing with his. "Good morning," he managed in a hoarse whisper.

Her breath hitched as he hiked her leg over his and let his cock rub the damp fabric between her legs. "I-I'm not dreaming?"

He chuckled. "With dreams like this, I'd never leave bed."

Bright blue eyes met his, her lids heavy with desire. "We're not in a bed."

"Do you want to be?" He realized a cold floor wasn't ideal, but the thought of moving before having her, before showing her the stars, was painful.

A shy smile met her lips, and she leaned forward and kissed one of his nipples. She swiped her tongue over its taut edge, and he knew she didn't want to retreat from their private haven any more than he.

Simon filled his palm with her breast and teased the tip through the fabric of her nightgown. Helen bit his nipple in a playful response.

"Vixen."

She bit him again. "I was sleeping. Minding my own business," she laughed.

"If this is how you mind your own business, I'd like to see you tending to mine."

Helen walked her fingers up his chest and wove them into his hair.

Simon had a strong desire to push her onto her back, but knew the cold floor would leave marks on her skin by the time they were done. No, he'd watch her above him. Watch her do whatever she pleased. He'd bring her pleasure any way she wanted. God's blood he prayed she'd gift him with a release buried deep inside of her.

Instinctively, Simon knew not to push her. Something about the way she'd pushed him away hinted of past pain. He'd never be that to her.

"Would you like me to tend to yours?"

Aye. "Only if I can tend to yours."

The silly grin on her lips tilted slightly and her eyes grew serious. Without another word, she lifted the hem of her nightclothes above her knees while straddling his chest. He could feel her heat and smell her desire. His eyes threatened to roll in the back of his head but he kept them on her. Simon's hands rested on her thighs as she crossed her arms over her body and removed her clothing.

Her skin was satin, smooth, and silky. Simon watched his hands as they traveled up her shapely thighs. He dipped his thumb over the crest of her hips and scented the glistening patch of hair covering her womanhood. Without touching her there, he skimmed his callused fingers over her stomach and up her trim waist until he held her perfectly luscious breasts in his hands. "I could touch you for years."

Leaning forward, Helen kissed him. She invaded his mouth like a vengeful army, taking no prisoners and leaving no spot untouched.

The heat of her core pressed down on him, his

erection jutting close enough to feel her folds.

Simon felt his control slipping. He broke away from her kiss and held her cheeks between his hands. "Are you sure of this, lass?"

Her eyes darted back and forth between his. "I'm straddling you naked, Simon. I think I'm sure."

"I need you. Now."

Her lips caught between her teeth. "Then take me."

Releasing a breath, he moved his hands to her hips and with little effort, lifted her over his length. With his eyes never leaving hers, he nudged her open and sank into the tight cavern of her beautiful body. Together they sighed, their smiles giving way to stolen breaths.

Helen's body gave him room and quivered around him, nearly undoing him right then. She moved her hips and he held her still. "A moment, lass. You're so tight."

She clenched him even more with his words.

He groaned.

"It's been a long time," she told him.

Good, he thought, no room inside her head for anyone but him. "I'll make you forget anyone before me," he vowed as he lifted her up only to plunge into her again.

"You're so sure of yourself," she teased.

Her eyes rolled up when he reached the back of her womb. "Us. I'm sure of us." Everything about their joining felt perfect, as if she were the missing part of his life.

Speech became impossible as they moved together. Their bodies in perfect sync with the other. Helen's hands roamed his hips, his chest. She set the pace and Simon willingly followed. He forced his body to stay alert and not give into the tsunami wave of pleasure building by being buried inside of Helen.

She leaned over him, the soft mounds of her chest slid over his, her fingers dug into his shoulders, and she reached higher. Simon kept the upward-thrusting tilt of his hips, giving more than he thought possible. Her breath hitched and when her orgasm crashed over her, he captured her lips to help keep her silent, knowing her pleasure would reach even higher. She spasmed, gripping him hard until her rocking body started to lax.

Unable to take more, Simon twisted her under him, positioning her back on the blankets. He cradled her hips and kept as much of his weight off her to avoid pushing her into the hard floor.

She snaked a leg over his hips and grasped his ass. "Don't hold back," she pleaded. "I won't break."

With her command, he drove harder, felt her surrender when his body tightened, and his release took over. All thought disappeared.

* * * *

A long time passed before either of them moved. Helen marveled in the weight of his body holding her firmly on the floor. She didn't even mind the pebble that wedged itself between her shoulder blade and her spinal column. Every limb in her body melted like butter in a flame. She couldn't remember a time she'd felt so safe, so wanted. So deliciously used and most definitely bruised. She'd wear the marks with a cat-sized grin and picture this moment for the rest of her life.

Considering her previous intimacies could be counted on a few fingers, and none of them worth remembering, Simon could easily play the role of 'world's finest' in her eyes.

"I'm crushing you."

"Yeah, but it's nice." And it was, their bodies still attached and slick.

He moved to his side but kept her gathered to him. It was as if he wanted to leave the warm, inviting place between her legs either. The offending pebble dislodged and fell away.

"Did I hurt you, lass?"

She nodded with a little laugh.

Simon grew serious and ran his hand over her shoulder.

"It's okay," she told him. "Very, very okay."

He kissed her nose and settled. "I shouldn't have

taken you here."

"Well, your room would have been off limits. The boys invaded your space last night to make room for one of your neighbors."

In fact, the room she'd been given was taken too and she and Amber were rooming together. The massive Koop was getting tight.

"I see. Mayhap I'll have a mattress brought up here."

She liked the thought but questioned the wisdom of spending every night in Simon's arms. After some mental math, she knew the timing was off for her to get pregnant, but that would change in less than a week. Birth control wasn't necessary in her sexless life back home, and it wasn't available here.

"I'm guessing that affairs aren't smiled upon in these times."

"Nay. Not with ladies of your standing."

She laughed. "I'm not a lady of any standing."

Simon placed a finger over her lips. "Yes you are, Helen. I'll not have anyone say or treat you otherwise."

She wrapped her leg around his hips and felt him start to harden inside her. "I noticed something."

He linked her knee with his hand and caressed the sensitive flesh of her thigh. "What might that be?"

"I noticed that ever since we came back here, to this time, you have a little more burr in your speech, a lot more sixteenth century language rolling off your tongue."

"Women like the accent. Makes them weep with desire."

Oh, how he knew exactly what to say.

"Do you use your talents often, *Lord* Simon?"

Helen felt his hand slide between their joined bodies. His nimble fingers found the perfect spot of pleasure and began to move.

"I practiced my talents enough in the past so I can please you."

Her body responded to his caress.

But what happens when I leave? He'll find *someone else to practice on.*

Helen forced the thoughts of Simon in the arms of another woman out of her head and lived in the now.

And right now felt pretty damn good.

* * * *

Simon's hunger drove them from their temporary haven. When they resurfaced, the first one to see them was Myra. With one look, she knew. As much as Helen thought herself an adult, she felt heat burn her cheeks and her feet fidgeted with the need to flee.

"My father is searching for you." She directed at Simon. "And Amber is asking where you spent the night." Myra's brows shot up, and she reached over and straightened the nightgown Helen wore. The breakfast meal time had passed, and from the sounds emitting from below, the day had commenced.

And I'm wearing a nightgown. Helen wanted to cringe. It was one thing to be intimate with Simon, quite another to announce it to the world. The MacCoinnich clan was large enough to be a small world.

Simon kept a possessive arm around Helen's waist and didn't answer Myra's concerns.

Wearing a kilt Simon had tucked into a hidden place in the wall of their private turret, he at least looked half dressed.

"Helen fell asleep upstairs. I'm escorting her to her room."

Myra, a sixteenth century lady, all prim and proper, wearing her floor length gown with long sleeves and a neckline that didn't plunge to even a freckle on her chest, burst out in a very broad grin. "Right," was all she said.

"I should get dressed." Helen moved out of Simon's grip.

"I'll make sure Helen gets to her room," Myra told Simon. "The men are in need of information only you can provide."

Simon glanced into Helen's eyes, asking if it was

162

okay for him to abandon her.

"I'm good. You go."

He brushed a knuckle to the side of her jaw and winked at Myra as he walked beyond them and down the hall.

The tease didn't even stop by his room for a shirt. He jogged down the hall and rounded the corner to the stairs. Once he was out of sight, Helen diverted her gaze to Myra who was watching her like a cat who'd trapped a mouse.

"What?" Helen asked.

"Nothing."

Both of them turned into Amber's room without another word and stepped inside.

"There you are. I was worried." Amber was out of bed and dressed with the cloak draped over her shoulders.

And she smiled. Helen couldn't recall if she'd ever really seen Amber smiling as she was doing now. Certainly not with this radiant grin lighting up her eyes, her face.

"You're...you're smiling."

Amber lifted the lapels of the cloak and shrugged her shoulders. "It doubles as a blanket. I slept a full night. I can't remember the last time that happened."

"Oh, Amber, that's wonderful."

"But you? You don't look as if you slept at all. Where were you?"

Helen stole a glance at Myra.

"Well?"

Myra saved Helen some of her embarrassment. "I found her and Simon walking down the hall. Together."

Amber's eyes grew wide. "Together?"

Myra nodded.

"Oh for crying out loud. We're both adults. Consenting adults." Helen wasn't a teen in need of scolding. Not that these women were scolding. "This is awkward."

"Really? Why?" Amber asked.

"Because..." Helen crossed the room to the washbasin and poured water in the bowl. "Simon is practically a brother to you," she said and pointed at Amber, "or a cousin at least. And a nephew to you."

"We've both known Simon since he was just a lad," Myra pointed out.

Helen brought a washrag to the water and wrung it out. She scrubbed her face and neck with more force than necessary. "Yeah, well, he isn't a *lad* anymore. He is very grown up." *With grown up parts that worked well. Very, very well.*

Helen felt her cheeks heat up again.

Someone behind her chuckled.

"Very grown up," whispered Amber.

"Relax, Helen. We're happy for you, truly."

When she turned around, Myra and Amber were standing side by side. The two of them looked so much alike with their long black hair touching their butts, both the same size and height, and eyes the perfect shade of chocolate brown. Back home, Hollywood would would've snatched them up in an instant.

"You are?"

"Aye."

Myra cocked her head to the side and her grin slid. "But you've met my father, right?"

Is this a trick question? Of course she'd met Ian. "Yeah?"

Amber glanced at Myra and her smile fell as well.

The hair on Helen's neck started to tingle and her skin started to pop with sensations. The same energy she experienced when her gift manifested. Her own personal indicator that information was about to arrive. "What?"

Myra motioned to one of the chairs in the room, encouraging Helen to sit.

Tendrils of power ran up and down Helen's arms. Sitting didn't make it better.

"Well?"

Myra gathered Helen's hand in hers and patted it

like she would a child. Her attempt at calm wasn't working. "If one of you doesn't start speaking I'm going to go bat-shit crazy."

"My father is um.... Well, he takes his role as leader of this family very seriously."

Fine, Helen had seen that. "So?"

"He takes in everyone who travels here with the stones as if they are his own. He offered his full protection to Tara, Lizzy, and Simon...even Todd."

Amber sat beside Helen. "He considers you his ward. His responsibility."

Funny, Helen thought Simon took on that role. But Ian was captain of this ship. She got that. "I appreciate that."

"He'll treat you as he would his own daughter. Protect you as such," Amber said.

"I'm not his kid. He doesn't have to do that."

"But he will. Does."

"He feeds me, keeps a roof over my head. I get it."

From the looks on Myra and Amber's faces, she wasn't getting it at all.

"When Tara and Duncan were found together, our father handfasted them within an hour—"

"And when Todd and I were found kissing, he promised to do the same to us if we continued," Myra interrupted.

Helen started to see the theme here. "And Lizzy?"

"Well, Lizzy..." Amber's voice faded.

"If we weren't risking our lives daily, he'd have forced Fin and Lizzy to marry, too," Myra told her.

Light flickered behind her eyelids. "So you think if Ian found out about Simon and I, he'd enforce a shotgun marriage?"

"Shotgun?"

Helen shook her head, forgetting these women didn't understand pop culture. "He'd force Simon to marry me."

Myra's mouth formed a perfect "O". "Aye, 'tis exactly what will happen."

It was Helen's turn to laugh. "He can try. But that ain't gonna happen. Besides, I've heard of long distance relationships, but living hundreds of years apart is bound to end in divorce." As she stood, the hair on her arms still hadn't gone down.

"You've been warned."

"Well thanks, girls. Message delivered. Now, can someone help me get into one of these dresses so I can go eat? I'm starving."

Amber and Myra exchanged a look and a knowing smile.

Helen knew she hadn't heard the end of this.

Chapter Eighteen

"So McNeil is after our women," Ian mused aloud.

"I didn't hear the name McNeil. In fact, I had the distinct impression a different leader led this band of warriors." Simon sat among the men and explained what he'd learned.

"Are you sure?"asked Ian.

"I'm not sure of anything. I'm relaying the information I heard. But—"

"But what?" Fin sat his ale down.

"Something didn't feel right."

"How so?" Duncan asked.

"Everywhere I perched I heard the same mantra. Almost like the practiced lines of an actor. Like a jester telling the same jokes. They're practiced and stale after a while, which was how these men spoke."

Todd stood and started to pace. "Brainwashed? *Drink the punch, my children, and follow me.*"

Simon shook his head but uttered the word, "Maybe."

"Manipulated. Like Grainna did to hundreds?" Ian's voice held a degree of concern.

"Grainna's dead. We all saw her die."

Duncan nodded. "It's not Grainna. We'd know if she'd managed to escape. But who could it be?"

"Someone who knows about us."

Ian tapped the edge of his desk with his fingertips in a slow, steady rhythm. "If a Highlander who wasn't Druid knew of us, he'd spread the word and all of Scotland would come to our doors to brand us as evil."

"So we're dealing with a Druid."

Simon nodded. "I think you're right, Fin."

Cian, always the staunch observer these days, pushed away from the wall and spoke for the first time since entering the room. "A Druid from the future."

They all turned his way. Simon wanted to deny the claim. He couldn't. There was always a possibility that someone from the future haunted them now.

"Mayhap."

Cian shook his head. "You said so yourself, a man from our time would flush us out as evil, as witches. A Druid with Grainna's knowledge would capture any of us and not focus on the women. But a Druid from the future—"

"Would notice the pattern of missing women in the future and assume the power belonged with them," Todd finished Cian's sentence.

"Precisely."

Todd shook his head. "I hope Cian's wrong, but I think he's right."

"What of McNeil?"

"A name picked at random? Or maybe whoever's behind this started their brainwashing with McNeil's men. Who knows?" The police officer in Todd shone through. He might not hold one Druid gift, but he vastly contributed to the family.

Ian sat back in his chair and sighed. "It just gets worse."

"We have to protect the women."

"And we will," Fin told his brother.

Simon sat forward. "I think I may have a plan for the women and children."

All eyes turned to him and he began to speak.

* * * *

The entire family, minus the youngest children, sat around Ian's study. Dinner had commenced and the main hall was changing shift. At least that's what Helen thought of it as. Twice a day, every day, the knights on watch would switch with those inside during the evening meal. The elders of the village would meet with

Lora or Tara to discuss the issues arising in the yard. Needs were attended to and addressed in the morning hours. The flow of the Keep ran like a Navy ship. Everyone had their duties, their place. Helen found endless hours with nothing to do. If she were honest with herself, she knew she'd never be a 'stay at home Mom' or anything the like. Now that Amber was feeling better, they started gathering the materials needed to make the time traveling stones into jewelry. Still, the days felt like an endless wait for doom.

Lizzy and Selma were the last to enter Ian's study. They sat beside Tara and Briac. The children exchanged a speculative glance.

Helen felt as lost as the kids. With them involved, something serious must have happened.

"We're all here, so let's start." Ian stood behind Lora who sat in his chair at his desk. Helen thought they'd be better suited with thrones. She was reminded constantly that as regal as Ian and Lora were, they weren't Scotland's royalty.

Helen found Simon across the room, perched by the fireplace. He watched her with sharp eyes that softened when she glanced his way.

"We have a lot to tell you, and little of it is up for discussion." Ian's eye was on Lizzy. "I know that won't settle well on you, Elizabeth, but please hold any comment until I'm through."

So Lizzy was the resident skeptic.

Good to know.

Ian took a full breath and let it out between pursed lips. "I'll start with information that just came to me. Information that none of you have heard."

Simon twisted his eyes to Ian. Obviously, her lover's Intel was not the information Ian wanted to share.

"Lora has had a premonition."

"Mother, that's wonderful," Amber said.

Lora's soft eyes tried to hold hope as she gazed at her youngest child, but they failed.

Oh, man. What the heck was going on?

Lora glanced around the room before speaking. "I thought after the fall of Grainna that we'd all live out our days here, together. Never once did I think Scotland wouldn't be called home to all of us until the day of our passing."

Everyone in the room tensed, breathlessly waiting for Lora to continue.

"I was wrong. My vision was as clear as they were during our battle with Grainna. And no less disturbing."

Why did she sound so ominous?

Lora's eyes leveled with you daughter. "Amber, my child, my joy. This cloak you wear will be the only thing keeping your mind from insanity."

Amber gasped, as did most of the people in the room.

Lora quickly continued. "But there is hope. Only your hope will not be found here."

"What do you mean?" Amber sat on the edge of her seat.

"A Druid awaits you in the future. This man, this warrior not unlike those here, will be the balm that saves you."

Helen felt her shoulders relax. So Amber's main squeeze wasn't living in sixteenth-century Scotland. So what? Seemed to Helen that half the people in the room found their spouse on a different continent. A different time.

"What are you saying?"

"You'll need to return with Simon and Helen when they leave...and stay."

And the shoe drops.

"For how long?" Amber asked.

"I see no end to your time in the future. I do see a void in your father's and my life when you leave."

"Forever?"

"'Tis hard to say, lass. Your mother's vision didn't go further."

Silence filled every corner of the room. Eyes started to brim with unshed tears. Except for maybe Cian, but then again, he bordered on creepy. *Hot* but creepy.

Lizzy, ever perceptive, broke the silence. "But this little newsflash wasn't what brought us all together tonight. What else is happening?"

Lora watched Amber as the news of her impending departure sunk in.

Ian continued.

"Amber isn't the only one who needs to travel to the future."

"What?" Tara asked, staring at her husband.

Everyone mumbled their surprise. Helen said nothing, all the while watching Simon.

Ian held out a hand to silence them. "Calm yourselves. Simon, why don't you explain what you heard."

"A band of warriors was stationed exactly where we thought. These are formidable warriors worthy of concern. Since they are the closest, my guess is they are the ones most likely to obtain whatever it is they want in the event we fail from keeping them at bay."

"They'll not win," Fin declared.

"Maybe not. Maybe so. We've no evidence and only faith in our abilities to guarantee the outcome of this conflict. The question isn't if we will win, 'tis why they are fighting to begin with."

"They're warriors, 'tis what they do," Myra said. "As a child you told us stories of battles such as these."

Ian tilted his head to the side. "Aye, I did, lass. This is different."

"This isn't another magical battle, though, is it?" Lizzy asked.

"Not exactly."

"I don't like the sound of that," said Tara.

Helen watched the tension mounting in the faces of the women. Simon raised his hands and motioned for the others to stop talking. "We think the man behind this siege is Druid."

Simon continued. "We believe he's Druid, and he came from the future."

Someone sucked in an audible breath. The kids sat taller in their seats. No one asked or said a thing.

"This band of warriors has one goal and one goal only." Simon locked gazes with Helen. "They're after our women. Namely, you." He slowly made eye contact with Tara, Lizzy, Myra, Amber, and Selma.

If Amber wasn't the only one returning to the future, and the enemy was after the women, then that meant—

"You're sending all the women and children ahead in time for their safety," Lizzy shoved out of her chair and shook her head, "and leaving the men behind to fight without us?"

"This fight never would have included you, love," Fin told his wife.

"Oh, don't you give me that bull. I'll fight alongside any man out there and kick some serious a...butt."

"Elizabeth, please."

Helen watched husband and wife fight. If the situation wasn't so dire, she'd like some popcorn to go along with the show. Lizzy riled was a sight. Fin got right in her face and didn't look like he was backing down.

With her eyes glued to Duncan, Tara said. "We're bonded. I'd not make the trip without you."

"True. Which is why only you and Lora will stay behind. Everyone else must go. We will evacuate you along the south-east channel the enemy isn't occupying. Everyone here will see you go. Tara and Lora will be hidden here." Ian rocked back on his heels as he spoke. The bold tone of his voice didn't leave much room for argument. Though Lizzy appeared ready to challenge him.

"Helen?" Ian addressed her.

"Yeah?"

"This home Simon spoke of in the future, will the mistress accept our intrusion?"

"Mrs. Dawson has the heart of a saint. She'd never forgive me if I said anything but 'yes'."

Ian nodded to Simon. "'Tis settled then. Simon and Cian will accompany the women and children and protect them there."

Lizzy started talking at the same time Myra began to argue. The children huddled together in excited anticipation of their adventure. Amber moved to sit next to her mother and grasped her hand.

Helen stood and lifted her hand like a third grade student. "Ah, excuse me?"

The kids looked at her but still murmured among themselves. Lizzy hurled a few feminist zingers at her husband, and Myra held a hand over her swollen belly.

"Excuse me?" Helen shouted.

The room fell silent.

"I'm sorry, but there's just one thing wrong with your plan."

"What's that, lass?" Ian asked.

"We don't have a way to get us back to the future."

Lora raised her voice. "In my premonition, I saw Amber and you both wearing necklaces matching the one that brought you here. The sooner you make the jewelry, the faster you'll arrive to your time safely."

"But what if the things disappear when we show back up in LA?"

"The necklace vanished when you arrived here the second time because it hadn't been created yet. The first time you arrived the larger stones hadn't produced the smaller ones. 'Tis safe to say that once the necklace is on your neck the second time, it will stay there."

In some twisted way Lora's explanation made sense.

"If Amber is staying in my time, how will everyone get back?"

Simon moved to Helen's side. "You and I will bring them."

Great. The amusement park time travel ride goes another round. Helen had fewer miles tracked on airplanes than she did time travel.

"I'll bring them." The stoic Cian spoke from behind

his father. "While Helen and Amber make their necklaces, they should make a dagger as well."

"Two. They should make two daggers. One for Cian, the other for us here. We'll need to summon our family home if they don't return on their own," Duncan said.

"Do you think the other stones, the bigger ones, will have stopped working?" Lizzy asked.

"We won't know unless we try to use them. We know for fact Helen's necklace worked."

Helen's head spun on her shoulders for the next hour while the family battled out the necessity of getting the women and children out of harm's way.

Tara questioned the need, but didn't want her children in the Keep during a battle no matter what the enemy was after.

Liz countered everything. She was pissed. A couple of times Helen noticed her body levitate off the ground. Now that was something one didn't see every day. Popcorn and a box of Jujus were called for.

Amber, obviously resolved in the need to leave, sat with glossy eyes, and watched the family fight.

Myra huddled with Todd as they spoke in soft tones.

While Helen witnessed the drama unfold, Simon moved to the back of the room and spoke with Cian.

The roar of bickering continued while Helen's mind began to wander. Whoever was waging war on the MacCoinnichs was believed to be a Druid. Okay, considering their past, this didn't sound too farfetched.

Helen's skin started to tingle.

A Druid from the future who only wanted the women. Why?

Helen raised her hand again, her brows pitched together.

When no one noticed, she placed her fingers into her mouth and blew out a stadium size whistle.

Everyone froze.

"Simon, you said these thugs wanted the women and that somehow connected this man to the future. Why?"

"Tara, me, and my Mom all disappeared without a trace. Myra, too—even Grainna, if we're being technical. A Druid from the future who had knowledge of our disappearance is most likely our enemy. *We* know the men are just as powerful as you women in ways of our heritage, but this man believes the power belongs to the women."

"And he wants the power why?"

This time Todd had the answer. "Tell me Helen, if Simon hadn't found you in the forest when he did and you were stuck in this time, wouldn't you try like hell to find your way home?"

She nodded. "Good point."

Ian raised his voice and put an end to the family meeting. "Amber and Helen have much to do in a short amount of time."

"Why the hurry?"

"A battle looms, lass. When it begins, all of you need to be miles and years away. We hope to spread word to the enemy that you've traveled south and hope they will follow. Then we can take the offensive approach and flush out the man behind this siege. The sooner you're out of harm's way, the faster we can implement our plan."

"We'll have to prepare the children."

"There's no time to make them clothing. Simon said the home they'll be in is secluded."

"It is. But Mrs. Dawson's clothing isn't going to fit anyone here."

Lora waved a hand in the air. "Don't fret. We know your time still uses gold."

Helen laughed. "Yeah, it was up to over a thousand dollars an ounce last month."

Todd whistled. "Wow."

"I know, the economy is in the toilet and gold is through the roof."

"You and your friend will have funds to support everyone," Ian said. "We need to act fast. No more arguments. If anyone has a legitimate concern we'll

175

discuss it, but the decision is made."

"Father?" Myra asked.

"Aye, lass?"

She ran her hand over her stomach. "We don't know if time travel is safe for an unborn babe."

Ian's shoulders fell, he walked around the desk, and gathered Myra's hands in his. "This child is part of you."

"But, 'tis never been done."

"We'll ask for guidance from the Ancients. However, would you risk staying and having this child while hiding above stairs? Todd will worry to distraction. We both know how costly that can be."

Todd placed an arm around his wife. "You're going to be fine. Besides, if you go into labor in my time they have amazing medication to take all the pain away."

"I can attest to that," Lizzy said.

"I know you're scared. Hell, we all are, but this is the right thing to do." Todd kissed the end of Myra's nose and gathered her in his arms.

This family was being torn apart and all because they loved one another too much to see anything bad happen to each other.

Helen's heart swelled deep in her chest. Her parents didn't care enough to stick around at all, good times or bad. Unlike many of the orphans she'd grown up with, Helen didn't harbor any fantasies about perfect parents who died unexpectedly. The people responsible for her birth discarded her. Simple as that.

Helen learned to live without a loving family, or responsibilities for another person. On some level that made her the lucky one. Only Helen didn't feel so lucky.

Chapter Nineteen

Helen was a photographer, not a jewelry maker. But since she was in possession of the piece for over a year, she knew exactly what it looked like. Unfortunately, she had no knowledge of how to create the piece from scratch. She didn't even know what the thing was made of. Only that there weren't any precious stones or metal on it at all.

Amber studied the sketch and asked questions. "Is this a Celtic knot?"

"Not in the truest sense. The weave was looser."

"Less perfect."

"Right."

Helen picked up the small sacred stone and turned it over in her hand. "It's hard to believe what this thing is capable of."

"'Tis hard to believe I'll be leaving here forever."

Helen put the stone down and gave Amber all her attention. "You have a great family. I can't imagine what you're going through."

In the days since the declaration of Amber's departure they hadn't spoken of leaving. Because the daggers they decided to make didn't have a predetermined image, they went to work on them first. They'd used a standard metal for the time to create the knife and were working on a sturdy handle for both. There was one small sacred stone left over with no clear purpose. They had no idea what to do with it. Not that it mattered. Amber and Helen hadn't finished the necklaces or even truly started work on them outside of their concept.

"When I was young, a child, I expected to one day marry. I knew the possibility of my husband taking me away from my family. Yet once Tara arrived, then Simon and the others, I knew leaving my family wasn't an option."

"What happened that made you think that?"

"I couldn't stand the touch of anyone, let alone a man not of my kin."

"Wow. No one?"

"Aye."

"Not one kiss?"

"Nay."

"That means you're a virgin."

Amber nodded. "Aye."

"I guess I should have realized that before now. Wow. That sucks."

Amber let a coy smile cross her lips. "You don't miss what you don't know."

"Yeah, but...damn. I'm sorry."

"So was I for a while. Everyone around me found love. Part of me yearns for that life."

"According to your mom, you're going to find it."

Amber shook her head. "My mother said a man will find me in the future, and that he will be the balm that saves me. Nowhere did she say I'd find love. Or even passion."

Helen watched a rosy blush creep onto Amber's cheeks with the last part of her comment. "When I think of a balm, I think of someone who makes me feel safe, warm, and taken care of." *Loved.* "I think the man behind this balm will be more to you than a blanket."

A knock on the door pulled them out of their conversation. "'Tis Simon."

Amber crossed the room and unlocked the door to let him in. He wore leggings and a white shirt that hung past his hips. For the first time in days, he appeared rested. "You look well," he told Amber.

"I feel much better."

"But you worry about the future."

"Aye."

Helen felt like a stalker watching the two of them talk. They were as close as brother and sister, and obviously loved each other deeply.

"You'll not be alone. We'll help. Won't we, Helen?"

"Of course."

Amber laid a hand to the side of Simon's cheek. "Thank you."

Simon patted Amber's hand and moved to stand beside Helen at the worktable. He stood close enough that she felt the heat of his body, the smell of his skin. Every part of her sparked into awareness and leaned closer. Simon didn't back away when her side rested next to his. He ran one finger on the back of Helen's hand and she knew he was just as happy to see her. "How far have you gotten?"

"Not far enough. You'd think this would be easy. I wore the darn thing all the time. The chunky details I remember. The chain was thick. This stone is supposed to be surrounded by a loose Celtic knot. But there's more to it, and this picture doesn't quite show the details." Helen waved at the book that managed to travel to Scotland with her. In frustration, Helen tossed the book on top of her backpack. "I know all the materials used to make the thing are virtually useless. No gold, copper, platinum. Just steel compounds."

"Like that of the knife?"

Helen nodded. "Right. Maybe that's what we need to use. The steel of the knife is less likely to rust."

"I seem to remember a backing to the stones, and six prongs holding it in place."

"I forgot about that."

Helen sketched the prongs in place on her drawing.

"It's still missing something," Simon said.

"If only I had a photograph." *My camera.* Helen scrambled to her backpack and grabbed her camera. "I had someone take a picture of me with an old guy wearing a kilt at a pub the first night I was in Scotland. I wore the necklace."

179

Amber moved to stand behind them while Helen turned her camera on. Thankfully, it fired up without incident. She scanned the images she'd taken. Landscape shots, people milling about the hotel. Old abandoned castles from a distance.

"What are those?" Amber asked.

"Cars."

"Moving carriages?"

Helen stopped scanning images and turned to Amber. It was then Helen realized just how awkward it would be to go forward in time. At least Helen knew enough about history to expect a lack of cars, computers, and technology. Sure, Amber had been told about the future, but she hadn't seen anything until now. "Motorized carriages. We call them cars."

A tiny fleck of excitement met Amber's eyes. Helen made a mental note to go through the pictures she had in the camera with Amber to help her prepare.

"Here we go." Helen found the photo and zoomed in. Memory of the necklace flooded her mind. "No need to guess anymore."

"This is amazing," Amber took the camera from Helen and stared at the display. "The image of you is perfect."

Something Helen took for granted everyday was a miraculous invention to Amber. "Here," she said, taking the camera from Amber's hands.

With a couple adjustments, Helen kept the flash from flooding the room and stood back. "Move closer Simon," she instructed.

"I haven't done this in years." He moved close to Amber and placed an arm around her shoulders.

"What are you doing?"

"Look over here," Helen told Amber. "Smile."

Amber's smile was as fake as they came. Helen took the shot anyway. After a couple, Amber started to relax and ask questions. "Are you taking our photograph?" Helen kept shooting.

"I am."

"But it only makes a small noise."

"But it does a big job."

Amber cocked her head to the side and the perfect smile lit her face.

"Got it."

Helen walked over to her subjects and revealed what she'd captured.

Simon glanced at the photographer with a look of serene pleasure while Amber held an expression of amused fascination. "'Tis me."

A soft chuckle fell from Helen's lips. "It is."

Amber placed a hand on Helen's arm. "Please take these of all our family. Our home. So that I might look back on them when I miss my family."

"Consider it done."

Without warning, Amber crushed Helen into a huge hug. "You've given me such a gift."

She glanced at Simon who winked at her. "I haven't done anything yet."

"You've given me something to remember everyone by. Not that I could ever truly forget, but this will make my leaving less painful." A tear fell off Amber's cheek.

Helen felt her eyes well up. "Oh, stop that. You're going to make me cry."

Pushing away, Amber picked up her skirts and hurried to the door. "Where are you going?"

"To tell my mother."

Then she was gone.

The second the door closed Simon placed an arm around Helen's waist and kissed the top of her head. "You've given her something money can't buy."

"It's just a picture."

He shook his head. "What does a family grab when their home is on fire?"

"Valuables."

"No, lass, they grab pictures. Snapshots of family memories money cannot replace."

"I didn't have family photos. Didn't have a family to take them with," she mumbled.

Simon took the camera from her hand and placed it on the table, then wrapped a second arm around her. "I'm sorry you've lived your life alone."

The hard armor built around the emotions of growing up an orphan started to crack. "It's hard to miss what you didn't know." Amber's words flowed from her mouth.

Simon didn't appear convinced.

He tilted her head and brought his lips to hers. His kiss was full of emotion. It stole her breath and plucked away at the steel around her heart. Her arms crept around his shoulders, but he didn't probe further, just took his time savoring this sweet kiss of promise.

Someone behind them cleared her throat and Helen nearly jumped back. Simon kept her from moving far.

They both looked at the door at the same time.

"Mom."

Lizzy filled the doorframe and smiled. "Don't let me interrupt."

Simon rolled his eyes. These two had such a healthy relationship.

"You know...?" She walked in and shut the door. "You really should lock this door."

"We were only kissing," Helen defended them.

Lizzy waved a dismissive hand in the air. "Not that. Your camera is sitting there, and the stones. What would someone think coming across them?"

"Amber just left."

"Yeah, I know. She said you were taking pictures."

Slipping out of Simon's embrace, Helen picked up her camera and took aim. "Amber wants pictures of everyone."

Lizzy slid beside Simon and smiled. "I would too if I were leaving."

"You are leaving," Simon reminded her.

"Only for a little while. Fin isn't getting rid of me that easily."

Helen managed several shots before Liz stopped her. "We'll get the whole family together before we leave. No need to do a bunch now."

After turning off the camera, she tucked it into her bag. Keeping it in the open was asking for trouble. "I should get back to this anyway." Helen started to weave the bands of metal together for the chain. At least that part should be easy.

"Can I have a minute with you?" Lizzy asked her son.

"Sure." Simon turned back to Helen. "I'll be right back."

* * * *

The family hall was vacant. Simon knew a guard was stationed at the top of the stairway, far out of hearing range.

"So, you and Helen?" Liz asked Simon.

This was new. His mother never took an interest in his love life. For all he knew, she wasn't aware he had one. Lizzy wasn't stupid. Pretending she was would be insulting. That didn't mean Simon had to share much in the way of details.

"Helen and I."

Liz placed her hands on her hips and attempted a scowl.

She sucked at scowling.

"I like her."

Simon smiled. "So do I."

"She's smart."

"I think so, too."

"Smart, but not completely prepared to be here...with you."

"What are you dancing around, Mom?"

"There aren't corner drug stores, you know, to pick up things. I had to raise you for the first thirteen years of your life by myself. It wasn't easy."

Ah, got it. His mother was giving him a delayed speech about birth control. Not that it existed much in this time.

Lizzy went on. "The way we all breed around here.... It's like it's in the water or something."

"It's in the sex, Mom."

She slapped his arm in a playful manner. "You do right by that girl."

"Do you really believe you have to tell me this?" In a way, he was offended by the conversation. His mom should know him better than anyone. They'd been through hell and back together.

"I'm a mom, I worry. I have a right to worry if I want to. Sex makes babies, not that I need to tell you this, and yours will be *my* grandchildren. You grew up without a father for a lot of years. I know you won't want that for your children."

"Mom?" Simon placed a hand on her shoulder and stopped her tirade. "Helen and I are adults. *We* will deal with whatever we need to deal with. If you know me so well, you know you *don't* have to worry about it."

"I still worry."

"And I love you for it." His smile turned into a scowl. "But don't insult me."

He met her shocked expression with silence.

"I didn't mean to insult you."

"But you did."

"I'm sorry."

"I know."

Simon left his mother in the hall and went back in the room where Helen worked. When she turned her smile on him part of his anger toward his mother faded.

However, her words didn't.

* * * *

The sanctuary Helen hoped to share with Simon for the remaining days they had in the sixteenth century was currently being renovated to house Tara and Lora. Much to her utter frustration, cornering Simon alone proved impossible. She was too exhausted to do much other than sleep anyway.

Finally, after only a few days of work, the necklaces were completed. With their completion, the reality that they'd be leaving soon crept in.

Helen managed to take pictures of the family in

various places of the Keep. From the high tower, she took shots of the surrounding hills. The final shots of the Keep would have to wait until they left. Nobody went outside the walls without a full escort and certainly not for a frivolous picture.

Pictures, especially digital ones, lasted forever. *Where will these end up,* she mused. Who would see them and what impact would they have on the future? Was she changing the future by taking them? Having never been the artsy photographer who took shots with hopes of landing them in the Smithsonian, Helen realized that these could end up on some government database of "X" files about the possibility of time travel. How she downloaded them, and where she put them, would have to be figured out, carefully. Every possible security considered. Every photo placed into a computer had a date stamp on it and location the picture was taken. Although that function probably wouldn't work in the sixteenth century. Even if it did, anyone analyzing the data would think a computer had screwed up.

Helen stood over a basin of water, splashing her face and neck. What she wouldn't do for a shower. The poor excuse for a bathroom stunk and was shared by too many people. She didn't have long to wait. Their return trip home was less then twelve hours away. Once night fell, they would ride out, find a secluded spot, and slip into the twenty-first century. They had darn well better arrive in Mrs. Dawson's backyard, or they'd all end up on the news as a band of misfits dressed in medieval garb.

The original plan was for Helen, Simon, Amber, and Cian to land in Scotland to intercept Philip and learn what he was up to. In light of the new and bigger problem, Scotland would have to wait until they tucked everyone in Mrs. Dawson's home.

Helen's poor friend was going to flip when they arrived. She'd love it. Every noisy inch of it. Mrs. Dawson always wanted children, but was never blessed with them. *Careful what you ask for*. A crash-course in being a grandparent was about to absorb Mrs. Dawson's life.

Frantic pounding on a door down the hall snapped Helen out of her thoughts. Her heart rate kicked in her chest as she flew to the door.

Shouts started to accompany the pounding. "We're leaving now."

Helen flung open the door and observed the chaos. Children ran to their parents with wide eyes and trembling lips. Simon, wearing only a kilt over his hips, pounded on doors as he ran down the hall.

Ian ran down the opposite way shouting orders. "Gather only essentials and dress quickly. You ride within the hour."

"An hour? What happened?"

"Their army is on the move," Ian explained.

"How soon before they get here?"

"Two days. We need you to leave and spread word once you're gone." Ian placed a hand to the side of Amber's cheek. "I'm sorry to have you leave like this."

Amber nodded and stifled a gasp when Ian turned and fled the hall.

"Okay, kids. You heard your grandfather. Get dressed and pack only what you can carry. Selma, Briac, help the others." Tara grasped Amber's arm and led her away.

Helen started to follow but Simon stopped her.

"Is everything okay?" she asked him.

The hall emptied in seconds, everyone scrambling to follow Ian's direction.

"I wanted to show you much more than the inside of these walls. But we've run out of time."

She sighed and leaned into his broad chest for one blessed moment. "Don't worry, Simon. The guy in the store said this necklace is good for more than one ride."

He chuckled and brought his hands to her face. After one deep, penetrating stare, he grazed his lips to hers and turned to follow Ian.

One simple kiss and her whole body rippled with pleasure.

"Helen?" Tara called from Amber's room, forcing her out of her daze.

Chapter Twenty

Rain pelted them on their ride across the Highlands. They rode for only two hours, but it felt like twenty. Sadly, Helen needed to ride with Briac so Simon could protect the women and children if necessary. Briac kept his seat despite the fact Helen nearly dragged him off on at least two occasions. Even with a death grip on the mane of the horse, holding on wasn't easy. She vowed never again to curse her car for its lack of speed or impeccable timing for breaking down. A car had a roof, heater, and cushioned seats. Black Beauty, or whatever the name of the horse they rode was, didn't even have a decent saddle.

Even with her internal complaints, Helen wasn't oblivious to the others. Myra didn't so much as squeak and the poor girl was seven months pregnant. Amber hadn't uttered a word since she left the Keep. They left the Keep with Lora, Tara, Duncan, and Fin, but the four of them were an escort, not part of the future-traveling party.

Watching Amber part with her father had been painful. Ian's eyes glossed over and his lip trembled when Amber mounted her horse. At least she would have some family with her for a while longer. But in the end, she would be left in the future without them.

Without realizing where her gaze landed, she was staring at Simon's broad shoulders as he led the small band of travelers through the dense wooded forest. Duncan scouted ahead and doubled back constantly. Fin kept with the bulk of them and Cian took up the rear. The sun had set and the last rays of light were fading.

The forest opened up to a meadow and Duncan stopped their party. "This spot will work." The rain eased to a small drizzle, which offered some relief.

With only twenty yards of open space, there was enough room to light a circle with all of them in it. Hopefully their plan would work, and Helen would be standing under pelting hot water within the hour. Without the threat of war, violence, or capture from the wacked out enemy wanting to steal the MacCoinnich women, Helen could finally let her guard down. Medieval life didn't hold a whole hell of a lot of appeal.

Rubbing her butt after sliding off the horse, Helen stood back as the family said their goodbyes. Duncan and Tara spent time assuring their children they would be together very soon. "Listen to Aunt Lizzy and Aunt Myra," Tara told them.

"Take charge when the men are absent, Briac." Duncan patted his son's shoulder as he spoke. Even though the kid was in his teens, he still had a tear in his eye. Dad did, too. Not that Helen would ever say she witnessed it. These Highland men had a very strict "no crying" creed built in. She couldn't help but wonder if they could lose an arm and keep from weeping. Something told her they could.

Tara had Amber in a deathly hug. "I guess I should have known things were quiet for too long."

Amber didn't hold back her tears. They ran down her face silently. "You had the courage to come to us, once upon a time. Now 'tis time for me to go forward. I suppose the Ancients might call it balance."

Helen opened her eyes wide to keep her own tears back. Duncan and Fin both held their sister and offered words of strength. Of hope. But when Lora stepped forward, it seemed everyone held his or her breath.

Lora held both of Amber's hands as emotion clogged her powerful words. "My lovely daughter. Every time the lord blessed your father and I with another child I had but one wish. I prayed that all of you would live long and happy lives. Duncan found the perfect mate in Tara. She's witty, strong, and brings laughter to our home. Myra would never have been happy with a man in our time. They simply weren't diverse enough for her. Todd is everything and more, the perfect husband and father. And Lizzy...." Lora laughed through her tears. "The things she says! God's blood, we all think them, but she has the courage to say them and make even your father listen. Fin is blessed to have found her and Simon. Our home is stuffed with healthy children and laughter."

Lora sucked in her lower lip, tears fell, but she kept going.

Helen wept openly, not caring. *It's not raining enough for people to think natural causes are to blame.*

Lora placed one hand to the side of Amber face. "But your laughter has been missing for some time. Every day my heart broke a little more. My beautiful baby was dying, and there was nothing I could do but watch." Lora's words sucked into a hoarse whisper. "But then Helen dropped in and offered us hope. Offered *you* hope. Even if I'm not able to witness your happiness, at least the Ancient's gave me hope that you would find it."

Amber pulled in audible breaths.

"If our paths never cross again in this lifetime, know that I will see you again in the next. I love you."

Amber threw her hands around her mother's shoulders and cried the wail of the grieving.

Helen had to turn away. Lora's love was strong enough to move mountains. At least Amber would always know that her mother cared.

Simon appeared at Helen's side, his arm wrapped around her shoulders. He placed his lips to her temple in silent understanding. Calm settled over her.

Although, the grief she witnessed was not her own, it still hurt. Helen vowed in that moment to be as much help to Amber in the future as she could. They would both be orphans in a sense. If there was one thing Helen knew, it was how to be a woman without a family.

Of that, Helen was the resident expert.

Amber and Lora broke apart, and more goodbyes spread.

When Helen turned around most of her tears were gone.

"Are you ready?" she asked Amber.

After removing the moisture from her face with the back of her hand, Amber forced a smile and nodded. "Ready."

Lizzy had helped Helen with the words to move them through time. Liz thought it would be stronger coming from the person wearing the necklace and had the forethought to consider that Amber would be too upset to talk.

She had been right.

Everyone traveling, all six adults and eight children formed a circle. The adults spread among the kids, easing their discomfort. Simon removed a knife from his waist. "We should shed a drop of blood," he told everyone.

But when he went to cut his own hand Helen's skin jolted. "No!"

He stopped his action and pitched his brows together.

"No. That isn't how I did this the first or second time I went through time." *And the kids didn't need any more stress than they already have.* Even though Cian held a time traveling stone in a knife at his waist, Helen looked to Amber for help.

"You and I."

Amber nodded.

Helen placed her palm out to take Simon's knife from him. He handed it over and stepped back.

Biting her lip, Helen grazed the knife to her palm and let blood seep. She handed the knife to Amber and watched her do the same.

Once the knife was safely in Simon's care, Helen grasped her hands together and then placed one directly on the necklace hanging from her neck.

Amber did the same.

Helen offered her hand to Briac at her right and Myra's daughter Aislin at her left.

"We need fire."

Duncan stepped up. "Allow me."

Without as much as a wave of a hand, a ring of fire four feet tall circled them. Helen had been told Duncan's Druid gift was fire, but she hadn't seen the extent of it until then.

"Thank you," she said.

Glancing at Liz for encouragement, Helen began. "In this night and in this hour, we ask the Ancients for this power. Send us now across the sea, to Mrs. Dawson if you please. May only an hour have previously past, since Simon and Helen had been there last. Keep us healthy, keep us whole, with all the children safely in tow. If the Ancients will it so, send us now and let us go."

A large crack of lightning scraped over the night sky. A roar of turmoil raged through every nerve of Helen's body. At the last second, she caught Simon watching her. A smile spread over his lips.

Then it fell in dread.

Nausea rippled through her body and surged to her throat.

Unlike before, this trip through time was painful.

This trip through time vanished mid-flight.

* * * *

When the world settled, Simon heard someone scream.

Helen and Amber were both crumpled on the ground in Mrs. Dawson's backyard. Simon lurched to Helen's side while Liz and Cian went to Amber.

She breathed, thank God.

"What happened?"

"I think they fainted," Cian replied.

"Simon? Simon is that you?" Mrs. Dawson called from the back stoop of her home.

"Aye. 'Tis me."

"Looks like you brought the whole clan."

Yeah, he had.

Helen wake up. The longer she lay there motionless,

192

the harder his stomach dropped.

He scooped her into his arms and walked into the house. Behind him, Cian held Amber while the others followed.

"Is that my Helen?"

Simon avoided saying the obvious. Mrs. Dawson's frantic voice caused his heart to skip a beat.

Amber stirred once Cian placed her on Mrs. Dawson's sofa. "Amber?" Liz called to her.

Simon met Cian's gaze. "Did you help her wake?"

"Nay."

Simon placed a hand to Helen's cheek, coaxing her to come around. "Come on, Helen. Your turn, lass."

Someone handed him a cool washcloth, which he placed on Helen's head. When her eyes twitched and started to open, he let out a shuddering breath.

"W-Where...?"

"We've made it. Mrs. Dawson is here."

"Is she okay?" Mrs. Dawson asked.

Helen started to move her limbs.

"She's fine."

Simon helped Helen sit up, his arm around her back for support. "Does anything hurt?"

"No. I think I passed out."

"You and Amber both."

Helen looked beyond him to Amber, who offered them both a wan smile.

Fiona, Tara and Duncan's daughter, offered an explanation. "I think the burden of too many people at once is the reason, Simon."

Helen shook the fog from her brain. "I think she's right," she added. "Next time we go a couple at a time."

"I'll put on some coffee. It looks like you all can use it."

"Thanks," Helen told Mrs. Dawson.

"We're sorry to have invaded as we have," Simon told Mrs. Dawson as she walked from the living room.

"I'm sure you have your reasons. I look forward to hearing them. I'm simply happy to see you back. After the first couple of days I started to lose hope I'd ever see you again."

Helen grasped Simon's arm. "The first couple of days?"

"You've been gone over two weeks, sweetheart."

"But I thought you said we could pick a time to come back?" Helen's pleading gaze met Simon's.

"I thought we could."

"Apparently the Ancients didn't want us returning when you desired."

"What about Philip?"

"Don't worry about him now."

Mrs. Dawson walked back in the room smiling. "I suppose I should find rooms for all of you."

"Oh, Mrs. Dawson I'm sorry. We had no choice." Helen stood, but Simon held onto her arm in case her head wasn't completely recovered.

Mrs. Dawson smiled at Helen. "You look lovely. I don't think I've ever seen you in a dress, much less one so grand."

Helen laughed. "It's all the rage in Scotland."

"Your hospitality would be greatly appreciated, lass."

Mrs. Dawson's cheeks grew rosy. "How could I refuse? My home is yours. Always. I don't think I have enough beds."

"Don't worry about that. We'll make do," Liz stepped forward. "I'm Liz, Simon's mom."

"Sorry," Simon offered his mother. "Let me introduce everyone." He started with the adults and made his way through the children, most of whom were busy looking around the room and mumbling to each other.

Mrs. Dawson greeted everyone with grace, her lips always in a smile. She did seem happy to have her home filled with people. For that Simon was thankful.

Even with the excitement of the evening, the youngest children were fading. Helen offered to show the kids where to sleep and left the room with Mrs.

Dawson and the women.

Cian stayed behind and milled about the room. "So this is your time?"

"I guess you could say that. With all of you here, it feels more like my time. Last month I wouldn't have said the same."

Cian ran his hand along a lamp. "Electricity?"

Simon nodded. "It runs nearly everything."

"Hmm. The home is warm but no fire burns."

"A heater. Probably run by gas. A different fuel source."

Cian moved to a wall and rapped the end of a knuckle against it. "How does the wood get so smooth?"

"It's not wood. I think it's plaster. You'll have to ask Helen or Mrs. Dawson. I was too young to care about how the walls were built when I lived in this time. There's a lot to take in." The aroma of coffee filtered in from the kitchen. "I'll get us some coffee."

"There are no servants?"

Simon laughed. "Actually, Mrs. Dawson has help, but they leave at night."

Simon left Cian alone and rummaged through the kitchen to find cups. He poured two and brought one in for Cian. Cian sipped the brew and nodded approval.

"Before the women return, I have something to tell you."

Simon glanced to the empty doorway. "What is it?"

"My knife is gone."

"Did you drop it outside?"

"I secured it inside my pack. Now 'tis gone."

Simon put his cup aside. "What does that mean?"

Cian's gaze moved to the floor. "I do not know. 'Tis safe to say Helen will be the one to take us all home when the time comes. Risking the loss of more stones would be too great."

Simon agreed, yet as he watched Cian move about the room, the loss of the knife didn't seem to alter his behavior. It was almost as if Cian had expected the knife to disappear.

Chapter Twenty-One

Helen found Simon sitting in front of a warm fire in Mrs. Dawson's library. Everyone was safely tucked in bed. Some were two to a bed, but the kids didn't care. They buzzed with excitement and questions that Liz and Myra answered until they were too tired to speak.

"There you are," Helen said as she walked into the room and closed the door behind her. She'd found a pair of jeans and T-shirt among the small stash of clothes in the room Mrs. Dawson said was hers. The dress may have made her feel the part of a lady, but to be out from under all those layers of material felt liberating.

Simon swirled a glass half filled with amber liquid and offered her a smile. He patted the space to the side of him on the sofa. Once seated, he wrapped a hand around her shoulders, tucked her into his side, and sighed. "I've missed you."

She wanted to remind him that they'd seen each other more than not, but knew exactly what he meant. "There isn't an army of men, or a clan of family telling us to stay apart now."

"No, no there isn't." He kissed her temple before taking a sip of his drink.

"What's in there?"

"Whisky, I think."

Helen removed the glass from his hand and took a drink. "It's smooth."

"I thought ladies didn't like the taste of whisky."

She tucked her feet up on the sofa and rested her hand on his kilted thigh. "I grew up with whisky and beer, not wine and sherry."

He smiled and said, "It's nice to enjoy this and not worry about an attack."

Helen blew out a breath. "I didn't realize how

stressed I was about the war until we arrived here and the threat was gone. I don't know how you live like that every day."

Simon stroked her shoulder as he spoke. Waves of pleasure tingled down her arm. "Before last year, everything was peaceful in Scotland. After Grainna that is. The MacCoinnich's trained me for war, trained me to be a protector. I wasn't sure I'd ever have to use those skills."

The distant look in Simon's eyes caused Helen to ask, "H-Have you ever killed a man?"

His eyes met hers. "Would it concern you if I had?"

"No, I guess not. Seems inevitable where you're from."

He moved his gaze back to the fire. "I've killed."

Helen swallowed. "Does it haunt you?"

"I think about it, but I don't dwell."

Their lives were so different. How they managed to find common ground was a miracle in itself. Helen watched smoke lift above the fire and leaned onto Simon's shoulder.

"I suppose we should find our beds. Tomorrow will bring new tasks to master."

Helen sat forward and frowned. "Beds? I thought we'd..." She clamped her mouth shut. There was no need to tell him she assumed they'd share a bed now that they were back in her time. In fact, Cian now occupied the room Simon had taken when they'd stayed at Mrs. Dawson's before.

"You thought what, lass?" His expression was stoic, but his right eye sparked a bit too brightly.

"Nothing," she said as she stood. "I guess I'll just have to find Mrs. Dawson's cat to snuggle against if you want to sleep in separate rooms."

"Are you asking me to join you?"

Oh, he was not going to get in so easily. "No, no. I'll find the cat. Goodnight, Simon."

Pivoting on her heel, she started for the door, ignoring Simon's indrawn breath and the grunt he made after she'd taken a half a dozen steps. But when a deep, rumbling purr filled the room, Helen couldn't control herself any longer and glanced over her shoulder.

In the middle of Simon's kilt and discarded shirt, stood a two hundred pound black panther.

Helen's heart raced to her throat. Even though she knew Simon and the animal were one and the same, a shiver of anxiety snaked down her neck. Reflected in the eyes of the predator was an untamed and unpredictable animal.

Simon lowered his panther head and let a low roar emit from his elongated jaw.

Helen couldn't stop from backing away. "Simon? What are you doing?"

He shook his head and took another step toward her.

She backed up again, found the doorknob, and turned it. "I said I'd snuggle up to a house cat."

His whole body shook with denial as he prowled closer.

Without thought, Helen turned and ran. She squealed with laughter as she found the stairs and fled.

Behind her, Simon gave chase.

She ran into her room, Simon close behind. Once inside, Simon nudged the door closed with his behind. His tail swished side to side. His cat eyes squared on her, and he licked his lips.

"Simon?" She stepped backward, her eyes never leaving his. "You're not playing fair."

He growled and Helen's knees hit the bed. She scrambled up onto the mattress, her heart kicked strong in her chest.

With one graceful pounce, Simon landed on the bed and straddled her frame.

If there was one place Helen never thought she'd be, it was lying under a lethal panther without one ounce of dread.

A long, wet, rough tongue licked the side of her face and she reached up and touched Simon for the first time. He was soft and warm and completely at ease in fur.

He licked her again.

"Okay, you can sleep in here."

He let out a soft roar, as if in approval, and changed. In only a few seconds, he was back in his own naked skin and kissing her.

Every muscle in her body started to relax and her arms wrapped around his waist and pulled his full weight down on top of her. His fingers ran down her side and nudged into the waist of her jeans.

Helen broke away from his kiss. "You couldn't do that with claws," she told him, nipping his ears.

"You're right. I'd rip your clothing off instead. Use that cat tongue to taste every inch of your delicious skin."

Heat shot to Helen's core. "That shouldn't turn me on."

Simon tasted the corner of her mouth and down her neck. "But it did."

"I didn't say that," she denied.

"You didn't have to. I smell your desire."

She wiggled against the bed, her jeans felt tight. "You can't smell that."

Simon grasped the edges of her shirt and pulled it off. He left her bra and moved to the button on her jeans.

"I was just a predator of monstrous size. I smelled your brief fear and your heat from across the room. I scented your sex, desired a taste. Those instincts stay with me long after the animal is gone."

He'd undone her pants and shifted them down her hips.

She panted, just like the cat. His words inflamed her more than they should. When her jeans made a soft swooshing noise as they met the floor, Simon smiled up at her as he nudged her knees apart.

Heady with want, he leaned into her thigh and sucked in a breath. "Will you let me taste you while the cat's instincts are still here?"

Her whole body wept with desire and her nipples hardened. He read her mind and dipped his head.

His tongue passed over one side of her sex, then the other, and Helen fell back onto the bed, her legs opened wide for whatever he wanted from her.

Simon chuckled, or maybe it was a purr. She couldn't tell. It didn't matter when his tongue found her. He lapped her up like cream. His tongue found places Helen didn't know existed. She felt her body grow moist as Simon hummed into her sex.

How could this man drive away all her inhibitions? She'd never been one to seek comfort from men in the past, certainly didn't initiate intimacy often, but with Simon, her world opened up.

The house was full of people, yet all she could think about was what she could do to please him.

She shouldn't be enjoying him as much as she was. Their time together was limited.

"Oh, right there," she softly cried, as her body reached toward his.

Something deep inside her body started to clench and build. Desire shifted to uncontrollable need. Just as her body started to peak, she felt Simon's tongue go slightly rough and pushed her over the top. Helen covered her mouth with her arm to keep from screaming out as her body shuddered with pleasure.

She hadn't begun to recover when Simon entered her again. His body covering hers, his erection buried deep. "You taste divine."

Unable to talk while his body rocked with hers, his cock found the back of her womb, making it want his seed.

He felt perfect. His body covered hers and kept her safe. All Helen could do was think of pleasing him, giving him everything she could. A tiny warning echoed in her mind, reminding her that this closeness would end up in emotional suicide if she wasn't careful.

Ignoring the warning, she wrapped her legs around

his waist and gave him more room inside her.

He groaned and took.

He wasn't gentle and she loved it. All the stress of the last week, of all the days back in his time drifted away as he blinded her with his passion.

Never in her life had a man made her feel so alive. Helen broke over the molting point a second time, and Simon caught her cry with his lips. She moaned around his kiss as he emptied inside her.

"Oh, Simon." She reached behind his back, holding him as his body stopped shaking and his breath started to even. "That was..." *Amazing, incredible.* "Magical."

Her body still shivered all over with zips of energy. The same feeling she got when her gift led her to what she sought.

Simon lifted his head and removed some of his weight. His deep, penetrating stare and a small lift of his lips told her he enjoyed her praise. He ran the pad of his thumb over her lips. "You're magical."

"Says the man with the cat-tongue," she said laughing.

His brows shot up. "You like?"

Her body shivered just thinking about it. "There should be a law against such pleasure."

"I'm sure there is, somewhere." He rolled to the side, tucked her into his body, and covered them with a blanket.

Simon stroked her arm and her eyelids started to drift close. "Simon?" she murmured.

"Aye?"

"It's okay isn't it? You being in here with me? I know your mom is—"

"My mother doesn't need to concern you."

"But isn't this frowned upon in your time?" She glanced into his eyes, gave a wan smile.

"We aren't in the past. Besides, my mother understands I'm a grown man." His expression turned thoughtful, stoic even.

"I don't want to put you in an awkward position."

"Do you want me to leave?" His body tensed. His head lifted from the pillow.

Reflexively, her hand gripped his waist. "God, no. I don't want anything to be weird for you. Lizzy seems like an understanding woman, but she *is* your mom. It seems like your family is really good at sticking their heads into everyone's business."

Simon slid his leg between hers and laid back down. "They care. 'Tis why they watch and comment on everything. Don't worry over my family."

Smiling, she snuggled back in his arms.

Simon felt Helen's body relax. Her arm lay over his hips, his leg tucked between hers. As her breathing evened out, and she succumbed to sleep, his mind was fully awake.

The woman was intoxicating. He lost all sense of direction when he was with her, except when it came to claiming her. As a cat, that need crawled up his back to the tip of his nose.

Having spent many hours of his life in animal form, there were times Simon lost himself in the ambitions of whatever animal form he chose. His sense of smell, sight, or hearing was stronger as a human because of it. He wasn't joking when he told Helen the animal in him didn't leave him completely when he shifted back to human form. A couple of years after he began shifting, he noticed the enhanced senses. Those talents molded him into the warrior he was. He could hear his enemy advance, smell their fear. Equally, he could smell the pheromones of a lover spike.

Helen emitted those like none other. Her scent drove him mad. He could also scent fertility much like an animal can with its mate. So why, when he scented Helen's, did he not bring her to completion with his tongue and dive away? Why couldn't he stop himself from claiming her with such primal force?

Why did he fill her with his seed knowing damn well the chances of it taking root and bearing his child was high?

Helen moaned in her sleep and dove closer into his embrace.

"I'm here," he whispered to her sleeping form. *I'm here.*

* * * *

Philip met Malcolm's icy stare through the glass. "She disappeared."

Malcolm grasped the end of the phone with white knuckles. "You've searched everywhere?"

Philip nodded, knowing the police recorded every word. Privacy in prisons was non-existent. "My secretary said she called while I was in Scotland, so I waited until I was back in the States to notify the authorities."

The last thing Philip needed was for the police to think he had anything to do with Helen's disappearance. The sins of his brother could very well float over to him if he wasn't careful. A missing woman abroad and the brother of a convicted murderer didn't bode well for Philip's freedom. As it was, the authorities had hauled him in for questioning twice. Each time the questioning took on a darker edge.

Of course, there was no evidence of foul play, no family to push an investigation. There were bandages found in Helen's bathroom trash with blood, but not enough to suggest a mortal wound. Someone in the apartment complex stated that they'd seen Helen after she'd flown to Scotland. She'd been with a large man who didn't fit Philip's description. Without anything other than his brother's crimes to go on, the police hadn't questioned him further.

Still, the entire ordeal unsettled him. Malcolm and his quest for freedom through Helen was what started this mess. Of late, Philip couldn't shake the feeling that Malcolm's freedom could very well mean Philip's incarceration. Trading places with his brother was not on his "to do" list.

Malcolm glanced over his shoulder to the guard standing at the door. "Was she in the States when she called? I thought she flew to Europe."

"She did, according to the flight records. Her return ticket is sitting with some of her things in Scotland so she didn't get back the way she left. The police said she called the office from her apartment. My secretary knows Helen as well as she knows me, she knows her voice. Still, she can't be in two places at the same time."

This meant that Malcolm's theory about how the stone worked might have a snowball's chance of being true. The spark in his brother's eye suggested Malcolm came to the same conclusion.

"If she called from the States, chances are she'll show herself soon. Have you checked with that old lady she spends time with?"

"Spoke to her on the phone. She sounded concerned about Helen's disappearance."

Mal's eyes narrowed. "You should check on her. She doesn't have family, right?"

No, which right now sounded like a blessing. Philip felt his own will bending toward his brother's. If Helen were in hiding, she probably would run to Mrs. Dawson's.

Philip had only met the woman once when she walked into the auction house in search of Helen. He had a terrible feeling the woman saw right through him, deep into his tarnished soul. He didn't want to repeat the experience.

"I'll call her tonight."

"A personal visit would be better."

Order delivered.

Philip forced a smile to his face. "Right."

Even behind bars, Malcolm managed to win. Philip knew what the man was capable of, and knew brotherly love wouldn't keep Philip above ground if he didn't come through for his brother.

"Call me tomorrow, two o'clock." Malcolm hung up the visitor phone and pushed the steel chair back. The guard behind him stood taller and nodded when Malcolm walked past him.

Philip slowly placed the receiver on the hook and watched his brother disappear. The farther away his brother walked, the less pull he had on him. But Philip was well rehearsed at releasing his brother's hold.

Others weren't.

Even the guard escorting Mal back to his cell couldn't be trusted. Philip might be able to push thoughts into the minds of the people around him, but Malcolm matched him with that gift, took it further, and erased a person's own desires as well.

When they were kids, Malcolm would practice his tricks on the teachers at school. It started off innocent enough. *I deserve an "A", Miss Benito* quickly morphed into *I was in your class all day*. On rare occasions, a teacher would break out of his brother's hold long enough to mark him absent. Those teachers always found themselves doing completely inappropriate things in front of, or to, students.

Philip remembered a thirty-something year old Algebra teacher, married and mother of two. Malcolm loathed her. Malcolm sat at the front of the auditorium during an anti-drug demonstration put on by the local sheriff's department and bent the teacher's will like a twig. Once all the students assembled, and the cops uncovered their contraband to educate the kids on what to stay away from, the teacher burst from her seat, ran to the table, and started popping all the pills she could grab. She screeched profanities as if she had Tourette's. The students howled in laughter while the police and school staff tried to restrain her.

The district fired the teacher and the police put her on a seventy two hour psychiatric hold before pressing charges. Malcolm never had to deal with her again.

Mal seldom dirtied his own hands. He'd have the bigger kids fight his battles.

But the bigger kids couldn't get his dick wet, and that's what landed Mal's sorry ass in jail.

Philip remembered the pictures and video of what his brother did to the woman he'd murdered.

Everyone on the jury would remember the pictures, too. No matter how hard Malcolm tried, he couldn't manipulate everyone's mind at the same time to get him acquitted.

Even still, a couple of the jurors had met with premature deaths since the trial. Philip would bet his soul his brother was behind their demise.

"Are you waiting for someone else?"

Philip shook his head to clear it, and stared up at the guard. *Smartass.*

Outside the penitentiary, he walked past the visiting families and made his way to his car. After sliding behind the wheel, he started the engine and turned on the heater to ward of the unseasonal chill in the air.

In the seat beside him, he picked up his father's journal. He opened to the dog-eared page, well worn from use, and read what he'd already memorized.

I found the stone hidden in a half-empty box of tampons. Fucking bitch thinks I'm stupid. Thought a man wouldn't go there. Thought I'd never look in that box. I'm not stupid. I know she uses it to see him. I don't know how yet, but I'll find out. One way or another, I'll find out.

Philip turned the page.

Came home from the club and found the bathroom in ruins. Claire was hysterical. She accused me of ruining her life. Me, the one who stood by her all these years—the one who raised her bastards as if they were mine. It's me she should love, not him. She'll never see him again. She'll learn to love me or die a bitter old woman.

The next few pages voiced the same sentiment. Philip's parents fought, and his mom fell into a depression—something Dennis Lyons hadn't seen coming. As much as Dennis loathed his wife's transgressions, he loved the woman...and hated himself for it.

She's back in the hospital. This time she locked

herself in the car and let it run with the garage door down. The doctors say she'll make it, but they want to take her to one of those crazy houses. I heard her mumble something about the stone while she was sedated. They gave her something to calm her down.

I've tried to make the fucking thing work. It won't. While she slept I put it in her hand, and the thing lit up like a goddamn star. I had to wrestle it out of her palm. When she woke she stared at me as if she knew.

I could kill the bastard who did this to her—who took her from me. I'll make this damn thing work if only to wring his fucking neck.

The pages after that were blank. Philip knew where the story ended. His mom successfully ended her own life by driving off a cliff. His dad, well, his step-dad anyway, ended up dying a bitter old man. Philip and Malcolm were ugly reminders of Dennis's wasted life. All of this happened before Philip's fifth birthday.

Malcolm remembered their mom, but Philip recalled nearly nothing. He remembered yelling and hospitals, and then the funeral. After that, a series of babysitters raised him and his brother. Mal manipulated every last one, much like his teachers. If he didn't approve, they didn't stay.

When Dennis died, Philip found the journal and a bag holding the stone. It was a rock, nothing more. Except the very same rock, or one exactly like it, sat around Helen's neck in the form of a necklace. The rock Dennis left him sat in a jail cell with Malcolm.

And now Helen had disappeared, just like his mother had from time to time before Dennis took the stone away.

In order to learn the stone's secrets, Helen had to reappear. Without any family of her own, she'd probably run to the only mother figure she had.

Philip buckled his seatbelt and shifted the car in gear.

It was time to pay Mrs. Dawson a personal visit.

Chapter Twenty-Two

Amber sat quietly on the back porch of Mrs. Dawson's home. With the exception of Mrs. Dawson, everyone had left early in the morning. The children were with Helen, and the others were finding suitable clothing and supplies to meet their needs during their stay in this century. When asked to go along, Amber waved them off. "I'll have plenty of time to explore. Besides, wearing this cloak might appear suspicious. We wouldn't want any unnecessary attention while everyone is here."

There was some legitimacy to her excuse for not accompanying them for the day, but the truth was, Amber needed time in her new world to adjust. Myra had warned her of all the modern conveniences and overall noise of this century. Her warnings didn't do justice to the reality. There were people all around them, strangers whose twisted emotions seeped through the cracks of Amber's protective cloak. She needed to find a more convenient means of protection. Wearing the cloak at all times might have made lifting her head easier, but it would draw curious eyes. From what Helen had said, the hot weather of California wouldn't lend itself to a long robe of any kind. Lizzy was searching for a garment that would suit Amber's needs so they could charm it before they were summoned back in time.

On a sigh, Amber picked up the empty cup used for tea and made her way into the kitchen. The smooth counters and ovens that didn't use fire to heat brought a smile to Amber's lips. She ran her hand along the ice

208

box and opened it long enough to feel the cool temperature inside. Multiple colored liquids sat in glass containers on the shelves. She felt as if she were violating someone's privacy by peeking inside so she didn't continue exploring the refrigerator.

Amber heard Mrs. Dawson's footsteps in the hall. "There you are," she said with a smile. "I was wondering where you might explore first."

Amber's spine stiffened. "I'm sorry if I overstepped—"

"Nonsense. Overstep all you like. How else are you to learn?" Mrs. Dawson slid onto a stool at the counter.

"You're too kind."

"It isn't every day I have the company of a beautiful woman from a century long past. I'll bet you have a question or two about everything in this room."

Amber glanced around. "Aye," she said.

"Then ask."

Smiling, Amber pointed to the first object she saw. "What is this used for?"

"It's a toaster. You put sliced bread into the slots, push down the button and in a minute or two, the bread is cooked on both sides."

She placed her fingers on the lever. "May I?"

"Of course."

Amber pushed the lever down and watched the inside of the machine turn red. "Amazing."

Mrs. Dawson proceeded to give everything in the room a name. A coffee maker, a can opener, a dishwasher—too many names and uses for Amber to process. It was all fascinating and a bit overwhelming.

How had Myra managed without the guidance of someone who understood where she came from? When her sister returned, she'd have to ask.

The telephone rang and Amber jumped.

"It's only the phone." Mrs. Dawson winked and reached to answer it. "Hello?"

Amber avoided listening, but Mrs. Dawson's body tightened as she spoke. "Oh, I'm sorry Mr. Lyons, but

I'm a bit indisposed at the moment. Would it be too much trouble for you to come back in an hour?" Mrs. Dawson placed a hand over the phone and whispered. "It's Helen's boss. He's at the gate."

"Why is he here?"

Mrs. Dawson shrugged. "Hold on, Mr. Lyons."

"What should we do?"

"He already sounds suspicious. If we turn him away, he might linger and be here when Helen and the others return."

"Is it safe to allow him in?" Only one maid wandered the grounds. Hardly any protection against a man.

"He's never threatened me." Mrs. Dawson placed her attention back to the man on the phone. "Come on in, Mr. Lyons. I'll have Amber meet you at the door while I find something suitable to wear."

After disconnecting the call, Mrs. Dawson waved Amber toward the front door. "Talk with him for a few minutes, see if you can use that extra sense of yours to find anything out. I'll call Helen and make certain she doesn't come back with him here."

Amber's heart jumped in her chest. She knew how to greet visitors, but this one posed a threat to Helen, or so they thought. By the time she reached the door, Mr. Lyon's knock sounded in the hall. She flattened her hand over her stomach and twisted the handle.

The man standing in the doorway wore a simple smile that brightened when his eyes met Amber's. "You must be Amber."

"Yes. Mrs. Dawson will be down in a moment, won't you come in?" Stepping aside, Amber let the man pass, ignoring the fluttering in her insides. It was common for women in this century to meet strange men without a chaperone at their side. The experience however, was new for her.

"Thank you," Philip said. "Are you Mrs. Dawson's nurse?"

Amber shook her head. "House guest."

He moved his head to the side. "Ah."

She would have offered to take his coat had he been wearing one. "Shall we wait for Mrs. Dawson in the library? She'll only be a minute."

"Fine."

Amber felt his stare as she led him into the dark room. "Can I get you anything?"

"I'm fine, thank you."

Philip stared at her after sitting on the edge of the sofa. Their conversation stalled and awkward silence filled the room. "What brings you here today, Mr. Lyons?"

"Mrs. Dawson and I have a mutual friend who has gone missing. I was hoping she'd have some information."

Amber couldn't tell if he was sincere with the cloak covering her shoulders. His dark eyes didn't hold his thoughts.

"Philip." Mrs. Dawson leaned on her cane as she entered the room. Amber eyed the stick, but didn't say a word about it. The older woman limped toward them and Philip stood.

"I'm sorry to bother you, but I was hoping you'd heard something."

"Nothing I'm afraid." Mrs. Dawson turned toward Amber. "Can you be a dear and ask Mavis to make tea?"

"I've come at a bad time. I won't be staying," Philip said. "I know Helen would want me to check on you." His gaze drifted to Amber. "But I see you have company."

"No need to worry about me, Philip, but thank you for your concern. Have you heard from the authorities?"

Philip hesitated before shaking his head. Amber wasn't sure if Mrs. Dawson noticed his hesitation, but she had. Trying to stay unnoticed, Amber pulled one arm out of her cloak and adjusted to the weight of anxiety surrounding her. Her heart started to leap and a small ache pulsed behind her right ear.

It didn't seem as if Philip would be staying long,

and losing this opportunity to read the man might not come again.

"They spoke with my staff and interviewed her neighbors."

"I somehow think she'll turn up."

Philip's eyes narrowed. "What makes you say that?"

"She's a resourceful girl. Maybe she's met a man who whisked her away."

How clever of Mrs. Dawson to offer a plausible explanation for Helen's disappearance.

"Don't you think she'd call if that were the case?"

Amber slid the cloak off one shoulder and took a deep breath.

"Have you ever been in love, Philip?"

"No, can't say that I have."

Amber grasped the edge of the cloak and allowed it to leave her back. The room pitched and swam, causing nausea to rise in her throat. Mrs. Dawson and Philip were deep in conversation, neither of them paying her any attention.

Amber hugged the cloak to her stomach. Mrs. Dawson's anxiety rose in Amber's mind.

Mavis, was questioning the sudden appearance of all Mrs. Dawson's houseguests, worried that they were there to steal some of Mrs. Dawson's wealth.

"Love makes a person do crazy things."

The pounding behind Amber's ear surged through her head and her palms began to sweat.

"Has Helen told you about a man in her life?" Philip asked.

"No."

Amber felt a twinge behind the word, telling her Mrs. Dawson lied.

"I hope you're right. That this search for her is in vain." Philip's words held the same twinge. He didn't want Helen to show up with a man on her arm. He lied, but why?

"Do you think she'll return with a suitor?" Amber asked.

Philip turned and fixed her with a stare.

Mrs. Dawson eyed the cloak and forced her concern away.

"As long as she returns, I really don't care who she shows up with."

Again with the lies.

Stepping closer, Amber smiled. "I hope you're right, Mrs. Dawson."

Every step closer to Philip felt as if she walked in mud. Something dark hovered over the man, but Amber couldn't read it. She let the cloak dangle in her arms. When she was close enough to the man, she pretended to trip.

Philip held out a hand to steady her. When his fingers touched her flesh the mud around his emotions splashed away and left dirty, readable water.

Philip Lyons was not an innocent man searching for a friend.

Helen would do well to stay clear of him.

"How clumsy of me. Much thanks," she told Philip before shaking his hand off. As much as she probably should have held on to learn more of his secrets, the pain of his presence was unbearable.

Mrs. Dawson pushed forward and helped Amber return the cloak to her shoulders. "You've hardly recovered from your cold, m'dear. You should keep this on."

As the cloak silenced the emotions in the room, Amber started to breathe easier.

"I should be going," Philip said. "Let me know if you hear anything."

"I will."

"A pleasure meeting you." Philip nodded toward Amber and walked beside Mrs. Dawson as they left the room.

Amber slumped into the sofa, exhausted from her brief exposure.

When Mrs. Dawson returned to the room, the cane was gone along with her limp. "My God, are you okay?"

"I'm well." Yet her hand trembled.

"You don't lie well."

"Nay, I suppose I don't. But that man does."

"Hold that thought. Let me call Helen and find something to calm your nerves."

* * * *

Two blocks away from Mrs. Dawson's house, Philip pressed an icon on his Smartphone and brought up the audio feed.

"Drink this," he heard Mrs. Dawson's voice.

Good, they haven't left the library.

"What is it?"

"It's stronger than wine. You look like you need it."

Philip remembered the washed out color on Amber's beautiful face. Something had spooked the girl.

"Better?"

"Aye. Much."

The thick accent of the girl sounded clearer than it had when he was in the room. Having just returned from Scotland, he recognized the lyrical tone.

"That man is not concerned about Helen's well being."

Philip held perfectly still.

"Are you sure?"

"He lied about the authorities. Lied about the desire for Helen to come home with a man. He's after her."

"Could you tell why?"

"Nay. But he won't let her leave his sight once he finds her. Of that I'm certain."

Philip fisted his palm.

"We need to warn her."

He hit the dash of his car. "I knew they were lying. Old broad knows where she is." He turned up the sound.

"They're on their way home now." Mrs. Dawson's voice sounded farther away.

"Is that safe?"

"Safer than if she were out there by herself. Here she'll have everyone's protection."

Who is everyone?

"Seems we've run from one battle to another."

"Philip is only one man. Not an army you've left behind. Come, help me in the kitchen. Baking always helps me calm down." Mrs. Dawson's voice drifted away as they left the room.

Philip tossed his phone to the side.

Helen wasn't lost after all. She was hiding.

The spooky, longhaired beauty knew his secrets.

That wouldn't do.

* * * *

"Now what?"

Helen ran her hands over her face. "I think it's obvious. I need to emerge from the missing or risk exposing everyone here."

"How will you explain your absence?" Myra asked.

"Mrs. Dawson's already done that. I met a guy. We had a wild fling. Now I'm back."

Simon winked her way.

"You have to keep Simon's name out of it," Lizzy said.

"I know. I'll make something up."

"You need to stay clear of Philip. The man wants more than your safe return." Amber's somber expression reminded Helen that this wasn't a game.

"He won't accost me in public. I can't see him accosting me at all."

"You didn't think him capable of breaking into your home, either. Yet, we saw him do so." Simon placed a hand over hers as he spoke.

The children were in the kitchen eating chocolate chip cookies with Mrs. Dawson. Cian stood by the door listening to the conversation, as usual, and offering nothing while Lizzy, Myra, Simon, and Amber helped Helen figure out their next move.

The kilts were tucked away along with the medieval swords. The only weapons at their disposal were their gifts. Though that might prove useful to Myra, who could move objects with her mind and Lizzy who could fly away if need be, Helen felt quite useless. Sure,

Simon could shift into an animal and take out an enemy, but that wouldn't exactly go unnoticed in a crowd of people. Even the kids could do some crazy-ass stuff.

Maybe it was time for Helen to try and flick a flame from her fingertips. She rubbed her fingers together with the thoughts.

"I'll take Amber with me to the office and have you or Cian wait outside for us."

"I don't like it."

"I can't hide forever, Simon. Besides, we need to know what Philip is after."

"He's after you," Amber insisted.

"He has had access to me for years. Why the sudden need now? There's something I'm missing here."

Lizzy kicked her feet up on the coffee table. "What do you know about the man's personal life? He's not married, right?"

"No."

"Family? Brothers, sisters?"

"No clue. I think he said something about his parents being gone. That's all I know."

Lizzy glanced at Myra. "I think I might need to call in a favor."

"Oh?"

"Todd's old partner, Jake. Only he's not old." Lizzy reached for the phone. "I don't know why I didn't think of this earlier. Man is he gonna flip."

"Is that safe?" Myra asked.

"Why wouldn't it be? It isn't like we can fake getting older. If he's still a cop, he'll have the ability to do a background check on Philip. See if there's anything in his past to point to what he's up to now."

Lizzy left the room with the cordless phone in her hand.

Helen shrugged and glanced at Simon. His jaw was set in a tight line, his expression grim. So much for worry-free days. "He's just a man," she assured him.

"We don't know that."

"I agree with Simon," Amber added. "The man felt familiar to me."

Helen tore her eyes away from Simon. "What do you mean familiar?"

"Strangers try to hide behind a mask of lies and a lack of expression but reading them is easy for me. I needed to lower my defenses to dig deeper into this man. He's guarded, as if he knows someone is peering into his soul. I think he's Druid." Amber pulled her cloak closer to her frame.

Simon stood and started to pace the room. "If he is one of us, there is no telling what he's capable of."

Helen didn't see the problem. Philip might be hiding something, but deep inside she didn't think he was dangerous. "Keep your friends close and your enemies closer. I've never thought of my boss as my enemy. The only way to figure out what he wants is to get near him."

"No."

Helen's head shot toward Simon. "Excuse me?"

"He's dangerous." Simon's tone was final. Good thing they weren't in his century or Helen might feel obligated to listen. As it was, she didn't.

"We don't know that."

"He's dangerous until we prove otherwise."

Myra, Amber, and Cian listened while Simon attempted to put his foot down.

"I think I know the man better than you."

Simon's jaw twitched. "You may know him, but we know Druids. We've seen what those who are evil are capable of. You haven't."

Something inside her shivered. Years of being on her own however, kept Helen from bowing to Simon's will. Sure, something about Philip had always bothered her. She'd chocked that up to the man's seeming interest in her as a woman. Now she knew it was deeper than that. Still, he wasn't dangerous. The only way she'd prove that is to get near the man and prove he wasn't going to do a thing to her.

Helen didn't realize how still the room had become until Lizzy stepped back in. "I left a message...ah, what's going on?" Liz slid to a stop and eyed her son before glancing at Helen.

Seconds ticked by without a word.

"Would someone please tell me what happened?"

Myra cleared her throat. "Helen wants to confront Philip and Simon was explaining how dangerous the man can be if he is in fact a Druid."

"I don't want to confront him, just spy on him to find out what he's after. I can't do that sitting around here hiding."

When Liz nodded, Helen thought she had the woman's support.

"The man broke into your apartment and followed you to Europe to spy on you. He isn't a choirboy. Doesn't mean he slices people up, but he's not innocent." Lizzy stood before Helen and broke some of the tension in the room. "I have a call into Jake at the station. With any luck, we'll hear from him soon and we can draw in more information. Laying low for a couple more days won't hurt."

"Unless Philip returns and finds me here. Then what?"

"Then you're surrounded by people who can protect you," Simon said.

All her life Helen only depended on herself. What happened when everyone in the room returned to their time? Who would be there to protect her then?

No, Helen could count only on herself. She'd learned a thing or two living on the streets. Some of the urban knowledge would come in handy now. "Fine." Let him think he won. From the look on Simon's face, they'd be arguing until dawn if Helen didn't relent.

Chapter Twenty-Three

"I can't believe I'm sitting next to you again." Jake Nelson stared at Simon's mother with his jaw on his chest. From what Fin had told Simon of the man, he wasn't sure how much he could trust him. Jake might have been as close to a brother to Todd at one time, but he hadn't made Simon's mother and Fin's stay in this century easy. According to Fin, Jake threatened to turn Liz and Fin into the police on several occasions, never believing their stories of time travel and magical powers.

Simon wondered what Nelson believed after he saw Fin and Liz disappear right in front of his eyes only two years ago. There was no denying his mother's or Myra's age. age, Myra's, whom Jake had met.

"We didn't think we'd need to return here either."

Jake's gaze swept over Myra's frame and settled on her protruding stomach. "Isn't it dangerous for you to...travel in your condition?"

Myra rubbed her belly. "We seem to be doing fine."

"Where's Todd?"

Worry filled Myra's face. "Home. For our safety, and that of the children, we needed to travel without him."

"Children?" Jake no sooner asked about them before several sets of footsteps ran down the hall and into the living room.

Fiona and Aislin sailed into the room at a run, Jake and Kyle fast on their heels.

"I tagged you!" Kyle hollered.

The ground under them started to shake when the girls came to a stop.

"Aislin, stop that," Myra scolded her daughter, knowing it was her making the earth tremble beneath their feet.

Aislin slid behind her mother's back and the room quieted. "Sorry."

Myra reached around her daughter and pulled her close. "We have company."

Jake and Kyle, both out of breath, stood taller and eyed Jake Nelson quietly.

"Jake," Myra called her son to her side. When he made it to her, she lifted her hand in the older Jake's direction. "Honey, I want you to meet the man your father and I named you after. Jake Nelson, this is our son, Jake Blakely."

Jake Nelson's speculative expression slid from his face like butter from hot bread. Little Jake was an exact replica of Todd and Nelson could see it. Todd's son proudly put out his hand for the other man to shake.

"My father speaks of you all the time."

"Does he?"

"Aye. Says you're the brother he didn't have."

Nelson pulled in a quick breath and blew it out slowly. "When you see him again, tell him...tell him I feel the same."

Jake nodded. "Yes, sir."

Liz encouraged the children to play in another room while the adults talked.

"So, you're Simon?" Jake said after the kids left the room.

Simon nodded.

"You realize you're supposed to be a teenage kid, right?"

"I was at one time."

Jake moved his gaze to Helen. "And you're the latest 'missing' woman. Am I to believe that every missing person on the books is a time traveler?"

"I wouldn't go that far," Liz told him. "We've been free of visitors for over a decade. Helen stumbled upon us. We didn't search for her."

"Are you a Druid, too?"

Helen shrugged. "So I'm told. Hard to argue with

the things I've seen in the last month."

Liz spent a little time bringing Jake up to date on the reasons for their twenty first century visit. When they broached the need for Jake's help, Simon and Helen took over the conversation.

"You want me to check this Philip guy for priors?"

"We'd like to know anything you can find out about him. Family, friends...places where he spends time outside of work."

"I'm not a private investigator. I'm a cop."

"He broke into my apartment. I saw him leaving."

"Did he take anything?"

"No," Helen said. "But then he followed me to Scotland."

Jake removed a small notebook from his jacket pocket. "Spell his name."

Helen rambled off the spelling and offered his place of business with an address and phone number. After Jake stuffed the book away, he turned to Liz. "I'll see what I can find. How long do you think you'll be here?"

She shook her head. "We don't know. But unlike before, we know we can get back and how. Helen has the key."

Jake narrowed his eyes in Helen's direction. "Seems to me if this Philip guy wanted to harm you, he would have by now. My guess is he's searching for something. Something you have."

"I don't have anything. Before my trip to Scotland, I was an open book to the man."

Jake stood and everyone in the room stood with him. "I'll get back to you tomorrow."

At the door, he stopped. "Do you plan on disappearing again, Helen?"

The hair on Simon's arms stood on end. Helen glanced his way with a flicker of uncertainty in her gaze. "N-no, not permanently anyway."

"Then you might consider coming into the station sooner than later. Tell everyone you're not a missing person and call off the search. Suspicion is higher when you're found. Considering you're the only one here with an identification that can be traced, it wouldn't work well for anonymity to be found here."

"Right."

Simon stepped forward. "I'll walk you to your car."

Jake's left eye twitched but he didn't argue as Simon led him out. The others stayed behind.

"What else can I do for you, Simon?"

Smart man. "About identification. Maybe you could give me a name of someone who can create such a thing."

"False ID would be illegal."

"We both know I'm not a criminal. I need to protect Helen and don't need to worry about being detained for deportation. Though I'm not sure where they would deport me to."

Jake snorted. "Don't you have some kind of special power that would help you get away?"

Simon flicked a finger in the air and a small flame shot in the sky. "A diversion wouldn't stop the police from searching for me. Revealing to the world what we're capable of would be catastrophic. We don't need reporters camped out here."

Reaching for the car door, Jake opened it and shifted one foot on the ledge. "I'll see what I can do. But you didn't get the information from me. I like my job, and have this crazy desire to eat. I was on probation for over a year after your mom and Fin disappeared the last time. I'm only helping because of Todd. But I have to look out for my kids first."

Simon nodded. "I understand. Any help would be appreciated."

He stood back as Jake slid behind the wheel and left Mrs. Dawson's driveway.

No one understood the need to protect a family more than Simon.

He turned back to the house, determined to protect his.

* * * *

Helen felt a bit like a teenage kid sneaking out of the house. A part of her loved having so many people around who seemed to care, but she'd always lived her life alone. Only abiding by the rules she made for herself and no one else...so waiting until Simon and the others approved of what she wanted to do wasn't in her.

One good thing about having a house full of people was her ability to play each against the other to sneak out. She told Myra she was with Simon, told Simon she was with Liz and told Mrs. Dawson that she needed a nap. Cian wasn't anywhere to be found, not that she'd say anything to him. The guy wigged her out. The strong silent type never did anything for her. Cian was all that and more.

Jake had called the day before to inform Liz that Philip's record was clean. Not one prior, not one juvenile offence. He had a brother, however, who was anything but clean. Serving life for a rape and murder charge without the possibility of parole. According to Jake, Philip visited his brother on occasion, but nothing appeared out of the ordinary. The police had brought Philip in for questioning a couple of times in regards to Helen's disappearance. With nothing more than a criminal brother to go on, they didn't hold him.

Philip wasn't the reason for her disappearance and didn't like the thought of the man being accused of something he hadn't done.

Armed with a story written in her head, Helen drove away from Mrs. Dawson's home ready to face her boss. It was Wednesday. Shipments came in on Wednesday so the auction house would have a few more people around than normal. Though she probably would have lost her job, she thought it best to act somewhat remorseful for her unexplained absence.

Her hands shook as she pulled into the parking lot and turned off the engine. "Here goes nothing," she whispered to herself as she slid out of the car. Not taking any chances, she walked through the front door, knowing the cameras pointed there were always running.

A shriek from the back of the building told Helen she'd been seen.

"Oh my freaking God." Lisa darted around the tables and embraced her hard. "I thought you were dead."

Guilt welled in Helen's chest. She hadn't thought she'd be missed. Not like this anyway. "Not dead."

Lisa moved away to look at her, and then pulled her in for a second hug. "You scared the crap out of me. Jesus, where have you been? Are you all right? Were you hurt?"

"I'm sorry I worried you. I met this guy—"

"A guy?"

"Yeah, an amazing Scottish yummy—"

"You've been missing for over two weeks. The police have questioned everyone. We thought you were dead and you were off with a guy?"

The concern in Lisa's face shifted to hurt.

"I know, totally irresponsible of me. He took me to this remote cabin. I lost my cell. It's been crazy. God, I'm sorry I didn't find a way to tell you I was okay."

"I hope he was worth it."

"Is any guy really worth it? I've probably lost my job, huh?"

Lisa crossed her arms over her chest and blew a strand of bleach blonde hair from her eyes. "You don't take a two week vacation without telling the boss. Philip has been worried like the rest of us."

Helen glanced beyond Lisa to the back of the showroom. "Is he here?"

"He was in the warehouse a few minutes ago."

Ignoring the pounding of her heart, Helen pushed around Lisa. "I better let him know I'm alive."

"You should do that."

As Helen made her way around the room, Lisa called out. "I'm going to want details about your Highland hottie."

Helen pictured Simon on his horse and wearing a

kilt. Something in her expression must have shifted because Lisa whistled and winked. "That good, huh?"

"I've had an unforgettable two weeks." There wasn't a trace of lie in her statement.

Helen heard voices in the warehouse before she rounded the corner and noticed Philip standing beside two men who were setting an early Regency buffet down.

"Philip," Helen uttered his name and waited for him to turn her way.

For a brief moment, Philip didn't look at all surprised to see her, but his expression quickly changed to one of complete concern. "Helen?"

She lifted her arms. "Back from the dead, apparently."

Philip strode her way and pulled her into his arms. She stiffened, never having had the man this close to her before.

The delivery guys watched the exchange.

Unable to avoid his brief hug, Helen patted his back and tried to push out of his arms. "I'm sorry I worried everyone."

He didn't let her go immediately and Helen's skin started to buzz. He tightened his hold and the realization that the man holding her was stronger than she was, made her question the wisdom of coming there alone. When he let go, he kept his hands on her shoulders and squeezed.

His touch was cold, his eyes dark. "Where the hell have you been?"

"It's complicated," she offered.

"Ah, Mr. Lyons, where do you want the rest of this stuff?"

Philip kept one hand on her shoulder and turned toward the men. "Set everything on the east wall. I'll have Lisa come back and finish the inventory."

The guys nodded and went back to work.

Philip kept a hand on Helen's shoulder and led her out of the warehouse and into his office.

He barked an order to Lisa and closed the door.

Some of the concern lifted and Philip's eyes crawled up and down her frame. They leveled on her chest briefly before returning to her face.

"I'm sorry, Philip, I should have found a way to call."

He leaned against his desk and waited for her to explain.

Ten minutes later, Helen had delivered her well thought out lie that sounded convincing even to her.

"I should fire you on the spot."

"I wouldn't blame you if you did."

"Did you tell Mrs. Dawson you're back?"

Helen nodded. "I called her when I arrived."

"What about the police? We filed a missing person's report."

None of what Philip was saying sparked any alarms, but the way his eyes kept a hooded stare on her made her heart leap. "I'll have to give 'em a call. I didn't think everyone would be so shook up with me taking a few days off."

"We wouldn't have if you'd told us."

He sounded sincere, and Helen started to feel guilty about her deception. Maybe Amber was wrong about the man, maybe he was only concerned for her well being. But then why had he been in her apartment snooping around? And why had he followed her to Scotland?

"Lisa told me you followed me to Scotland."

Philip pushed off the desk as he spoke, his eyes leaving hers. "I thought you'd like the help. I didn't think I'd be interrupting..."

"It wasn't like that."

He waved her off. "I don't want the details."

He closed himself off and slid into his chair. "I'm sorry."

"Do you know the police questioned me?" A spark of anger edged with his words.

"Why you?" Now was the time to ask some questions. Maybe find out why he was at her apartment.

"I'm your boss. We were both in Scotland when you disappeared."

His explanation was plausible.

It was time to stretch some of the truth. "I talked to one of my neighbors today, they said they saw someone who looked like you at my apartment right after I left."

His hand hesitated as he reached for a pen on his desk. "I went to your apartment after you went missing. They must have seen me then."

Helen shook her head. "That's funny, they said a guy in a suit was there the day after I left. They must have you mixed up with someone else. But you're the only one I know who wears a suit."

Philip's eyes found hers and held.

They were cold, piercing.

Helen shivered.

"It wasn't me."

"Okay."

But it wasn't okay.

"I should be going. Let the police know I'm not missing."

Philip lifted his chin. "I'm glad you're not dead."

Helen's skin started to buzz and her hand reached for the necklace. It was warm in her palm and reminded her of who waited for her at Mrs. Dawson's home. She really should get back before someone came looking for her.

"I'm sorry."

"You should be. I'll have to think about your job."

"I thought I'd be fired."

"I should fire you. Not look back."

Any other boss would. The fact he didn't told her he needed her for something.

"I'll be in touch." His voice stopped her before she left the room. "The next time you end up missing, people aren't going to search hard to find you."

It was a warning. Or maybe it was a threat. "I'm sure you're right."

Chapter Twenty-Four

"Where the hell is she?"

Simon was frantic. He'd searched the house and hadn't found Helen anywhere.

Her car was gone.

"I'm sure she's fine," Myra said as she slowly made her way across the room. "Probably just needed some air."

"She would have told one of us if that were true." No, Simon had seen something in her eyes earlier that day. She'd been quieter than normal.

Amber placed a hand over his. "She wanted to confront Philip. Do you believe she'd go alone?"

Damn he hoped she wouldn't be blind to the threat the man posed. But he knew how determined she'd been the other night. "Aye. She would."

"Helen's a smart girl, if she did go to him, she wouldn't have met him alone." Mrs. Dawson picked up her phone and started to dial.

The room grew silent while Mrs. Dawson made her call.

"Hello Lisa, dear. It's Mrs. Dawson."

She paused and nodded. Then smiled. "So she was there?"

Simon's shoulders fell. At least he knew that much.

"Oh, okay. Well, can I speak with Philip, then?"

Mrs. Dawson's lips fell, her back stiffened. "I see."

The room felt cold.

"Okay. Be a dear and tell him I called, will you? Fine." Mrs. Dawson hung up and set the receiver down. "Helen was there. She told Lisa the story about her fling and spoke briefly with Philip before leaving."

"So she's on her way back?"

Mrs. Dawson's eyes grew wide. "She left over an hour ago."

Liz stepped forward. "How far away is the office?"

"Thirty minutes."

Simon reached for his broadsword, but his hand only met the denim on his hips. "Where was Philip?"

"He left shortly after Helen. Told Lisa to lock up."

Everything went still inside of Simon's head.

She should be back by now.

Something was wrong.

* * * *

The rural road that led to Mrs. Dawson's home seldom had drivers; it was one of the things Helen liked most about the location of the house.

She rounded the curve and slammed on her brakes. A car sat crossways, blocking both lanes.

Her compact car came to a screaming halt, missing the front bumper of the sedan.

Adrenalin rushed through her veins, her body buzzed with unleashed anxiety. With both hands on the steering wheel, Helen gripped it hard and stared out over the hood. The seatbelt held her in place and kept her from flying through the windshield. Good, lord, leave it to her to nearly die in a simple traffic accident. She could travel through time, come against a bunch of burly men wielding swords in the forest, but meeting the number one guy because of a stalled out car was just stupid.

Helen leaned her head on the steering wheel and caught her breath.

After a few seconds, she lifted her gaze to the car in front of her and ignored the itching under her skin. She undid her seatbelt and slid from the car, wondering if someone was unconscious in the front seat of the other car. Why else would it be sitting like it was without anyone in sight?

Without thought, Helen ran to the other car. "Hey,

is anyone in there?"

There wasn't an answer.

She reached the door and peered through the glass.

The seat was empty.

Gravel slid along the pavement behind her. Before she could turn to see what caused the noise, splitting pain met the side of her head.

The world weaved in front of her eyes and the dark dash of men's dress shoes met her field of vision as she slid to the ground.

* * * *

Maybe there was more of his brother's blood flowing in his system then he gave credit. Philip watched the rise and fall of Helen's chest as she breathed. He hadn't meant to hit her so hard. He wanted her stunned, but her deep sleep that followed concerned him. Maybe he'd already caused damage enough to make her useless.

With bound wrists, and a gagged mouth, she wouldn't be difficult to hold once she woke. *If she woke*.

Thanks to the lousy economy and constant evictions, he found an abandoned home not far from where he'd picked Helen up.

He'd parked his own car in a garage at a different home several blocks away.

Now all he needed was for the crazy bitch to wake up.

He needed answers.

Malcolm needed answers.

Thankfully, the bank realtor felt it necessary to keep the house water running and the electricity flowing. Philip sipped water from a plastic bottle and kept half an eye on his captive.

He knew, somewhere deep inside, that Malcolm needed this woman to survive. The fact that she'd lied straight to his face, saying she'd just arrived back in the States after a hurried liaison with a man, made something inside him boil with rage.

All women were liars.

First his mother. Now Helen.

And to think, at one time he would have considered fucking the woman.

Not now.

He hated liars more than anyone.

Philip had listened to several conversations over the past few days from Mrs. Dawson's home. Whoever spoke in the room had entirely too much knowledge about him, about his brother. They knew he'd been in Helen's apartment. Knew he needed something from her. But they didn't know what.

Every one of them sounded foreign. Ignorant. They asked the most stupid questions about simple things like the television or computers. Any first grader knew what Google was.

Out of the corner of his eye, Philip noticed Helen stir.

He kept to the shadows and waited.

Helen moaned and wiggled on the carpeted floor of hallway. Philip placed her beside the back wall and shut the doors to the rooms. He kept a small light on in the bathroom, allowing only a small amount of light into the hall.

Her eyes blinked open. Her body stilled.

Philip laughed.

Helen pulled against the restraints until her back was against the wall. She searched the darkness but Philip knew she couldn't see him.

Her breath started coming in short pants as panic set in.

He tapped the wall with his foot.

Every muscle in Helen's body tensed. Her eyes shot in his direction. Fear rolled off her in waves that Philip could actually feel. It warmed him and sent a shot of excitement up his spine. It was sick, he knew, but he liked it.

"You should have listened to your ignorant friends and stayed away."

Helen moaned behind the rag in her mouth.

"I'm going to remove the gag, Helen. You will not

231

scream." He held up the taser he had in his palm and squeezed the trigger. The snap of current and beam of light filled the dark corners of the hall.

Helen's fear soared higher and Philip felt blood pump to his groin.

Chapter Twenty-Five

Her skin burned, sizzled, and popped. Her head throbbed. Philip ripped the gag from her mouth along with the duct tape holding it in place. The pain in her cheek wouldn't compare to the pain of the taser. She didn't scream and test him. His hand was far too steady, his stare entirely too comfortable.

"Why?" she choked out of her raw throat.

"I despise liars. Can put up with just about anything other than a bitch liar."

How did he know she'd lied? And what lie was he referring to? "Please, Philip, let me go. You don't want to do this."

He touched the cold metal of the taser against the flesh of her cheek and ran it down her jaw.

She braced herself for the shock that didn't come.

"I didn't. But *you* didn't leave me a choice. Now our time is running out and I need to know how this thing works."

He tapped the taser against the stone on her necklace. It wasn't possible for him to know the power of the stone, yet he stared at it now in morbid fascination.

"W-what are you talking about?"

"I think you know," he said as he lifted the stone from her neck and rubbed it with his thumb. The stale garlic scent of his breath mixed with hers as he peered closer.

"I don't."

Philip wound his fingers around the pendant and yanked the chain. The force jerked her neck, and the metal bit into her skin. Piercing pain rippled down her

233

back.

With her moan, Philip smiled.

Helen could feel his grip on reality starting to crack. She wasn't sure how she knew his psyche was crumbling but it was. Every time he touched her in some sinister way his smile became more of a sneer, his eyes lost more focus.

"Please."

"Please, please," he mimicked. "Just tell me how it works, Helen, and I'll be happy to let you go." *Said the spider to the fly.* So she could run to the police and send his ass to jail? *Not likely.*

"I don't know what—"

He slapped the words out of her mouth. She tasted blood.

"You flew to Scotland, checked into the hotel, and were back in the States within a few hours, calling the office from your apartment. How did you do that Helen?"

Her mind scrambled for a way out of his grip. Dammit, she should have learned to light the man's ass on fire so she could run. *Simon!* He would know what to do. The sisters and all their magical mojo would know how to get the hell out of this impossible situation.

"That's not possible. I was in Scotland."

"Briefly."

"Let me go," she begged.

"Not until you tell us how it works."

Us? Who the hell was us?

"How what works?"

He moved his hand holding the taser a few inches from her skin and squeezed the button.

Nausea burned in the back of her throat. She struggled with the restraints binding her hands. If she had her hands free...

"It was an accident. It only works for me," she finally said.

He pressed his lips to her ear and leaned his frame into hers.

Every muscle in her body held perfectly still.

"Now we're getting somewhere."

He pulled in a deep breath, as if drawing her scent into his body before pushing away.

A long-suffering breath escaped her lungs when his body heat no longer mingled with hers. With some distance, her mind scrambled again. Behind him, a hallway loomed. Her voice echoed around her, giving the illusion that the house was empty. She moved her feet out in front of her, restoring some of her circulation.

"I don't know if I can get it to work again," she lied.

"Pain is a great memory aid."

She could get it to work. A little blood, a simple chant. Then, pop, she'd be back in Scotland.

She closed her eyes and relief swelled in her chest. She'd be back in Scotland and away from Philip.

"If it only works for me, why commit a felony to understand its secrets?"

Philip glanced up at the ceiling. "A felony? Huh, guess you're right about that. Must run in the family."

Helen pulled her feet under her and started to inch up the wall.

The snap of the taser kept her seated. She'd need her hands free to touch the stone and move time. Being unconscious would nix her escape.

"This isn't like you, Philip. You're not your brother."

Slowly his eyes drifted to hers and dark spears of anger rolled off him.

"What do you know of my brother?"

God, why had she said that? "I- You said something once...I think."

He shook his head. "Try again, Helen, that lie doesn't work."

"I'm not sure where I heard it then."

"I never speak of Malcolm. There are no family photos around for anyone to see."

Malcolm? Where had she heard that name before?

"You're not him," she insisted. "You don't want to hurt me."

He reached her in two long strides and pulled her to her feet with the edges of her shirt. His whole body pushed against hers, pinning her to the wall. The hard line of his cock slammed against her stomach and a completely new set of fears washed over her. Memories of old men in foster homes swam into her memories. She'd always managed to got away from them. She'd get away from Philip.

"I don't know about that. Your skin trembles and the stink of fear dripping from your pores..." He ground his hips into her.

"No," she whispered. *Simon. Please help.*

With one hand, he reached up and circled her neck with long fingers. "Tell me how it works."

She nodded. "I'll show you."

His fingers squeezed.

"I need my hands free."

She coughed and tried to back out of his hold.

"If you're lying..."

"I'm not."

His hands left her neck and dipped down the front of her blouse and around the swell of her breast. She closed her eyes and blocked the feeling. He kept moving until his hands wrapped around her waist and pulled her away from the wall.

His nose nuzzled her neck as he reached behind her.

"No."

He laughed. Like lightning, he twisted her around, pressed her chest against the wall, and wrestled the tape from her wrists.

Her skin burned as it tore and bled from the abuse.

"Slow movements, Helen."

It was a warning. Not that she needed it.

It took him a moment to move away from her, making her wonder if his motivations for her abduction were changing.

With him a few inches away, she wasted little time rubbing her bloody wrists against her palms. She closed a fist around her pendant and felt it warm. *Only me.* She pleaded in her brain.

"Turn around," Philip barked.

He hadn't moved far enough away, she realized. The chances of him traveling with her were too high. "You need to give me some room."

One step back was all he allowed.

"Show me."

"It might not work."

"Show me." His jaw tightened.

"Fine." She glanced up and down his frame. "You're too close, but it's your funeral if you get caught in the current. It doesn't hurt me, but it burns what's around me."

He gave her two more steps of freedom.

It would have to do.

She started in a silent whisper. "In this day and in this hour—"

"What? What are you saying?"

"I ask the Ancients for this power." Though she spoke louder, she didn't think Philip picked up every word.

The hair on Helen's head started to swirl with the force of wind picking up in the room. Flames started to spark around her.

Philip twisted around, then pinned her with a glare. "What the fuck?"

"Take me now across the sea," she said louder over the noise of the room.

Philip stepped forward and Helen lifted a hand up in an effort to stop him from coming closer. A zap of electricity flickered from the vortex starting to engulf her body and slammed her enemy against the far wall.

"Back to Simon's family."

As the world fell away, Philip's face lost all expression.

Helen lifted her middle finger in a silent wave goodbye.

Chapter Twenty-Six

Simon found her car only blocks away from Mrs. Dawson's home. He shifted from falcon to wolf in an effort to pick up Helen's scent. It didn't work. Wherever she'd gone, it wasn't on foot. Pavement didn't lend itself for leaving marks in the road to follow. A big drawback of this century as far as Simon was concerned.

He took to wings again and searched the road for any sign at all. As the sun dipped over the horizon and the heat left the surface of the earth, part of his soul drifted with it.

He hadn't protected her. His new family. Searching for love never entered his mind since becoming a man, yet he'd found it with Helen. Found it only to lose her. Maybe if he'd told her that she might be carrying his child she'd have acted with more caution.

What ifs and maybes would plague him until he found her. But where was she?

As he made his way to Mrs. Dawson's home, he plotted the demise of Philip. The man Simon knew in his gut was behind Helen's disappearance. The warrior in him wanted to call the man out, finish him with a clean swipe of his sword. After he found Helen of course, but finish him in the end.

They'd call Simon a murderer.

He'd call it justice.

Then he'd be forced to return to the sixteenth century or live in the twenty first as a wanted man. No, he couldn't risk that.

Helen might not want to return to his time.

The question was, could he return without her?

* * * *

Philip's cell phone was at his ear as he made his way out of the vacant house. The shaking of his knees pissed him the fuck off. The lying bitch vanished into nothing. Nothing!

He made it to his car and squealed out of suburbia. In minutes, he'd managed to get the night guard at the prison to put Mal on the phone.

"Well?"

"She disappeared, again."

Mal pushed out a breath. "How?"

Philip picked his words carefully. Knowing the guards would listen to every word.

"I'm not sure. She held *it*..." Philip didn't speak of the rock, assuming Malcolm would know what *it* was. "Then spoke to the air. Asked for power." He sounded crazy, he knew.

"Back up, she said what?"

"Something about asking for power."

"You're not making a whole hell of a lot of sense, Phil, how about from the top."

Philip slammed his fist against the steering wheel as he sped through a red light. "She said, *I ask for this power. Send me across the sea, back to Simon's family.*"

There was a long pause. He thought maybe the phone went dead.

"Mal?"

"I'm here."

"Did you get that?"

"Yeah. I got it. What happened then?"

That's where he was fuzzy. "I don't know. A fucking hurricane inside the house shot out of nothing and poof. She was gone."

"Like magic on a stage?"

"Without the mirrors." Philip pulled into the back lot of his warehouse and shoved the car in park. Anyone checking for Helen would go there first. Philip needed to grab a few things and disappear for a while. He didn't even know why. It wasn't like Helen had a ton of family searching for her the first time she disappeared. Chances were Mrs. Dawson wouldn't ask about her so soon. Still, the way his skin itched he knew he needed to skip town for a couple of days. Then it dawned on him...if Helen could vanish as quickly as she had, she could return just as quickly. Lead the police to the house he'd kept her. His DNA was probably littering the place.

Sonofabitch! What had he done? And why?

"If you figure it out," Philip said to his brother. "You need to come back for me."

Mal chuckled. "If I ever make parole, I'll come to you. Where else would I go?"

The line clicked and went dead.

* * * *

Helen slumped to the ground the minute the wind stopped blowing and sat on the tips of her toes. She wasn't sure where she'd land, but wasn't going to be unprepared for an attack.

The familiar stone walls of the Keep, and the moist, dark interior met her senses.

Behind her, someone took in a sharp breath.

Helen peered into the dark for the source of the sound.

"Helen?"

Tara. *Thank God.*

Helen lowered her hands, not even realizing she'd placed them in front of her face defensively.

Tara and Lora sat up in bed, poised for flight.

When everyone in the room recognized a lack of threat, Helen moaned. All the adrenaline and fear of the last few hours threatened to manifest into a scream.

"Oh no. What happened?" Lora's voice penetrated her thoughts and a warm arm covered her trembling shoulders. The two women helped Helen to her feet and to a chair by the fire.

Tara pushed a glass of water into her hand. Helen took it and greedily quenched her thirst. Lora's fingers brushed over what Helen was certain were bruised and bloody features on her face.

"I'm okay."

The worry in the ladies eyes, however, didn't fade.

"Everyone else is fine."

Tara's shoulders slumped with relief. "Then what happened?"

Helen thought of Philip, his hands on her body, the stench of his breath against her face.

A small knock sounded on the door of the tower room.

Lora hurried to it, opened the door quickly, and let Ian in.

Ian stared, his fists clenched at his side. "Are you sure you're okay, lass?"

Helen nodded, not quite used to the fact that Lora and Ian could talk to each other without voicing the words aloud. Lora had obviously called him to the room with their special bond. "Bruised, but not broken."

"Who did this to you?"

"I should have listened to Simon. He was right." After a deep breath, Helen detailed Philip's abduction, his crazed behavior.

Ian listened from a distance. Lora held her hand and Tara stroked her shoulders.

"All of this in only a few hours?" Ian asked.

"What do you mean? We've been in my time for four days."

"You've only been gone half a day for us."

Helen shook her head. "We wanted to arrive back in my time close to when I left. That didn't happen. I thought the stones moved you at your will."

"The Ancients have the ultimate power over the stones. There must be a reason for the delay on your end and the quick return on ours," Lora said.

"Has the fighting started here?"

"No," Tara told her.

"A few of our enemy's men were captured, but nothing else has happened."

Helen shivered. "With Philip acting like his homicidal brother Malcolm, and all the crap going down here, I don't know where to go."

Tara squeezed her shoulder.

Ian snapped his head up. "What name did you say?"

"Philip, my boss."

"Not that one."

"Ah, Malcolm? That's Philip's brother. The one in jail for murder."

Helen could see the wheels of thought twisting in Ian's head. "Malcolm?"

"Right. Why? Does it mean something to you?"

"Mayhap. Tell me again, from the beginning, everything this Philip said to you."

This time when Helen relayed the traumatic event, Ian sat on the edge of a table and appeared to hold his breath with the anticipation of her words.

"Philip knew about the necklace, but not its true power."

"That's what I got out of it. He kept talking about himself in the plural sense. *We* need this and *us* that. He's crazy."

"Mayhap. Or, he's Druid as is his brother."

"You think? I never noticed anything special about him. He's charismatic, seems to get what he wants in life, but other than that...nothing." Outside of the past few hours, Helen would bet money Philip wasn't capable of hurting anyone.

She'd have been wrong.

"I didn't know I had a gift until I came here," Tara offered. "This guy could be just as clueless."

"He didn't act clueless."

"And he was after the necklace."

"No, see, I didn't feel that. He didn't try and get it off my neck. He had plenty of opportunity when I was out to hack it off had he wanted to."

Lora lifted her gaze to her husband. "He might have gotten a hold of one of the other stones in the future."

Every nerve ending in Helen's body sparked. The hair stood on her arms. "Yes. Of course, that has to be it. His brother is in jail and not going anywhere according to Jake. Malcolm could use the stone and escape."

Ian rubbed his jaw. "The man leading the warriors against us...his name is Malcolm."

"Oh, God. I led him right to you."

Ian waved her concerns away. "He was here long before you, lass. Even if it is the same man, his actions are not your fault."

Helen stood on unsteady feet. "I've got to go back, stop Philip from telling his brother anything."

Lora grasped her hand. "You need to rest. You appear about to fall over."

"Lora's right, Helen. Besides, there's no way to undo what's happened. The Ancients warned us about traveling in time to change the past," said Tara.

"But Simon and the others. They don't know what happened to me. They'll be—"

"Worried sick, I know. Relax. They can always return here using Cian's knife."

With a frantic shake of her head, Helen debunked that plan. "No, they can't. Cian's knife wasn't in his pocket when we landed."

"What about Amber's stone?"

"It's still there."

"Then they have a way."

Tara draped a blanket over Helen's shoulders. The weight of the fabric felt safe and her body started to melt into the thought of sleep. Damn she was tired. More than she'd ever been in her life.

"One night. We'll have a clearer vision of what to do in daylight."

"My wife is right, lass. Besides, if Simon were to see you now, he might find himself in the jail you speak of."

"I look that bad?"

Tara offered a bleak expression. "You don't look good."

Helen let out a small chuckle, which quickly moved to tears.

Tara wrapped her arms around her. "It's okay. We're here."

"I thought he was going to kill me." *Rape me.*

"He didn't."

Helen grabbed hold of the other woman and let the emotion of the day roll over her.

Chapter Twenty-Seven

The first time his cell phone rang, Philip ignored it. In the pre-dawn hours, he removed his car off the highway and onto a desert gravel road. The location looked as if it was used by weekend dirt bike riding families who camped unplugged from the rest of the world. Suited him. He didn't want to see anyone, didn't want to talk to a soul. He stepped outside his car long enough to piss before crawling into the passenger seat. He glanced at the blinking green light on his phone and gave in.

The message was from the night guard at the prison.

Malcolm was missing and they knew Philip had spoken to him earlier that night.

"Come in on your own, or we'll come in search of you. Your choice."

It was a threat.

Philip buried his face in his hands. "Better fucking come back for me, Mal. You better fucking come back."

In the last hour, a bone-deep peace he'd lived with all his life had vanished. Maybe it was the connection with his brother, maybe it was reality being a bitch and taking a massive sized chunk of his ass in a bite. Whatever it was, Philip knew his life wouldn't be the same. "Should have known that when I yanked Helen from her car." Yeah, he'd known then his life would alter forever.

Yet as the morning rays of light started to filter in the sky, he tried to grasp onto one bit of logic.

Remorse. Did he fell that? Not completely.

Under it all was an exhilarating thrill he'd experienced as he pushed his taser against Helen's skin, as he felt her trying in vain to hold still. Just thinking about it hardened him all over again.

He eased his seat back as his eyes drifted closed. He'd know what to do after a few hours of shuteye.

A little sleep and ho'd be good.

* * * *

Every muscle in Helen's body screamed in protest when she woke.

"Aspirin," she mumbled from her prone position.

"All I can offer is tea," Tara replied from across the room.

Helen popped one eye open and shut it quickly. *Sixteenth century. No toilets, long dresses, big, bad men in kilts.* One of these days, she'd like to wake not thinking of anything other than when she was going to drink her morning coffee or maybe take a run around the block. Damn, when was the last time she'd done that?

A month.

"Tell me it has caffeine."

Tara chuckled. "Not sure if it does or not. Tastes good though."

Helen wiggled her other eye open and winced as she sat up.

"Well, I'd like to say you look better."

"But you'd be lying." Already she could feel the stinging skin around her lips where the duct tape had held her gag in place and the tenderness over her eye where Philip has struck her. Even the back of her head hurt like hell. Oh, yeah, he'd knocked her out to begin with.

What a helpless sap she'd been. A stupid rabbit waiting for a fox to pounce.

"Here." Tara handed her a cup. She graciously accepted and placed to her lips.

What it lacked in sweetness, it had in taste. The warmth trickled down her throat like a balm. "Thanks."

"I wish I had some ice to put on that eye."

Helen brought her hand to the right side of her face and let out a little moan.

"That bad?"

"I'll live."

"But it hurts?"

"It does."

Tara's hand sat on Helen's leg in comfort. "If Cian was here, we'd have you fixed in a minute."

Funny, Cian didn't seem the healing type. Yet she knew of his gift to heal others. "Where's Lora?"

"Oh, uh, she and Ian left the room about an hour ago. I think they're trying to figure out what to do next."

"What's to figure out? I need to go back and try and stop Philip from...from..."

"You can't change the past. If Malcolm has already made it to this century, there is nothing you can do. Too many events would be wiped out if the Malcolm behind these attacks is the same as in your century."

"It might not be too late."

Tara shook her head. "Let's assume Philip's brother is the one here. He's been sending men after us for over a year. Simon wouldn't have been fighting in the Highlands the day you accidentally fell through time. You might never have met. The men chasing you might have—"

"I get it." Oh, did she get it.

"One of the reasons we didn't use the stones over the years was the fear that we'd screw up something catastrophic and void something important. It wasn't like I didn't miss pizza, or a bar of chocolate." Tara's gaze drifted back in obvious memory of said delight.

"The point is we avoided all travel. We thought it was for the best."

"Well I sure as hell can't stay here, and your kids can't stay there."

"Of course not. But you can't undo what's been done. One phone call, one instant message, and Philip will have informed his brother how to use the stone. If he's Druid, he'll slip away. If he isn't…"

But Helen knew already that Philip's brother Malcolm and the Malcolm raging war on the MacCoinnich's were the same guy. She'd bet her next nonexistent paycheck on it.

"It's the same guy."

"You don't know that."

"Yes, yes I do." Helen's body vibrated with the knowledge. It was her Druid gift dammit, and she knew when it was singing to her. Right now, it was hitting a high 'C'.

"Even if it is you can't change it."

This was all Philip's fault. He should be the one here fixing this and not the MacCoinnichs.

A warm rush of calm washed over her. "Of course." Bring Philip here. Make him stop this stupid war.

"Of course what?" Tara's eyes met Helen's.

Helen kicked back the blankets and shifted to get out of bed. "Come on. I need you to help me look presentable."

"Why?"

"I'm going home."

* * * *

The grandfather clock in Mrs. Dawson's hall chimed the noon hour.

Simon pushed out of the chair and started for the stairs.

"Where are you going?"

"I've waited long enough, Cian. She's out there somewhere. I need to find her."

Cian stood poised between him and the door, blocking him. "Amber said she didn't sense her anywhere."

"Amber could be wrong."

"When has that ever happened?"

Never. "There's a first time for everything."

"Not in this. Patience."

"Fuck patience." His woman was missing and sitting around doing nothing wasn't finding her.

Cian's gaze shot to Simon's.

The air stilled around them and neither spoke.

"You love her."

Simon started to deny the charge.

He couldn't.

Cian shifted his gaze.

"We'll go together to find her."

"Someone needs to stay with the women."

"You make it sound as if they're weak. We both know they out power both of us." Cian turned away.

"Neither one of us knows how to drive a car and a horse would prove useless here."

Cian shrugged. "'Tis time we learned the ways of this century, or be hostage to it. I'll find our host and we'll borrow her transportation."

A plan, they had a plan.

Simon made his way to the back of the house and Mrs. Dawson's kitchen, where he'd found her more times than not feeding one of the many hungry children in the house. A plan, they had a plan. He heard Selma's voice scolding one of the children at the same time he noticed a flash of light from the back window.

"Cian," he bellowed, rushing toward the light.

He ran past a dazed Mrs. Dawson and gawking children as the light swirled in every color of the rainbow.

Outside, the wind had kicked up, sending leaves to the ground.

Simon felt the presence of his family behind him as the wind settled and a lone woman stood in the center of light.

She turned to him and his heart skipped a beat.

Helen.

He didn't take a breath until she was locked in his arms, her body flush with his. "Tell me I'm not dreaming."

"Not dreaming," she mumbled. Her arms held him tight.

"I thought I'd lost you." He shifted back long enough

to stare deep in her eyes. That was when he noticed her face.

Everything inside him turned stone cold. "Who did this?"

She stiffened. "I'm okay."

"Who?" He'd kill the person responsible for marring her face. Simon brought a finger up to the purpling bruise under her eye and cringed when she winced under his soft touch.

"Calm down."

"Do not tell me to calm. Tell me who dared to touch you, lass."

Helen grasped hold of his hand. "Not until you swear to wait to do anything. Ian told me you'd kill him."

"Aye, Ian would be right."

"Ian also agreed that we need Ph…we need the man who did this to take back to your time. To stop the war."

Simon blinked the red from his eyes and focused on Helen's swollen lips. He could see the harsh lines on her skin where someone had bound her. What else had she suffered?

Simon placed his lips on her temple, wishing he could heal her with a kiss. Though he felt nothing but tenderness for the woman in his arms, inside his body rage ruled. "Who, Helen?"

"Ian and I both believe that Philip's brother Malcolm has somehow gotten a hold of one of the stones. We think he's the one in your time raging war. We need to capture Philip and drag him to the sixteenth century."

"Philip did this?"

Helen's lower lip trembled, her gaze met his. "We need him alive, Simon."

He had his answer.

Every nerve in his body shimmered in the need to shift…shift into anything, any animal that could take him to the man who'd touched his woman.

"We'll find him. No one wants him tied and

quartered more than me. But we do this right."

He wanted to argue, but needed Helen to elaborate on where Philip might be hiding. Simon had already cased the man's home and office and found nothing.

Simon tightened his jaw.

Helen relaxed in his arms, slumped into him really. He kept her from falling and placed a possessive arm around her waist.

He'd honor Ian's request.

Philip would return to the sixteenth century alive.

Barely alive.

* * * *

Unlike any time before, Simon sat in the circle with the women. The flickering of light cast from the glow of candles shot their silhouettes on the walls. His palms itched with inactivity. It took his mother over an hour to come up with the right words in hopes of finding Philip before he had the chance of running too far.

"Are we ready," Lizzy asked.

"Yes," Simon barked.

Helen shot him a stern look.

"Let's hurry this along." Myra rubbed her protruding belly. "The baby's active tonight."

"You're not in labor, are you?"

Myra shook her head. "Heavens no. Simply tired."

Lizzy and Amber sighed.

Simon's gaze fell to Myra's stomach and without thought, his gaze moved to Helen's thin waist. *Is she carrying my child?* It was too soon to tell.

Helen reached for his hand and his gaze traveled to her once battered face.

His stomach twisted and his grip tightened.

"I'm okay."

So she said. Cian may have healed her wounds, but there was still a haunting behind her eyes.

"Let's begin," Amber said.

Simon captured Amber's hand and waited for the others to join. Amber's fingers twitched in his and he saw her eyes flitter between Helen and him. Her lips turned up briefly, before her attention moved to his mom.

Cian stood beyond the circle observing along with Mrs. Dawson. The furniture in the living room had been swept aside and candles sat in a circle around them. One solitary candle sat in the center for them to focus on.

Once Myra grasped Lizzy's hand, the flames around them grew an inch. Even without words, the power crackled in the air above them.

"Picture Philip in your head as we search," Lizzy instructed. "Ready?"

"Yes."

"Aye."

Simon brought up Philip's image in his mind and rested his gaze on the flame.

"In this day and in this hour, we ask the Ancients for this power. Help us find our enemy, wherever he's gone wherever he may be."

The flames around them rose, the center one by a foot. Soon the center flame balled into a sphere and in it, the image of Mrs. Dawson's home appeared. For a brief moment, Simon didn't think the image would change, making him think that Philip was nearby. Then the picture shifted and rose before it headed east away from the setting sun. The lights of the city drifted behind and the cactus trees of the desert dotted the landscape.

They started to levitate off the floor.

"Do you know where this is?" Simon asked Helen.

"Could be anywhere."

The image weaved over and around the hills until it came upon a rocky bluff. All movement in the images stopped.

"It's too dark." Amber peered forward.

Movement darted before their eyes.

"Coyote," Helen murmured.

Simon tilted his chin and closed his eyes. He pictured the coyote hunting in the dark with nocturnal vision. *Come back into view*, he coaxed the animal with his head.

"There it is again."

"Simon, can you reach it?" Lizzy asked.

He felt the cold of night nipping at his nose and felt the familiar heartbeat of a wild dog. "Yes."

"Reach what?" Helen asked.

Let me in. Simon spoke to the animal through the connection the Ancients had given them while Lizzy explained to Helen what he was doing.

"Simon can speak to animals, see through them. He's had to do this once before in a circle. If he can get into its head, maybe we can find out where it is."

As his mother finished speaking, Simon felt the animal's will move aside and his own jump in. Simon shook his head and opened the coyote's eyes. The world spun in muted black, white, and grey but the images were sharp. He picked up the scent of oil and campfires. Simon turned the animal around in search of light. His gaze landed on a lone car sitting in an unoccupied campground.

The coyote inched forward, ears alert and eyes sharp.

A loud click stopped his movement.

The passenger side of the car opened and a foot stepped out, then two.

Simon forced the animal behind a bush and watched.

His nose twitched with a scent more familiar than any before. Helen's scent.

"Found him."

A growl rose in Simon's throat and Philip froze.

It would be easy to make the coyote attack, leave the man for dead.

"Where is he?" Helen's calm voice asked.

Simon forced the coyote to still and then back away. "Simon?"

"I'm looking." Once Philip felt the threat was gone, he continued over to a small campfire he'd built and

Simon forced the coyote to leave. Following the scent of cars, he found a path many had been on until he saw a paved road and a sign. "Red Rock Canyon."

"I know where that is." Helen's voice was hopeful.

Simon moved the coyote off the main road and released his hold on the animal.

He blinked open his eyes, saw black and white, then closed them again.

"Simon, are you okay?"

He nodded. "I'm fine." A couple shakes of his head and his vision cleared.

Lizzy thanked the Ancients and closed the circle with a soft puff of air that blew out the candles. Slowly they lowered to the ground.

"How far is Red Rock Canyon?"

"Couple of hours without traffic."

Simon helped Helen to her feet. "Get a coat. We need to go now, before he moves on. We'll take him from there to Ian and return here when we're done."

"Be safe," Lizzy said.

"God's Speed." Cian shook Simon's hand.

Chapter Twenty-Eight

Only half the moon lit their way once they turned off the main road and into the canyon where they expected to find Philip. Helen turned off the lights of the car and cut the engine. Simon sat beside her, eyes closed.

"He's still here."

Simon must have been using one of the nocturnal animals to stalk their prey. Helen shivered, knowing Philip didn't stand a chance.

"I'll secure him. Call for you when I'm done."

"He might have a weapon."

Simon's eyes caught hers. "A gun?"

Helen lifted her hand to her throat. The memory of Philip's knife scraping her skin brought on a wave of fear. "I don't know about a gun. Certainly a knife."

Simon captured her hand and ran a thumb along her jaw. "I would kill him with the knife he used against you."

Without a doubt, he would. "We need him alive."

Simon coaxed her lips open with his thumb and leaned in and captured them. His heated kiss was brief, but felt into the core of her soul. "He will regret ever touching you, lass."

Swallowing hard she said, "I know."

"Lower the window and listen. But stay here until I call."

"Be careful."

Simon raised an eyebrow and winked before removing his dirk from his side and sliding from the car. The dome light barely flickered and he was out the door

255

and several feet away.

The call of a coyote had Helen twisting in her seat. Another high-pitched scream from the wild animals sounded in the opposite direction. A chorus of howls ripped through the silence of the night, masking any sound Simon made on his approach.

Helen smiled despite the severity of the situation and resolved herself to wait.

Not two minutes had gone by and Helen gave up.

Patience was *not* her thing.

She crawled out of the window to avoid the light filling the empty sky. Feeling a tiny bit like the stupid woman who runs into the basement knowing the boogieman was down there, Helen kept her eyes wide and her ears open. For some reason, sitting behind the wheel of her car felt more dangerous. If being with the MacCoinnich clan had taught her one thing, it was to trust her instincts. She had a gift, one that kept her safe more than not.

Sending Simon toward a lunatic alone wasn't sitting well with her. She knew arguing the point with Simon wouldn't get her far. He was all medieval about some things and so very modern about others, it was one of his personality quirks she loved the most about him. Like how his accent thickened when he was in warrior or lover mode. She loved it.

Helen stopped and placed a hand to her chest.

No, she loved him.

And as soon as life slowed down she'd tell him.

If only life would cooperate.

* * * *

Philip paced on the side of the small campfire. He was cold, he stunk, and he didn't care too much for the coyotes roaming the desert night.

Where the hell is Malcolm?

They'd spoken of this canyon long before they knew what the stone could do. Before their life turned to shit, they'd visited the canyon with their father. He shook away the painful memories and stared into the fire.

What the hell was he going to do?

The police wanted to question him about his brother's disappearance. And if Helen ever appeared from wherever the hell she'd vanished, the police would want to do more than talk with him.

He ran a hand through his hair and blew out a frustrated sigh. Jesus, what was he going to do?

Another coyote howled in the distance, a little closer than the others. He twisted on his heel and narrowed his eyes in a vain attempt to see where the noise came from.

A chorus of howls called from behind him, answering the first animal's cry.

Were they surrounding him? Philip stood a little taller, gauged the distance to his car, and relaxed. Only a few yards. Nothing he couldn't manage easily if the animals wanted to attack him.

He turned back to the fire and placed his hands in front of his body to warm, to think about his situation. Usually he was the levelheaded one, the one to count on in a crunch. Yet when he'd snatched Helen, a surge of power he hadn't known he possessed welled up from nowhere. Damn he was screwed, really and truly fucked. Even now, days later, his cock hardened and his pulse raced as he remembered the fear in her eyes. "You're one sick mother," he said to himself. Still, his lips twitched into a sick grin. Maybe this was where madness began, in the dark of a desert night surrounded by coyotes and cold autumn air.

Maybe... He froze, his body doing its best impression of a wooden board, as the hair on the nape of his neck prickled. With his hand slowly reaching to his right hip pocket where he kept the knife he'd held against Helen's throat, his gaze drifted with slow, calculated ease. Beyond his right shoulder, by his car, was a sight that made his breath catch.

Blocking Philip's escape was a fierce coyote. He stood at attention, hair standing on end, and a growl rolled low from its gut.

"Oh, screw me," he murmured as his hand slowly removed the knife. What was the protocol for chasing off wild dogs? Was he supposed to make himself big and yell, or hold still and wait for the dog to consider him a non-threat and move along?

The coyote stared him straight in the eye and pulled his lips back to bare his teeth. The growl and ensuing yip-like bark frightened Philip more than he cared to admit.

"Go!"

The coyote continued to yip and pierce the night with sound, becoming more fierce with every passing second.

Philip took an unconscious step back.

A noise behind him made him stop.

Another coyote paced to his right.

Movement to the left indicated more of the pack wanted to play.

Fear reached up and squeezed his neck in a death grip. He wouldn't get to the car without injury.

"Fuck off!"

The animals stepped closer, slowly.

He shoved the knife in front of him like a sword. A useless tool in his current situation. The animals would have to be on him to use it.

He twisted to his left and the coyote there lifted his face to the sky and cried. Each step away from the animal brought Philip closer to the fire. Any closer and he'd be licking burns along with the bite wounds he undoubtedly would be suffering soon.

"How does it feel to be the hunted and not the hunter?"

The question came from behind him, close to his ear, in a voice so low and deadly, Philip felt his bladder spasm and the warm liquid spilled down his leg, puddling in his boots. He spun in a circle, intending to gut the man behind the words. But with lightning speed, the man towering over him removed the knife from his grip and held it against his throat.

The night grew still. Within the sudden eerie silence only the breath Philip expelled from his lips in short, staccato pants made any sound.

He recognized the man holding the knife to his throat. He was one of Helen's friends, one Philip remembered from casing Mrs. Dawson's home.

"What do you want?"

The knife pushed closer to the pulsating vein in his neck.

Philip went deathly still.

Hatred rolled off Helen's friend with physical force. He could almost feel the man's piercing eyes drill holes into the back of his skull.

"You. Are. A. Dead. Man."

One of the coyote's snarled and caught the man's attention.

"Simon?"

Philip heard Helen's voice but didn't dare move his head and risk having the knife slice into his flesh.

"I told you to wait in the car, lass." The coyotes started to snarl.

"Call 'em off," Helen said from the darkness.

Simon glanced beyond Philip, and the knife slipped away from his neck. It could be the only chance Philip had to escape. At the distraction, he ducked and twisted, catching Simon off guard.

He managed only two yards before the force of a freight train tackled him to the ground with a warrior cry.

The world spun. A fist smashed into his face. Everything threatened to go dark. Coyotes filled the night with sound, and another fist pushed his stomach up somewhere near his heart.

Simon shoved off Philip. "Get up."

Philip was out of his league. With one look into the man's eyes, he knew Simon would kill him if given a chance.

"Simon? C'mon. We need him alive." Helen stood a couple feet beyond them, her voice soft. Her eyes shifted from Philip then quickly back to Simon.

Philip didn't press for reasons.

Simon reached down and grasped Philip by his shirt, hauled him to his feet, and shook him until his teeth rattled. The fierce expression on Simon's face slowly slid into a grin. "We won't need you for long, Philip."

Helen moved behind Simon and placed a hand on his back. "We should go."

"Aye. Let's take this bastard where he'll learn what happens to men who accost defenseless women." Simon put his hand to Philip's neck and grasped tightly. Only when Philip sputtered did Simon ease his grip.

As Simon waved his free hand around in the air, fire from the pit spread into a circle, surrounding them, and Helen started to chant.

* * * *

They arrived at the Keep in the dead of night. The main halls were littered with men, most of whom slept while the guards kept watch.

Simon changed into proper clothing and donned his sword. The weight of the weapon felt right on his hip. Philip had been gagged and bound, waiting for Ian to assemble the right men to accompany them outside the Keep.

Fin met them and approached from the bottom of the stairs. "'Tis good to see you, lad."

"She's fine," Simon offered before Fin could utter his unspoken question. "They are all fine."

They embraced briefly.

Fin nodded. "I wondered after Helen arrived, battered the way she was."

"She was the only one who suffered at his hand." And Simon swore no one else ever would.

"Yet he lives."

"A necessity." Simon tilted his head to the side. "For now."

Fin grasped Simon's shoulder. "We will finish this battle and call our family home."

...and Helen will return to her time. Simon didn't want to think of that now.

"Fin!" Ian's voice called from above stairs. They both looked up and saw Ian wave for them to move upstairs.

They kept silent until they made their way to the small, hidden chamber the women used. Duncan and Todd were inside with the ladies. Helen had found a gown, her hair was now fixed in the traditional braid.

"We have a problem," Ian announced the moment he closed the door.

"As always," Helen muttered as she slid to Simon's side. He automatically wrapped his arm around her.

Duncan stepped forward. "Seems the man we captured from Malcolm's camp has met with an unfortunate accident."

"Accident?"

"Seems he fell on one of the guard's blades while trying to escape."

Simon dropped his head with a sigh.

"What does that mean?" Helen asked.

"He's dead, lass."

"No, not that, Simon. I got that. What does it have to do with finding Philip's brother?"

"We've no way to do it. Our prisoner was our beacon," Fin explained.

"Simon found him before—"

"I found small parties of men who worked for him, but not the man they called Malcolm."

"Didn't the prisoner give any clues where to look?"

Duncan laughed. "A man of loyalty doesn't divulge his laird's secrets."

Helen pinched her eyes together. "Well don't you guys torture in this time?"

Simon shot Helen a smile. "Bloodthirsty, lass?"

"Well there has to be some benefit to living in this time."

"The man wouldn't speak, lass. Hard as we tried to loosen his tongue," Ian explained.

"Now what?" Tara asked.

"We find him. How hard can finding one man be?" Helen turned to Ian.

"If it were only so easy. The Highlands are vast, Helen. What you say is not so easily done."

Simon noticed the frustration mounting in Helen's stance. Her hands ran over her arms and her fingers dug into her palms.

"I found Simon on a different continent and in a different time. I'm sure I can find Malcolm in the same neighborhood."

"You can do that, lass?"

"Sure. Why not?" Helen shrugged her shoulders and glanced around the room to astonished eyes. "Why the looks? We all have a gift. Mine just isn't often useful...well, until now."

Ian let a rare smirk spread over his face while he glanced to his oldest son.

Duncan shrugged and turned to Fin.

"How can we help?" Fin asked as he rubbed his palms together.

She hesitated. "I guess a picture of the guy is out. No personal affects. I could talk with Philip—"

"No!" Simon shouted the word.

"It's not my first choice, either, but he does know the guy."

"What else can you use?"

Helen placed her palms together and brought them up to her face, taping her nose in thought. "We believe Malcolm had one of the stones, right?"

"Aye."

"The smaller stones came from the larger ones. Where are those?"

"Hidden about the Keep," Ian told her.

"Bring them to me. I have an idea."

Ian nodded to Duncan. Fin and Duncan quickly left the room to retrieve the stones.

Simon leaned close to Helen's ear. "You think you can truly do this?"

She smiled with only a hint of hesitation. "Hey, I'm a time traveler. I have the 'finding people' thing down."

He chuckled, running a hand over her soft cheek. "'Tis good to see you smile again."

Helen leaned into his touch. "We'll get through this."

Chapter Twenty-Nine

With every ounce of bravo Helen could muster, she placed the stones in a line and concentrated. Her fingers tingled, whether from anxiety over the past days, or her gift kicking in, she couldn't tell.

She stroked the necklace hanging from her neck and pulled in a deep breath. Her skin tingled until she hovered her hand over the stones, feeling the vibration of one. She lifted the stone and placed it to her side.

"Is that the one?"

"No, that one gave me my necklace." The feeling was absolute as she moved to the next. She envisioned Amber and quickly removed the stone on the far right. "Amber's"

She thought of Cian. But when she lifted that stone she didn't add it to the elimination pile. "This is Cian's. But we don't know if his knife drove Malcolm here."

Staring at the remaining stones, her vision blurred. Helen spread her fingers wide and closed her eyes.

Malcolm, buddy boy, which one are you?

She smelled a fire and rain. At first both hands tingled, making her wonder if she'd narrow her search to one. Soon the overall sensations muted and heat took its place. A cold gush of air met her palms as she moved them over the stones on her right. Keeping her eyes closed, heat emanated from one. When she rested her palm on it, the sizzling of her skin singed all the way to her skull. "This one."

Everyone in the room sighed.

"What now?" Lora asked.

Helen lifted the stone in her hand and smiled. "We

264

go find the bastard and make him stop."

"We? There is no *we*." Simon corrected from behind her.

"Excuse me?"

"It's too dangerous for a woman to—"

"Save it, Simon. I don't have a death-wish or anything, but unless you can use this thing as a laser pointer to Philip's brother, you don't have a choice but to take me with you."

Simon placed both of his massive hands on his hips, ready to fight her.

"The lass has a point."

Fin stepped forward. "And if she's anything like your mother arguing with her will only waste time."

Helen smiled.

"I don't like it." Simon glared at his father. "The battlefield is no place for a woman."

"Agreed," Ian said.

Helen opened her mouth to protest.

"Don't bother," Tara told her. "They'll kick this around for a few minutes, grumble about the weakness of our sex, and then fold."

Duncan glared at his wife.

"What? Did I stutter?"

Lora chuckled under her breath.

Ian shook his head. "The lass is right. No use pretending we can do this without Helen's help. We'll keep her safe, Simon. No harm will come to her as long as I have breath."

Todd, who had kept silent through the whole exchange backed away from the door. "I'll gather Philip and meet you in the courtyard. I don't know about you, but I miss my wife and kids. Let's get this done."

"Good point," Fin moved to Todd's side. "I'll help."

Helen glanced down at her gown. "I need to get out of this."

"Dammit," Simon muttered as he led her from the room to change clothes.

* * * *

Rain drizzled against them as the horses plucked their way over the green hills. Ian used his gift repeatedly driving the heavy rains away. Helen was still soaked.

Simon sat behind her on Kong, the two of them leading the way. Helen ran her hand over the stone she'd tucked into the waistband of her pants. Her skin tingled and pulsed, the stone acting as a compass. She lifted her hand and pointed to the west, the rest followed.

Their small party had left the Keep as dawn broke. It was past noon now. They hadn't seen another soul since leaving, and from the expressions on the men's faces, they worried.

Helen glanced over at Fin. He led another horse that carried Philip. Draped over the ass end of the animal, Philip was anything but comfortable. Many times in the first hour of their trip, Helen noticed Philip attempting to watch where they were going. Trying to keep his head up must have been too difficult and now he simply hung there. She wanted to muster an ounce of sympathy for him, but then remembered the terror he'd put her through.

Half a mile later, the stone went cold and a chill went up her spine. "Stop."

Simon reined in his horse. "What is it?"

Something was wrong. They were headed in the right direction, but the air changed and every fiber of her body told her to stop.

"Shhh," Fin whispered.

Everyone stilled. Even Philip had the good sense to hold perfectly still. Ian waved his hand to the East. Todd and Fin urged their horses forward slowly.

Simon moved Kong to the nearest patch of trees and grasped the reins of Philip's horse from Fin as he rode by.

Ian and Duncan circled around the opposite side of Fin and Todd. Ian's falcon soared into the sky. The men in stealth mode was staggering, quiet. They knew something was coming. Like waiting for an earthquake, but having no idea when it would strike.

When the ground shook, it came by way of horses. Over two dozen riders, all split up to attack each party.

She'd led them to their death, Helen was sure of it.

Huge, fierce men with raised swords and shields to protect their bodies screamed out as soon as they were spotted.

Simon's arm squeezed her even tighter.

Philip wiggled on top of the horse, his eyes big as saucers.

Helen leaned forward, watching what was sure to be a massacre. They were outnumbered.

Behind her, Simon murmured under his breath. Suddenly a few of the horses charging Fin and Todd abruptly stopped, tossing their riders to the ground, evening their odds.

Simon shifted his attention to Ian and Duncan, and again half a dozen riders were thrown. The men scrambled to their feet and lightning split the sky.

Duncan sliced his sword over the head of his enemy. Blood sprayed in an arch over his head.

Helen squeezed her eyes shut against the brutality of the field, but couldn't sit in darkness long. Though she shuddered, she had to keep watching. The falcon screeched and dove at one of the enemies.

Simon kept to the shadows of the trees, keeping her from harm's way. He helped in the way he could. Helen noticed his body flinch and his eyes focus on the horses their enemy rode.

One by one, each man fell from his mount, whether by Simon's hand or one of the MacCoinnich's, Helen didn't know. Everything was moving so fast. Men were bleeding everywhere, bodies falling to the cold, wet soil to die a slow and painful death.

Bile rose in her throat and threatened to erupt. This was medieval life and the death Simon had spoke. How did he live with these memories so vivid in his mind? How would she?

Fin yelled above the striking steel. "Hold on," he warned.

Simon grasped her tighter. "Hold, Kong," he muttered to the horse.

The ground shook under them with the earthquake Helen anticipated.

The horses that no longer carried riders, bolted away from the fight. The others attempted to follow, some with riders successfully, unable to gain control.

Bodies littered the ground and a paltry few warriors remained. Sword met sword, then flesh until only two men stood. Their retreat was swift.

Only once they rode over the western slope did Helen breathe a sigh of relief.

Her whole body shook as she watched the men who had somehow become part of her family return to their side.

Duncan rode his horse their way and bolted past them. Kong sidestepped and Helen grasped Simon's waist.

Behind them, Duncan drove into the trees and returned fifteen seconds later with Philip dangling off the ass of his horse. Throughout the battle, Helen hadn't noticed that Philip had fallen from his horse and was attempting to get away with bound hands.

Duncan tossed him to the ground after stopping among them. He hit hard, his head shot up and he glared at all of them.

"We need to follow those who fled," Ian told them.

"Isn't that dangerous?" Helen asked.

"Aye. They'll likely lead us to the man we seek. The risk is one we must take."

* * * *

Philip was losing his mind. His stomach was pushed up against his shoulders and his right eye was swollen shut. Death would be a better companion then this. After the brutality of watching men running other men through with swords, he didn't think things could get worse. Then, for a brief moment after he'd slid from the horse, he thought he'd find freedom. Not that he'd know where to go or had a clue as to how to survive, but it had to be better than this pack of barbarian men were.

Helen sat beside her lover smug and content. Philip wanted to tear her to tiny pieces. She was the reason for his pain. The reason he'd fallen into the strange world. He'd heard only tidbits of information from his wardens. He knew they were searching for someone and they thought he'd be useful when they found them. It was safe to say the small army of men with their guts spewed all over the wet hills were part of the other man's army. He hoped the rest of the army was better skilled.

It didn't escape Philip's notice that these men had other tools at their disposal. A magical arsenal. He'd seen the large man, who'd lifted him as if he were nothing, shoot fire from his hand. How the hell was Philip going to combat that? Earthquakes and perfectly timed lightning only happened on the silver screen. He was fucked with a capitol "F".

"We're almost there," Helen announced. "Over that hill."

One of the men broke away. Philip managed to see him gallop by before holding his head up to watch became too much trouble. Either he blacked out or had managed to fall asleep, when the horse he rode on came to a sudden stop.

Two of the riders, the leader and one of his sons, rode ahead while the other two took the opposite direction.

Smoke billowed from a short distance away, providing proof of a camp.

Simon helped Helen off the horse and she stood a short distance away. Without ceremony, Simon pushed Philip until he hit the ground, jarring his hip and causing pain to shoot down his thigh.

Above them, the predatory bird Ian carried like a weapon, soared. Simon stood still, staring at the animal as it flew toward the smoke filled camp.

Helen's gaze shifted from Simon to Philip and back again. She glanced at the sky but kept quiet.

Without words, Simon left the horses standing alone, grasped Philip's arm and pushed him forward. "Move," he yelled, forcing Philip to walk in front.

Helen walked behind Simon, her eyes searching the horizon.

"Is he there?" Helen asked.

"Aye. Ian is explaining his options."

They walked a few more yards, each step jarred Philip's sleeping limbs.

"We've come to negotiate. End the bloodshed." Ian's voice penetrated the damp Highland soil.

A large tent sat in the middle of a small clearing. Several fire pits littered the ground. Well-armed men held massive swords and crouched low as if ready to fight. Philip wouldn't stand a chance, tied as he was. Even loose, he wouldn't live long if these men decided he wasn't useful.

"I've grown used to bloodshed." A voice rose from inside tent. The men surrounding it stood ready for a fight.

"What is it you fight for? Land, gold...or are you a mercenary?"

The faceless man laughed, his voice gruff with age. "Hardly that anymore."

"Then what?" Ian kept asking questions.

Philip watched.

Simon urged him forward but kept Helen slightly sheltered by his body. The mist started to turn into droplets of rain, adding to the misery.

"I want what your women can provide."

Fin laughed, but Philip noticed Fin's hand tighten on his sword.

Helen tucked behind Simon. Dressed as she was the men in the camp wouldn't mistake her for a woman. At least not from a distance.

"*Our* women? There are plenty more littering the Highlands."

"Not the kind of women you have. We both know what I speak of."

Philip's mind scrambled. Something about the voice sounded familiar. Maybe it was the fact that it wasn't laced with a Scottish accent, or maybe it was the verbiage used.

"Our women are of no use to you."

"That's debatable."

"Still, they will not be a part of our negotiations." Ian glanced over to Simon who gripped Philip by the arm and took two steps forward. "The bloodshed ends today, Malcolm. They do call you Malcolm?"

Philip lost his footing. Simon righted him and kept him moving.

"How do you know my name?"

"Not all of your men died quickly," Ian explained.

"The bloodshed ends when I get what I want. You're outnumbered here. I'll be a good sport however and give you a few minutes head start."

Ian laughed and the sky rumbled. "'Tis you who will need more men."

The voice inside the tent laughed as well and then the man behind the voice stepped into view. He held a crossbow that was pointed at the ground. Long grey hair touched his shoulders. Weathered skin ran over taut muscles on his forearms and chest. Philip's skin crawled and his heart sped up. *It can't be.*

"My bow will remove you first."

A loud click broke the silence. All eyes turned to Todd.

In his hand was a twenty-first century gun.

Malcolm went deathly still.

"You recognize the threat, don't you?"

Malcolm nodded, his face turned in Philip's direction.

"Set the bow down," Todd instructed. "My bullet will hit you faster than any bow can travel."

"Son of a bitch," Philip murmured.

"We have someone who might convince you to find a

271

new sport." Ian nodded once and Simon shoved Philip down the short embankment.

Philip tripped and tumbled several feet before managing to stand again. When he did, he was a few yards from the tent. A few yards from his brother. "Mal?"

Malcolm's face twisted into a look of horror. Recognition flooded his features and his anger rose to the boiling point. "How the fuck?"

Philip could say the same. Malcolm looked sixty years old. Yet when Philip had seen him only a couple of days before he was a thirty-year-old man in his prime.

"Jesus, you're old," Philip said, not filtering his words.

Mal stormed forward and grabbed Philip by his shirt. He moved him left, then right. Philip couldn't steady himself with his hands tied behind his back. "And you're not."

"How?"

"Damn rock sucked me from prison and into this hellhole. Thirty three years in this God forsaken land."

"Why not just go back?"

"Don't you think I thought of that, dumb-fuck? The stone disappeared. We need one of their women to take us back."

Philip swallowed and glanced behind him at Simon. "They have one with them now."

For the first time in years, Philip opened his mind to his brother and allowed the other man's thoughts to enter into his mind willingly.

Malcolm's gaze lifted and followed Philip's to Helen.

* * * *

Helen's blood grew cold in her veins. All eyes were on her even as Simon shoved her behind him.

Fin moved in tighter, Duncan did the same.

"I don't want to harm her. Just use her to go home. Once I'm gone, the bloodshed will end."

"If you mean no harm, instruct your men to stand down," Ian said.

Malcolm lifted a hand, the men at his side eased their stance, but they didn't put down their arms.

Ian shifted on top of his horse, restless. "Not good enough."

"This is my camp. My rules."

"Has living on our soil taught you nothing? You are on *my* land, have murdered *my* men. You will do as *I* say." Ian's tone straightened Helen's spine.

Malcolm's gaze shifted to Todd briefly before he placed Philip between the gun and himself. Philip attempted to move out of the deadly path, but Malcolm gripped his arm and held him in place. Philip's face took on a grey tone.

A small lift of Malcolm's lip expressed his disgust. He closed his eyes.

Noise from behind her had Helen spinning on her heel. A dozen men sat at her back and from nowhere many more emerged from the shadows of the trees, some on horseback, others on foot.

Duncan and Ian twisted their mounts so their backs were to each other. Fin and Todd did the same.

Ambushed.

Simon took Helen's hand and pulled her tight to his frame.

By the time she glanced back to Philip and his brother, one of Malcolm's men tore at Philip's bindings.

"My camp. My rules. Give me the woman and the rest of you can go."

Helen's hand grasped onto her necklace. She might be able to escape, but the others would be lost.

There had to be another way.

"Helen?" Philip called her.

"You cannot have her."

"We're outnumbered," Helen whispered to Simon. "Even if we did manage to kill them, we could be hurt or worse."

Simon's grip grew fierce. "Nay."

There had to be a way out, a way to escape using the rules placed by her enemy. In her head, she thought of Lizzy and of the conversations they'd had about shifting time. The nerves on Helen's hand started to jump. *"Never attempt to return to a time where you've already been. Elise, the Ancient who appeared to us warned us against it."*

That's it!

Helen turned to Simon "Do you think his hold on these men will dissolve once Malcolm's gone?"

"Yes, but—"

She placed a finger on his lips. "Trust me then."

"Let's go, Helen."

"The lass goes nowhere," Ian yelled.

"Ian," Helen called out. "Remember the wise words of Elise?" Helen hoped that by saying the name the others would follow along. "...wise woman, visited you some time ago?"

"She can't help us now, lass."

Helen glanced at Malcolm, who grew restless.

"I think she'd approve of my sacrifice for your lives."

Malcolm smiled at that.

Fin started toward them. An arrow shot in front of his horse, stopping him.

Helen raised her hand. "It's okay." She grabbed hold of Simon. "He comes with me."

"No," Malcolm yelled.

Helen took a deep breath, filled her lungs, and blew it out slowly. "I have no reason to believe you'll treat me with any respect at the end of our journey. Simon comes or the two of you can go to hell."

"We'll just kill her and cut the necklace from her neck," Philip said.

Well damn, she hadn't thought of that. It was time for some of her earlier years of bullshit to work. "Nice visual, boss, but it doesn't work that way." She fingered the necklace on her neck. "This is branded to me. I'm the only one who can make it work."

"Is she telling the truth?" Malcolm asked Philip.

"How the fuck am I supposed to know?"

"Simon comes with me."

"Do you know what you're doing?" Simon whispered.

"Yeah. But it's a risk. No telling what will happen when we land."

Simon pulled her into his frame, his body molded to hers. "We take the risk together."

God she was hoping he'd say that. She really didn't want to land in the wrong time without him by her side. She nodded.

Together they walked hand in hand down the hill.

"Simon?" Fin called.

"It's okay, Dad. Elise was a wise woman. Have faith."

"I don't like it," Ian grumbled and lightning split the sky, spooking the horse.

"Just take care of these men here," Simon suggested as they kept walking.

Helen kept her eyes glued to Philip.

Once she could smell the stench of Malcolm's skin, she stopped.

She reached between the folds of her clothing and removed Simon's dirk. Malcolm surged forward to grab her arm but Simon intercepted with lightning speed. "Relax. I just need a little blood." The edge of the knife scraped against her finger.

Philip winced.

"Wussey," Helen told her ex-boss.

She dripped the blood in a small circle around them, hoping it was enough to move them in time without standing the touch of either man. When she was done, she nodded to Simon who lit the ring. She grasped Simon's hand and started to chant.

Malcolm shifted from foot to foot with nervous energy.

"In the day and in this hour, I ask the Ancients for this power." The familiar shift in the air and heat from the rising fire ring started to ground out her voice. Instead of lifting her voice high, she kept it low so only she and Simon could hear. "Let's go back to the United

States," she lowered her voice even more. "Back to nineteen seventy eight. If the Ancient's will it so, take us now and let us go."

The year specified was before Simon or Helen had been born. A time when Philip and Malcolm were only kids.

Helen glanced over to Philip, who watched the swirling vortex surround them. Malcolm was pulling a knife out of his pants, a smug smile on his face.

Weightlessness surrounded them, knocking the other men back. Helen held onto Simon's side, her eyes never leaving her enemy.

A rush of air emptied from the circle, forcing Philip and Malcolm to the ground.

Everything stopped. Malcolm scrambled to his feet but before he made it far, he grabbed his gut and doubled over. The knife in his hand dropped.

"What the fuck did you do?"

Philip never made it off the ground. He grasped his head and his eyes shed tears of blood.

"I took you b-back," she stammered, unbelieving of what she saw.

Helen lifted her eyes from the dying men. It was dark, the distant sound of traffic pointed to a road being nearby.

"The canyon," Simon suggested. The same canyon they'd been in before.

Philip rolled onto his back screaming in pain. His cries penetrated the night. Hair fell from his head in chunks and skin receded from his nails.

"You bitch," he managed before words were no longer possible.

Before her eyes, Philip's skin stretched and folded in on itself. The stench of burned skin singed her nose. Both men writhed in place until they couldn't move. She buried her face into Simon's shoulder, unable to watch any more.

When the noise stopped, Helen blinked and noticed a small pile of soot. Within seconds, a wind came from the north and blew the ashes of both men all over the cold, desert floor.

The intensity of the day, the month, shook inside her as she trembled in Simon's arms.

He stroked her hair, whispering calming words in her ear. "We're okay."

"I know."

"He'll never hurt you again."

"I know."

"How did you know they'd die?"

"I didn't. Not really." She pulled away and glanced at the ground where the two men had lain only moments before. "Your mom told me about Elise, the Ancient who came to you after Grainna died. She said not to use the stones to go back to a time where you lived before."

Simon nodded. "She didn't say we'd die if we do."

"Your mom said it would be painful for any of us to be in the same time with our younger, or older selves. I thought if we could shift Philip and Malcolm back to a time when they lived, we could disarm them, bring them to justice." The memory of Philip's melting flesh swam in her head.

She shivered. "I didn't know they'd die."

Drawing her in his arms again, he said. "It wasn't your fault. You didn't kill them. Mayhap the Ancients decided to serve justice to their old souls, and leave their child souls alone. They'd be children now, if we truly are in nineteen seventy eight."

The patch of desert was dark, hardly a moon lit the night.

"What do you think happened to Malcolm's stone, the one he used to travel back to your time?"

"If Malcolm lived in my time for thirty years, he arrived long before the small stones evolved from the larger ones. They didn't exist. The fact that you and Amber have stones stayed with you during travel, proves you're the only ones who should possess these stones during your lives. Cian's disappeared, proving he isn't meant to travel in time at will."

"Are you sure?"

"No." Simon laughed. "I know only what I've seen." His gaze traveled back to the tiny specks of ash on the ground.

"It's over," Helen whispered.

Simon ran his hand over her hair, kissed the top of her head. "It's over."

Now they could get on with their lives.

Chapter Thirty

Helen transferred a few of the MacCoinnich's at a time to take them home. On her final trip back, to retrieve Simon and Cian, Ian and Lora asked that she take them with her to say goodbye to Amber.

It was all happening so fast. Helen hardly had time for goodbyes herself. Lizzy embraced her and reminded her they were but a thought away if she ever needed them. But living in the sixteenth century simply wasn't a sacrifice Helen could make. Besides, Mrs. Dawson needed her. Amber needed a friend and mentor. Her place was in her time, not in Simon's.

The two of them didn't speak, the inevitable parting brought tears to her eyes every time she thought about it.

With the majority of MacCoinnich's safely deposited in the Keep, Helen took Ian and Lora back.

When the vortex cleared, Lora noticed Amber first. The two ran toward each other and embraced.

"God's blood I've worried about you."

Lora pulled away from her daughter, glanced down her body and back up. "These clothes suit you."

"They feel strange," Amber admitted.

"They won't forever."

"Are you sure? Must I stay?" It was the only time Helen heard Amber come close to a complaint about her fate.

"Aye, lass. Your happiness will be found here."

Amber stared at the ground.

"You must be Laird and Lady MacCoinnich. I'm Mrs. Dawson." Mrs. Dawson walked down the back steps and interrupted them.

"I'm sorry, Mrs. Dawson, I should have introduced you," Helen said.

"You've had a lot on your mind, m'dear. Don't fret. Please, let's come in out of the cold. You don't have to rush back, do you?"

Ian glanced up at the home and over to his daughter. "A few minutes."

"Good, good. Come in."

They walked through the back door of the house. Ian's head snapped back and forth. "Cian, show me this fortress. Tell me what it lacks."

Instead of going with them, Simon stood by Helen's side, his hand on the small of her back guiding her to the sofa where he sat beside her. Ian and Cian disappeared around the corner.

"I don't think anyone has ever called my home a fortress." Mrs. Dawson chuckled.

"And never will again I'm sure."

"Can I get you anything?"

Lora's eyes scanned the room and marveled at the modern delights. "Thank you but no. Helen tells me that you've welcomed our daughter into your home as if she were your kin."

Mrs. Dawson patted Lora's hand. "I wasn't blessed with my own children but always prayed for them. Seems God has given them to me a little late. First Helen, now Amber. Though I know they aren't mine, they are welcome to all I have and any protection I can give."

Lora grasped the older woman's hand. "I cannot measure my gratitude."

"It's my pleasure."

Helen glanced at Simon who watched the two women talk, the expression on his face unreadable.

Ian stepped back into the room. "The structure is strong. Bound to withstand Finlay's earthquakes."

"It's been through a share of those. Mr. Dawson insisted on an earthquake retrofit in seventy-one. We had a bomb shelter placed in the basement in the sixties." Mrs. Dawson went on.

"I didn't know you had a basement," Helen said. She'd never seen it before.

"Couple of secret rooms, too. Those panic rooms were popular about twenty years ago."

Helen glanced around, wondering where such a room could possibly be.

"It isn't in here, dear. I'll show you. Might as well let you know about Mr. Dawson's gun collection while we're in there."

"Mrs. Dawson, I had no idea."

"I loved my husband but he was a bit paranoid at times. Guess that happens when you serve in a war or two, which he did. Then we had the arms race, the Cold War. We all thought we'd be nuked then."

Lora's eyes lit up.

"Don't you worry. That's all behind us now. Our economy is going to pot quickly but we'll be okay."

"Are you sure Amber won't be a hardship?"

"Please. How much can one girl eat? We'll be fine. Mr. Dawson left me quite comfortable." Mrs. Dawson smiled into the thoughts of her late husband.

Ian removed a pouch from the satchel around his waist and handed it to Mrs. Dawson. "This should help."

Mrs. Dawson waved him off but he placed it in her hand with a final word. "'Tis yours. She is our youngest daughter."

Without looking in the bag, Mrs. Dawson set it on the table. "She's safe here."

"Aye, that we already know," Lora told her.

Ian glanced at his wife. "We need to go."

Lora nodded and stood.

Their goodbyes were brief. Amber's tears misted as she embraced her brother, Simon, and her parents. "I love you all."

For one final trip back, Helen shifted time. Either she was getting better at it, or the Ancients were showing pity on her for her efforts. This final time felt easier somehow. Less taxing.

Ian gifted Helen with a rare smile and thanked her for all she'd done. Lora hugged and kissed both her cheeks. "God's speed, lass." She really didn't have a clue what that meant, but everyone tended to say it as if it was a blessing so Helen smiled and thanked Lora for the sentiment.

The children said their goodbyes and went to their rooms, their grandparents leading the way. Tara and Duncan said goodbye next, then Myra and Todd. When only Fin and Lizzy were left in the room, Helen said a tearful goodbye for the last time.

Simon couldn't keep his hands to himself. He kept Helen close, never more than a foot or two away. She was so good at shifting time that he worried she'd disappear in the blink of an eye.

They hadn't had a moment alone since they'd returned after Philip's and Malcolm's demise. Their time together was running out.

Helen faced his parents, tears in her eyes, "Thank you for everything," she told them.

"We've shown you nothing."

"That's not true. You've raised a wonderful son." Her eyes rested on his, glistening with tears. "Without him I'd have died that first day."

Simon saw his mother's solemn expression as she looked at him.

"Simon is a man who makes his own choices, forges his own life," Fin added. There was pain behind his father's gaze.

"Yeah well, where I'm from when someone doesn't have decent parents, they end up being all kinds of nasty."

Lizzy laughed at that, and some of the rising tension left the somber mood in the room.

"And you're the one who told me to trust in my gift, believe in it. You helped me believe in myself, Lizzy. For that I'll always be grateful."

"There's no reason for all these tears. You can come visit. If there is one person in the universe who can, it's you."

Helen glanced around the room, her eyes shifting to the floor. "Yeah, I guess." She swiped at the tears on her cheeks and turned to Simon. "I need to go."

Pain rippled through him as he stared into her swollen eyes. He could do this. Life was about sacrifices and about making the right decisions for the many and not the few.

His mom and Fin stepped back but didn't leave the room.

Simon pulled Helen close, his heart thick in his chest. "I love you, lass."

She sobbed into his chest. "I love you, too."

The words were music to his soul, making everything else around him fade. "We don't need to be apart."

Helen kissed him, stopping his words. He forgot his parents, the room they stood in, and simply felt the desperation behind her kiss. When she pulled away, she forced a fake smile to her lips. "I can't stay here, Simon. And I love you too much to ask you to leave. Your family needs you."

He nodded and smiled. "Aye. My family does need me."

Helen sucked in her lower lip and stepped out of his arms.

Then, because his time was at an end, he turned to his parents.

Lizzy sobbed and threw herself in his arms. "I know. We all know."

Simon hugged her and stared at Fin.

"Lora had a premonition," Fin explained.

"I don't understand," Helen said from behind them.

Simon kissed his mother and embraced his father before turning to Helen. "You're my family now, Helen. 'Tis you I need to be with. You I wish to be with."

Helen's mouth gaped open. "You mean you're

283

coming with me?"

"Aye. If you'll have me."

Her arms wove around his neck. The tears filled with pain changed to those of joy. "I'll have you," she laughed.

"As my wife," he informed her.

She stopped kissing him and stared into his eyes. "Was that a proposal?"

It's a demand.

He glanced at his mother. The woman who taught him everything he knew about modern women. "Aye, it was."

Helen kissed him again, this time melting into his arms.

"You approve?" he asked when her lips left his.

"Of course, I approve." She pushed away from him and hugged Lizzy one last time. "Unless something stops us, we'll visit."

Lizzy nodded. "I know."

Simon hugged his parents a final time. "Tell the others goodbye."

"We will."

Fin and Lizzy stood back, giving Helen room.

His future wife whispered under her breath, barely breathing the words to move them through time. Everything Simon had known, his loving parents, his family, his world, drifted away. As the vortex surrounded them, He stared into Helen's eyes and saw the brightness of her soul.

"I love you, lass."

"I love you, my Highland shifter."

Epilogue

Ian and Lora met Fin and Lizzy as they left the upper chamber where Simon and Helen had left.

Ian's heart squeezed in his chest, feeling the empty place that would never quite be the same without Simon's presence. "They've gone?"

"Yeah," Lizzy pushed away tears. "They were so happy. Sad in some ways, but happy."

Lora swung an arm around Lizzy's shoulders in comfort. "'Tis for the best."

"I know. It just hurts."

They started down the stairs, talking as they went.

"Do you think she knows about the baby yet?" Ian asked.

"I doubt it," Lizzy answered.

"Simon knew," Fin told them without a hint of a doubt in his voice.

"What makes you say that, son?"

"The way he said *family*. He knew she was pregnant."

Lizzy sighed. "You don't think he's marrying her because of the baby, do you?"

Lora squelched that thought. "Simon loves the girl. Did long before any child was conceived."

Lizzy nodded. "You're right. I know you're right."

"Let's drink to another generation." Ian poured them drinks when they reached his study and lifted his glass for a toast. "May our children be happy in their new life..."

As his glass rose in the air all sounds in the house went completely silent.

The hair on Ian's nape stood on end. He dropped the goblet from his hand and reached for his sword before swinging around.

There, standing in the middle of his study, was a huge man dressed completely in black. The clothing clung to his skin, weapons of all kinds covered his body. His penetrating gaze landed briefly on the women before moving to Ian. Seeing Ian's sword unsheathed, he stripped a gun from nowhere and aimed it at Ian's chest. It looked like Todd's weapon, only different.

From Ian's side, Fin let loose his dirk. It flew through the air but instead of sticking in the threatening stranger's chest, the man spread his hands in the air and an iridescent stream of light surrounded him. The knife bounced off the light and onto the floor.

"Where is she?" he yelled.

"Who?" Ian asked stunned at everything this man was doing.

"Where is Amber? Where is my wife?"

Other Books By CATHERINE BYBEE

Time Travel Romance

Binding Vows

Silent Vows

Redeeming Vows

Highland Shifter

Contemporary Romance

Wife by Wednesday

Married by Monday (coming 2012)

Paranormal Romance

Before the Moon Rises

Embracing the Wolf

Soul Mate

Possessive

A word about the author...

Catherine Bybee has been addicted to books for as long as she can remember. With the love of reading romance novels came the desire to write them as well. Creating worlds where passion and intrigue collide gives Catherine the perfect balance. Catherine currently lives in Southern California with her husband and two growing sons.

She loves hearing from her readers and encourages everyone who enjoys her books to follow/friend or even annoy her on:

Twitter: http://twitter.com/catherinebybee

Facebook:
http://www.facebook.com/pages/Catherine-Bybee-Romance-Author/

Goodreads:
http://www.goodreads.com/author/show/2905789.Catherine_Bybee

Catherine's Blog: http://catherinebybee.blogspot.com/

Visit Catherine at www.catherinebybee.com

CPSIA information can be obtained at www.ICGtesting.com
Printed in the USA
LVOW121950180612

286644LV00019B/7/P